"We are gathered here today..." the priest began.

The words were powerful, but Alinor could scarcely hear them. Her whole body was alive with danger.

Kavian had said he would not allow her to marry another, and she knew he would keep his word. But how would he stop the wedding now?

Nothing the priest said could penetrate her ears. Where were they in the marriage service? How much time did she have?

Then she heard a rustle of astonishment amongst the tiny congregation.

"Well, Alinor," demanded a voice behind her. "Do you confess that you cannot marry another while you are my wife?"

Alinor whirled. He stood in the doorway, a figure swathed in desert robes, his hands on his rifle, in the spread-legged possessive posture she knew so well. She could be in no doubt about what he meant to d

Kavian Durran, the Crow had come to claim her.

D0967996

Dear Reader,

Welcome to another month of powerhouse reading here at Silhouette Intimate Moments. Start yourself off with Lindsay Longford's *Renegade's Redemption*. Who doesn't love to read about a rough, tough loner who's saved by the power of a woman's love?

Move on to Susan Mallery's *Surrender in Silk*. This sensuous read takes a heroine whose steely exterior hides the vulnerable woman beneath and matches her with the only man who's ever reached that feminine core—the one man she's sure she shouldn't love. Alexandra Sellers plays with one of the most powerful of the traditional romantic fantasies in *Bride of the Sheikh*. Watch as heroine Alinor Brooke is kidnapped from her own wedding—by none other than the desert lord who's still her legal husband! In *Framed*, Karen Leabo makes her heroine the prime suspect in an apparent murder, but her hero quickly learns to look beneath the surface of this complicated case— and this fascinating woman. Nancy Morse returns with *A Child of His Own*, a powerfully emotional tale of what it really means to be a parent. And finally, welcome new author Debra Cowan. In *Dare To Remember* she spins a romantic web around the ever-popular concept of amnesia.

Read and enjoy them all—and then come back next month for more of the most exciting romantic reading around, here at Silhouette Intimate Moments.

Yours,

Leslie Wainger
Senior Editor and Editorial Coordinator

Please address questions and book requests to:
Silhouette Reader Service
U.S.: 3010 Walden Ave., P.O. Box 1325, Buffalo, NY 14269
Canadian: P.O. Box 609, Fort Erie, Ont. L2A 5X3

BRIDE OF
THE SHEIKH

ALEXANDRA
SELLERS

Silhouette
INTIMATE™MOMENTS®

Published by Silhouette Books
America's Publisher of Contemporary Romance

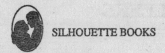

SILHOUETTE BOOKS

ISBN 0-373-07771-8

BRIDE OF THE SHEIKH

Books by Alexandra Sellers

Silhouette Intimate Moments

The Real Man #73
The Male Chauvinist #110
The Old Flame #154
The Best of Friends #348
The Man Next Door #406
A Gentleman and a Scholar #539
The Vagabond #579
Dearest Enemy #635
Roughneck #689
Bride of the Sheikh #771

Silhouette Yours Truly

A Nice Girl Like You
Not Without a Wife!

ALEXANDRA SELLERS

was born in Ontario, and raised in Ontario and Saskatchewan. She first came to London to attend the Royal Academy of Dramatic Art and fell in love with the city. Later, she returned to make it her permanent home. Now married to an Englishman, she lives near Hampstead Heath. As well as writing romance, she teaches a course called "How to Write a Romance Novel" in London several times a year.

Because of a much-regretted allergy, she can have no resident cat, but she receives regular charitable visits from three cats who are neighbors.

Readers can write to her at P.O. Box 9449, London NW3 2WH, England.

Prologue

He sweated as he slept, his face beaded with heavy drops of it, his dark hair, loosely curled, clinging to the damp skin at his temples, falling back elsewhere to reveal a broad white brow, finely carved cheeks, arrogant nose, a proud, strong mouth.

He sweated and moaned, as if he were ill, but there was no nurse at the bedside, no one to ease the tortured heat that his anguished brain produced.

He tossed. The rough blanket that he wore as a covering shifted, and his naked arm and chest passed within the glow of a chink of light falling through a gap in the wall of cloth. He was powerful, muscled, hard; the night was jealous of the light's touch and covered him quickly again with her embrace.

"Nuri!" he cried then, as though sensing the night's banishment of the light, for in his language the word meant "light." "Nuri!" he cried again, yearning, desperate, but the night determinedly shrouded him. Until the sun rose, he belonged to her. She would not give him up to the lamplight, whatever his cry.

In his dream, it was not light he sought, but his light, the woman of that name. He strode through the fortress, eluded always by the film of cloth, the flick of grey silk that moved around a corner, through a door, just ahead of him. Now he followed it, now he searched blindly, opening doors onto empty rooms, turning into empty halls, catching hold of a drapery to find that it was only a veil or a curtain against a window or wall, not a woman's dress.

Always, the wind blew. He felt it against his temples, he saw it billow in the hint of gauzy fabric he pursued and never caught. He knew that the wind came from the centre of the fortress, that the woman, however many wrong turnings he took, was leading him there.

Now at last, he was close upon her. A door shut just within reach, the draperies trailing for a second out between the double doors and then disappearing as they banged to. For a second he even glimpsed her face. He reached out, pushing the doors wide as he strode inside.

She was there at last. She both stood at the centre, and was the centre. The wind lifted her hair off her face and pressed the grey silk against her body, and yet she was the wind.

For a moment he could not move. He stood watching her, while his heart beat in wild possession, knowing there was no exit to this room, save the one that his own body blocked. He watched her, his head high, knowing she was his, his passion intolerably stirred by the thick, pale hair that the wind barely lifted, by the perfect body revealed under the grey gauze and the wind's firm caress.

So would be his own caress—firm, shaping her, leaving nothing to chance or imagination, discovering and creating her in the same moment under his hands.

She smiled and held out both hands, like the ancient goddess of the waters, pure, true, undefiled.

She both was, and was not, his own. His body leapt with a passion like death, and his heart with a love like fear.

He overcame fear and death both to approach her, and then he embraced her, and she was all his, she was human, his wife, sworn to his love, perfection with flaws, fire with ice, water with drought, light.

"Nuri!" he cried. "My light!"

He wrapped her tightly in his arms, so that she would never escape again. "Nuri!" he cried again, his intent ferocious, passionate, all-consuming.

She opened her mouth to speak, and he paused to listen. But no sound came from those full lips that he had, for a fatal second, delayed kissing. She smiled, and her gaze drifted from his, and then, like smoke, the vision faded and the firm shape of her was air.

He awoke with a cry of desolation. Outside the tent, the wind was rising, but though it beat against the tent it did not make its way inside. A voice called out in question, and he raised himself on an elbow, reaching out to the bed beside him to be sure that he was, indeed, alone, for the dream had been powerful.

"Did you call, Lord?"

"A dream," said the man.

"Of victory, please God."

"I dreamt of Victory," the man agreed, for she was victory to him. He did not say that she had eluded him.

"May God's ears be present," said the watchman, and passed on into the night.

The rain was starting. The dreamer heard its first faint taps against the tent wall under the hammer of the wind.

Chapter 1

"Ladies and gentlemen, ah, this is the captain." Alinor Brooke, sitting by the old-fashioned oval window in a dream state induced half by the drone of the ancient propellers and half by the scenery far below, stirred a little to listen. The captain cleared his throat. "We're now passing just to the eastern border of the Kingdom of Parvān; we're over the Great Central Desert at the moment, and if you look off to the right, in the distance in a few minutes you'll be able to see the capital, Shahr-i Bozorg, up in the foothills of the Kohishir Mountains."

Alinor turned obediently to peer through the scratched, moulded plastic, striated with a thousand tiny lines that each caught the blinding light of the sun in a hair-fine sparkle. Narrowing her eyes against the glare, she gazed out across the miles of desert towards the rugged, snow-topped mountains in the distance. They were actually flying at a level below the highest peak, Shīr, the mountain which gave its name to the whole range; a fact which made the ancient but serviceable propeller plane seem fragile, a fly that the tons of rock might at any moment reach out to crush.

Alinor shivered. Koh-i Shīr. She whispered the name to herself. Lion Mountain. Milk Mountain. The name, like so much else in the Kingdom of Parvān, was ambivalent, and so perfectly apt. "Lion" certainly described that crouching, menacing, yet noble presence that dominated the whole landscape. And "milk" described not only the unchanging white of the mountain's highest reaches, but also the plenty that was to be found below, in the country's rich, protected, high valleys so unlike the sweep of desert beyond. What other language had a word that could cram so much into one short syllable? *Shīr.* Masculine protection, feminine bounty. The Great Mother and the Great Father in One. "The Lion/Milk belongs to us, and we to the Milk/Lion," he had recited to her, the first time she saw the mountain. *Shīr ān-i mā hast, o mā ān-i shīr...*

Alinor shook that remembered voice from her head and focused on what her seat partner was saying. "Will your fiancé meet you at the airport?"

"Oh, yes, I think so." Of course he would. Gabriel was the perfect English gentleman, and anyway, his connections with the embassy would be needed to speed her progress through immigration. Kaljukistan was still nervous of foreigners. For decades, under Soviet rule, they had seen virtually none. With the breakup of the Soviet Union had come a few years of easy borders, and then the war with Parvān had closed the border again to casual foreign traffic. Add to that the fact that Kaljukistan was now officially an Islamic state, and she was a woman travelling alone. Gabriel would certainly meet her.

"This is a view, by the way, that hasn't been seen very much until recently," the captain said a minute later, as the mirrored great dome and the towers of Shahr-i Bozorg came into view, sparkling in the distance. Alinor stared at the sight against the bright sun until her eyes hurt. Parvān.

"Commercial aircraft are now flying over the Great Central Desert again, after several years when the war between Kaljukistan and Parvān made it too dangerous. For those of you who aren't aware, out there somewhere in that desert is the border, and only the locals know exactly where it is. During the war, anyone who strayed into this airspace might get shot at from either side, or both at once, as I can tell you from personal experience.'' There was a smile in his very English voice, and a ripple of laughter among the foreigners aboard. ''Peace between the two nations has cut two hours off your flying time this morning, and we'll be landing at Shahriallah, the newly renamed capital of Kaljukistan, in just over half an hour.''

Alinor blinked. *Shahriallah.* Yes, of course. For a moment, dreaming, she had forgotten. Somehow she had been expecting him to say that they were going to land at Shahr-i Bozorg, as though she had lost years in time, or slipped into another lifestream, one in which she was flying home...

No, not home. Alinor's jaw tightened. It had been many things, Parvān, but never *home,* whatever he had said. With a jerky movement she reached for her carry-on bag and dragged it onto her lap.

''Have you dropped something?'' said a soft voice, and she looked up into the face of the stewardess, the exotic, hooded, slightly slanted Mongol eyes proving her unmistakably a Kaljuk. As she spoke she bent and picked up a small folded sheet of paper that had flipped into the aisle from somewhere as Alinor picked up her bag, and handed it to her.

Someone's details, perhaps, that had slipped out of her address book. It didn't look familiar, the crumpled square of faded white, but in the hectic last days before her departure much had been happening. With a smiled word of thanks, Alinor reached for the paper.

As her fingers closed on it, she was filled with a sudden sense of dread, and an almost overwhelming urge to deny all knowledge of the paper, to refuse to take it. But the stewardess had already let go and was bending over another passenger a row away.

After a moment of staring at it, Alinor unfolded the paper, one simple fold.

Return to your home.

Alinor gasped and glanced nervously around her. Was the note meant for her? Who could have dropped it? She tried to remember who had passed her seat during the course of the flight, but her memory was a blank. She only remembered the stewardesses, offering coffee and the exotic snack that had reminded Alinor more sharply than anything else could of what part of the world she had come to.

The Kaljuk woman beside her had apparently noticed nothing.

"I think this must be yours," Alinor said to her seat partner, offering the paper to her.

The woman's smile stiffened as she glanced at the paper. "No," she said. "I cannot read it."

Most educated Kaljuks were still unfamiliar with the Arabic script, which had been reinstated with the establishment of the Islamic state after decades of Soviet rule. This had had the effect of rendering most of the educated secular class of the country illiterate at a stroke. Only the Mullahs now could read.

Parvān, on the other hand, had never fallen under Soviet rule. This had produced the curious contradiction of Kaljukistan, a newly re-Islamicized post-Communist state, trying to force Parvān, which had never given up either democracy or Islam, into a fundamentalism it neither needed nor wanted. The kind of contradiction the East was full of. The sort of thing that had always used to charm her... "Not every Western mind can appreciate the ways of the East," he had said to her, his eyes dark and glittering with admiration. But she appreciated the ways of the East no longer. He had seen to that. Now she hated it all, the contradiction, the lying, the hypocrisy...and the complete contempt for any theory of woman's shared humanity with man.

The note might have been there before she even sat down, Alinor told herself restlessly. But she could not hide there. She would have seen it when she set her carry-on bag down....

Her bag! Could she have brought it aboard herself? Had it been slipped into a pocket of her bag somewhere in the whirl of humanity at Samarkand airport, and fallen out here?

Return to your home. It might mean nothing, no more than the passing rage of someone who hated the presence of foreigners in their country. But then, why her? her brain asked relentlessly. There had been hundreds of foreigners at Samarkand, and there were at least a dozen on this plane, sparsely populated as it was.

Bar gard beh mīhanet. Alinor read the words of the beautifully curling Arabic script again as the truth forced its way into her brain. There were three things that proved the message was meant for her. The first was that the command was written in the personal, familiar form. The second was that the language was not Kaljuki, but Parvāni.

It must be for her. The note could only be for her. Because the third was that she had seen such a note once before, long ago, and far away, and passed to her in the same mysterious way....

And the meaning then, as now, had been not *go* home, but *come* home. *This is your homeland now,* he had said, more than once. *Alān īn mīhanet ast...*

A chill crawled over her skin in the plane's rarefied air. Who had given her the note, and when? How close was the messenger now?

And how much of a fool had she been to come back into his orbit, even after so many years?

The men, sitting at the front, got off the plane first. It was a rule even foreign airlines had to follow nowadays, flying into Kaljukistan: the sexual segregation of passengers. Men at the front, women at the rear. All for the protection of women, of course.

The woman beside Alinor was using the waiting time to adjust her headscarf, and Alinor turned to the business of pulling out her own silken square and tying it around her head to disguise the thick, pale ash hair that swept well below her shoulders.

Her seat partner examined herself in a compact mirror and clucked irritably. "There are more women than men in Kaljukistan now," she observed disgustedly to Alinor in English. "So many killed during that stupid war. But still we let them do this to us."

When the men had departed and there was no chance of the sexes rubbing up against each other and inducing uncontrollable lust in the men, the stewardess who had stood with her back to the women turned and beckoned them, and they all began to file out into the gangway.

Outside the heat was appalling, a dry, merciless fire on the skin and in the lungs. A stewardess led them down the ramp and across the tarmac into the small, bomb-damaged terminal building that once, perhaps, had been air-conditioned. Now, with one corner of the ceiling torn away, and enclosed only with scaffolding, no air-conditioning was possible.

The line-up for immigration was not long, but it was slow. When a man reached the head of the line, he would turn to signal, and from the ranks of the women waiting behind, his wife or daughter or other property would detach herself and step forward to be guided through the immigration process.

Here was where Gabriel should have met her, on the other side of a customs desk, to vouch for her reasons for being in the country. Alinor could see no sign of him. The line moved slowly. She passed a sign that said, in English and in the new Kaljuki, that there was a charge—"aerprot entry taxe" in English—of five pounds sterling, ten dollars U.S., or twelve dinars to be paid. No roubles rate was given, she noted.

Her turn came at last, when there was only a handful of unescorted women left. A dark, heavily sweating man with a gun lying negligently behind him in the booth deftly slipped the five-pound note from her passport and spoke to her in awkward English. She resisted the impulse to reply in Kaljuki.

"I'm getting married tomorrow to Gabriel Horne. He's with the British Embassy," she repeated, trying to remain calm in the face of the bland deliberate stupidity in front of her.

"Tomorrow. He is your fiancé? Do you know him?"

Nervously she watched as he began to flip idly through the pages of her passport. She smiled and refused to show anger. "Oh, yes, we met in England, where I was a student of Kaljuki," she said brightly, hoping desperately to distract him from his browse. If he saw the Parvān stamp... Again Alinor cast a desperate glance into the airport beyond the Immigration desk. Gabriel's fast talk and presence was supposed to prevent this, for no one could predict the response of a Kaljuk immigration officer to the presence of a pre-war Parvān entry stamp in a foreigner's passport. "We'll blind them with paperwork," Gabriel had said. "Best if he just doesn't go on a forage through your passport at all."

Her heart began to beat in loud, heavy thuds. Where *was* Gabriel? Was something wrong? Had there been an accident?

The official—she gave him the title in her mind, though with the two days' growth of beard he looked more like a desperado—only grunted and continued to paw through the pages of the passport. She suspected that he was part of the new class of desert tribesmen who had inexpertly taken over the bureaucracy since the advent of the new Islamic government. "He should be here with the paperwork," Alinor tried again.

"Peppervorrk?" He glanced up. So he was a bureaucrat at heart, in spite of the exterior, Alinor thought. The thought of more paper excited him. "Vut peppervorrk?"

"Our special licence from the Archbishop of Canterbury," Alinor said. Permission had been needed for a marriage to take place in the tiny Church of England in Shahriallah. She had filled out the form that requested the licence, and the licence had been sent directly to the priest here.

Have you previously been married? the form had asked. Alinor had thought a long time before answering that. *You were never really married, it was not a true ceremony....* In the end she had answered No. To do anything else would have opened up a complication there was no way of resolving.

"Miss Brooke!" said a harassed voice beside her. "I'm terribly sorry, we got our wires crossed, I'm afraid I thought you were arriving tomorrow."

She looked up to see an Englishman in a crushed beige linen suit, already talking with an air of apology to the official in bad Kaljuki. But at least he had a sheaf of papers, and she watched as the immigration man dropped her passport and reached for this.

"Gabe's been called away rather suddenly, I'm afraid," said the Embassy official in an aside as the other waved his hands importantly over the papers. "It was only when my secretary pointed out that the *wedding* is tomorrow that I understood that you must be arriving today. So sorry."

The Kaljuk's glance brushed the Englishman with a flick of astonished contempt that he should apologize to a woman, confirming what Alinor had suspected about his origins. But the fact of a man's presence, however unmanly he might be, had an effect on the official, and with a little more bureaucratic posing, he stamped her passport and handed it and all her papers to the Englishman. Safe in masculine custody now, Alinor stepped past his desk and officially entered Kaljukistan.

Chapter 2

The Embassy was a small but ugly concrete building in the socialist realist style, and the inside was exactly what the exterior promised.

"But there was really nothing else of suitable size and location available," Margaret, the new ambassador's wife, assured Alinor, leading the way into a hot, boxy bedroom on the second floor. "One of my husband's first tasks, when diplomatic relations were established, was to find quarters for the Embassy. He didn't enjoy that very much. Thank you, Abdul."

The Kaljuk porter put down Alinor's bags and departed while Alinor lifted the long garment bag she had carried herself and hung it on a hook on the back of the door.

"Is that your dress?" asked Margaret with real interest. "May I see?"

Alinor couldn't resist the other woman's appeal. She slipped the zipper all around the bag's long seam and carefully drew out the soft, heavy folds of the dress.

"How absolutely lovely, my dear!" breathed the ambassador's wife. "Where did you find such a beautiful thing?"

They stood gazing at the creation in shared feminine wonder. In a kind of determined statement of her origins, Alinor had decided to be traditional, and very, very Western. The dress was made of thick, lustrous raw silk the shade of antique ivory, deeply ruffled around a neckline that left the shoulders bare, smoothly tight over the bodice to a low-set waist that formed a V in front and back, and then flaring from the hips in yards of fabric over thick, thick tulle to the floor. It was the dress of a princess bride. A dream.

Looking at it now, and remembering her crazy determination that a wedding in a distant Eastern country should not rob her of a bride's legitimate trimmings, Alinor felt a little foolish. Coming all this way with such a dress, when there would be no family or friends, no one but Gabe, to appreciate it! What had possessed her? A simple silk suit would have done as well, and been more useful afterwards, too.

"My dear!" the ambassador's wife breathed again, and Alinor wondered if the cool upper-class tastes of the Englishwoman were offended by the extravagance of the creation. If so, Alinor would never know it. "And what are you wearing on your hair?"

That was the most outlandish extravagance of all. "I can't show you," Alinor said. "It's all packed on ice, and I'm not to open it up till tomorrow."

Margaret blinked. "Goodness! Well, I'm sure you'll look charming!" She was safe saying that, whatever might be "on ice," because the child would look charming wearing sackcloth and ashes, she told herself. She was a very appealing combination of fragility and strength, not unlike ivory herself, her slender, wandlike figure exhibiting the kind of grace one usually only met in Indian women, or sometimes the Japanese. And that thick, pale hair sweeping her shoulders, as smooth and liquid as water, must draw the men likes flies, especially in this part of the world. And what eyes! A deep grey-green... "Gabe's a lucky man," she said absently.

"I'm a lucky woman," Alinor said softly. And she was. Gabe was so gentle, so honourable, so...safe. He was the sort of man who would cherish a woman, keep her, and protect her...a man to take his marriage vows seriously. He had insisted on the traditional form of the marriage service, all those old vows. "Except of course that you won't say obey, my darling," he had written.

Fleetingly Alinor wondered whether she would be better off vowing to obey Gabe. If she were ever to be tempted to do something wild...to run away, perhaps...to throw off the thin veneer of her Western training and...what would there be to prevent her, to make her think twice? Perhaps, if Gabe ordered her, and she had sworn to obey him, that would have made her safe...

"Well, we must get down to the church for the rehearsal," Margaret was saying, her practical voice cutting across Alinor's imaginings. Alinor shook her head. What on earth had she been thinking? Run away? It must be the effect of the East on her mental processes, even here, deep inside one of the ugliest building shapes ever produced by Western thought.

"One of Bertie's assistants has volunteered to stand in for Gabe today," Margaret went on cheerfully, leading Alinor out of the room and back down the stairs. "I'm terribly sorry to rush you, I'm quite sure you need to rest, but I promised them we'd get in before Evensong."

The ancient little church was at the end of town, in what had been the foreign quarter sixty years ago, before the Soviet takeover. It had clearly been serving a non-religious purpose during some part of the sixty years, but restoration was now underway. The big leaded-glass window behind the altar had never been destroyed, but all along the walls the leaded glass in the tiny pointed stone windows was new. The new windows were almost garishly modern, with slashes of bright, primary-coloured glass very much at odds with the quiet, powerful beauty of the magnificent red rose at the cen-

tre of a white octagon bordered with blue which made up
the main window.

If she had any doubts about marrying Gabe, they disappeared as she gazed at that window. *Whatever happens here
must be right,* Alinor thought, in a quiet part of her mind
removed from ordinary cares and worries. She could trust
herself to that window, and she knew that she had done the
right thing in returning to this part of the world to marry
Gabe, frightening as the thought had sometimes seemed. It
would all be right for her. The window seemed to promise
it.

Allahu akbar, allahu akbar, allahu akbar... Alinor's
blood kicked suddenly to life, hearing the high, wailing un-
dulations of that call for the first time in over three years.
The mosque was some way away, but the mournful voice
was unmistakable. *God is great. Come to prayer. Asr,* the
afternoon prayer, had begun.

The late sun pouring in through the rose window told her
that the church faced southwest, towards Jerusalem, and
therefore... It was a second before Alinor realized that she
was unconsciously casting about to discover which way lay
Mecca. So great was the pull still, so deep had her training
gone, so strong her desire to find God through that other
path, that even along the distance of three years it reached
for her! She shivered in the heat of the little church, shook
her shoulders, and refocused as the young priest explained
what she must say tomorrow, and what Gabe would do.

It was all so different from last time. So comfortingly and
reassuringly different.

Alinor saw the mosque later, from her bedroom window,
its newly repainted green dome sparkling in the setting sun.
She dressed for dinner to the sound of the call for evening
prayer. It was to be a small engagement party for them, and
Alinor expected that Gabe would come to her room first, so
that their reunion would not have to take place amongst a
lot of strangers. She waited, sitting by the window looking

out as the sun set behind the mosque, until it was clear that to wait any longer would make her late, and then went down the hall to the ambassador's private apartments.

"Well, here's one of the guests of honour, anyway," was the way Bertram Willard introduced her, at the doorway of a large, beautifully furnished sitting room. There were a dozen or so guests—English and North American by the sound of it—who all looked up to greet her with friendly smiles. "I'm afraid we've just had a message, Miss Brooke, to say that Gabe can't return tonight. He'll meet you at the church in the morning."

"Oh!" She was more shocked than they knew. It wasn't like Gabe, somehow. Something in her moved quickly to hide and protect her real feelings, and her natural softness of manner stood her in good stead. Her step had faltered, but Alinor was so graceful that it had seemed more of a polite pause to listen. "Is everything all right?"

"The line was bad, I'm afraid. He did ask to speak to you before he rang off, but the connection died. However, he had time to promise he would meet you at the church in the morning."

"Terrible that Gabe had to be away at all," someone said ruefully, shaking her hand. "I'm amazed you couldn't have sent someone else, Bertie. What's it all about, anyway?"

"Not Embassy business he went on," Bertie said amicably. "Something of his own. He got a message of some kind and went straight off."

A drop of cool sweat slipped from her neck down the line of her back underneath Alinor's loose-fitting silk shirt. She glanced up at the ambassador's rather cherubic middle-aged face.

"Really?" she said calmly, although the information amazed her. While she had thought it was Embassy business that took him away, it was surprising enough. This was almost inexplicable. Gabe had told her he knew no one here, she was sure of it. She spoke for the ambassador's ears alone.

"I didn't know Gabe knew anyone here outside the expat community."

"It was a surprise to me, too, but he must know them quite well, because he was determined to go at once."

"How *awful* that Gabe can't be here today of all days!" exclaimed a woman a few years older than Alinor, as Bertram stopped by her to introduce Alinor. "Never mind, he'll be here tomorrow, and that's what counts, isn't it?"

There was no way back to the other conversation without making too much of a thing of it. But Alinor had a constant battle with restlessness throughout the meal and the evening that followed.

"I hear you're already fluent in Kaljuki," said an Australian, also recently arrived in the country. "How did you manage that?"

"I spent a year out here before the war," she explained. "While I was doing my university degree."

"Really? In Kaljukistan?"

She hesitated. She should have realized that there would be a lot of questions tonight, and hardened herself to the lies she should perhaps be telling. But she had expected to discuss it all with Gabe first, decide what to say...waiting for him, she had simply forgotten this part of it.

"I was attached to Shahriallah University," she temporized. The cold facts were true enough, though the implication was false. "The University of London set up an arrangement as soon as Kaljukistan declared independence, but it was only in effect for a couple of years before the war started. I was lucky enough to make it through that narrow window of opportunity."

Lucky, did she call it? Perhaps if she had done what the university expected she might have considered herself lucky now. As it was, it was amazing that a lie so hot didn't burn her tongue. Lucky? It had been the worst year of her life. If she out-lived Methuselah she would never forget it.

She had never attended a class at the University of Shahriallah, nor spent a day in Kaljukistan. But she had become fluent in the language. That much was true. Kaljuki wasn't all that different from Parvāni, not much more different than Scots from English or Canadian, in spite of the very different histories of the two countries over the past few hundred years.

"And what are you going to do while you and Gabe are here?" asked the man on her other side, to Alinor's relief. "Having the language will be a tremendous advantage, one that not many Embassy wives have." He smiled and corrected himself. "Spouses, I mean, of course."

"If it doesn't mean stepping on anyone's toes, which Gabe isn't sure of yet, I'd like to do something in women's education," Alinor said. "The literacy rate among tribal women wasn't high even under the Soviets, and now that they've switched alphabets it's really dropped."

"Tribal women! These days even the middle classes are floundering!"

"Are they?" She had heard as much from Gabe, but she meant to tread very warily.

"But I wonder how the Mullahs will feel about a foreigner teaching the women. They might suspect your motives."

"Yes, I won't do anything in a hurry," Alinor agreed calmly.

"The wrong thing could sabotage Gabe's career, I suppose."

"Well, I won't do that."

But she certainly would find something useful to do. She couldn't bear to be only an "Embassy wife," wrapped up in the expat community, not seeing beyond her own nose.

Fatigue hit her as she walked back to her bedroom an hour or two later. Then she realized that she had been up for nearly twenty-four hours, and that her body clock had lost several hours. The last few steps seemed impossible, and just for a moment she felt that she needed to sleep a week, that she couldn't possibly get married tomorrow.

Alinor heaved a sigh and turned the key in the lock. She

missed Gabe, that was all it was. She was tired, she had expected to rest against his chest, to be told that he had everything in hand. And instead he had gone on a mysterious mission that no one, including herself, understood the reasons for.

Just for a second she wondered if he would be there tomorrow. Perhaps he had changed his mind as the time approached, and couldn't face telling her? Then she shook her head. Of course he would be there. If there was a man you could count on, Gabe was that man. She had been mistaken before, but she knew she wasn't mistaken in Gabe. Even if he had changed his mind, he was far too honourable to take this way out.

The room was in darkness, and Alinor frowned as she felt blindly for the light switch. Surely she had left a light on when she went out? The one by the bed. The bulb must have blown. But where was the wall switch?

A draft of cool air reached her in the darkness, and she shivered. Certainly she had not left the window open. She was very sure of that. Margaret had warned her that at this time of year dirt and sand could get carried in on the strong winds. With a sudden premonition, a thrill of fear, Alinor found the wall switch at last and flicked the lights on.

A curtain blew gently in the breeze from the open balcony door, lightly caressing the silk of her wedding dress on the closet door, but there was no one in the room, and nothing had been disturbed.

It was several seconds before she saw the note pinned to the pillow.

Chapter 3

It was written in Parvāni, but she had known it would be before her trembling fingers touched it. A thin piece of white paper, like the one aboard the plane. She should have known then. She *had* known then.

Thou art my wife. I will not allow that thou marry another.

Alinor shivered and whirled as a gust of wind blew in the open balcony door. But there was no one there. Whoever had left the note must be long gone. Even with the official hostilities at an end, no Parvāni would want to be caught breaking and entering in Kaljukistan.

Thou art my wife. Zanam hasti. Only one man could have written such words, though she had once been assured that she had never been his wife. Even in her fear and trembling, she marvelled at the possibilities of ambiguity: the Parvāni word for "wife" was exactly the same as that for "woman." *Thou art my woman.*

Maybe he had thought so once, but ten months after that day when he had pretended to marry her in good faith, he had divorced her. She was no one's wife, no one's woman, except Gabe's.

A movement flashed abruptly on the edge of vision. Alinor lifted her head in a sudden chill, and met her own eyes in the mirror across the room. She expelled breath on a weak laugh. Her face was white with horror. She looked as if she had been punched in both eyes. Where was Gabe? she wondered wildly. What was the message that had so abruptly and unexpectedly taken him out of town in a country where he hadn't had time to make friends among the citizenry?

In the hot desert night air, she shivered. *I will not allow that thou marry another.* Suddenly she knew who had drawn Gabe out of the city, and why. And she knew as if it had been written in the note that he would not be at the church tomorrow. They had got to him. Prince Kavian of Parvān was holding Gabe prisoner, to prevent her marrying him.

"My dear! How lovely!" said the ambassador's wife.

Alinor sat at the mirror, fixing the wreath of delicate flowers into her long pale hair. The flowers, palest pink and a blue that tinted her grey eyes blue, had been shaped into a thick circlet that, resting against her pale forehead, gave her a medieval look. Her bouquet, lying on the bed, was equally thick and heavy, a mass of blooms that would reach almost to the floor against the heavy white silk of her dress.

For nothing. It was all for nothing. For a man who might even be dead. But she had to keep faith. He had said he would see her at the church, and she had to go through the pretence, because what else was there to do? There was no one here she could tell the truth to, or at least, not until it was a proven thing that Gabriel Horne had disappeared.

Alinor put the last hairpin in place, and stared at her reflection. The bruises hadn't disappeared from under her eyes overnight. Of course she had hardly slept, every creak of the floorboards, every breath of wind waking her to the electric certainty that Kavian had come for her, and the conviction that if he did, no one could stop him.

"You're nervous," said the ambassador's wife with a smile. "How charming. I didn't think brides were nervous anymore, but I assure you, my dear, Gabe is a wonderful man. We've known him for years, he's been almost a son to us. You know my husband has specially requested Gabe on his last three posts. He's definitely heading for ambassadorial status one day."

"Yes," breathed Alinor. She put a last touch of colour on her bloodless lips and stood up. The silk rustled over the tulle, exactly as she had meant it to, a distinctly Western rustle, nothing like the whisper of gold lamé over fine green silk that she had worn last time, at that wedding that had not been a wedding.

"You are beautiful!" said the ambassador's wife in a half-whisper. "Let me see you with the bouquet."

Obediently Alinor took up the heavy flowers, not yet beginning to wilt after their long confinement on ice. A cascade of pink and blue and white and green from her waist to the floor set off the rich silk to perfection.

"You're like a pagan fertility goddess!" said the ambassador's wife, in a flight of fancy that was completely unlike her. Those wide, slanting, grey-blue eyes. The thick, pale hair pouring over her bare shoulders, the rich silk, the flowers...the child was a masterpiece, thought the ambassador's wife. Botticelli should paint her.

She bent to pick up her own bouquet, a lovely spray of white that was meant to go with anything. She was going to be the matron of honour for this marvellous child with the haunted eyes. With eyes like that, if it were anyone but Gabe, the ambassador's wife reflected gravely, she'd have said, *don't do it. Think it over.* But Gabe loved her, and the woman Gabe loved would always be safe. Whatever this child had suddenly begun to fear—and the ambassador's wife knew the pair hadn't courted long, because Gabe had been posted so suddenly—was unfounded. She would find out soon enough that she had made the right choice.

"Have you seen Gabe this morning?" Alinor finally summoned the nerve to ask, but she couldn't look the ambassador's wife in the eye as she did it.

"Not before I came away, but Bertram will make sure he's at the church." She glanced at her watch. "They must be there by now. I told him we'd be setting out by eleven and that if he hadn't got Gabe away by then he was to come and let us know."

Alinor was on automatic pilot. Whether Gabe was or was not at the church, she had to go there, she had to go through the motions. To whom could she say, *I'm afraid Gabe's been kidnapped by a man to whom I once believed I was married?*

There was a limousine waiting for them outside in the sweep driveway. The sun was already hot with the intensity of a summer morning in a desert city, but the car was air-conditioned, and its coolness embraced her like a friend. Alinor sat in the back seat, her wonderful dress spreading around her in unconfinable abandon while the ambassador's wife insisted on taking one of the fold-down seats facing her.

"I refuse to crush that fabulous silk!" she said, when Alinor protested and tried to draw her skirts closer. "It's only a minute or two in any case."

Alinor never knew how long it was, she only knew that the church was there too quickly for her peace of mind, the fear building up in her so that she could scarcely breathe. If Kavian had kidnapped Gabe, everyone would think she had been left at the altar. She would have all that humiliation to go through before she could make herself understood. Would anyone believe her if she said that he'd been kidnapped by her ex-non-husband? "He divorced me by the *talaaq* but I later learned we'd never legally been married anyway"? How would she get through the awful explanations?

The little church looked so real in the sun, its windows glowing, its brickwork holding it firmly to the earth in a promise of stability. Alinor slipped out of the car into the bright heat and smiled as she saw the young priest waiting for her at the top of the stairs in his bright robes of office. Behind him stood Bertram Willard in grey tails, looking as wildly incongruous against the desert backdrop as Alinor herself. She flinched as she saw him. This was it. He could only be waiting to tell her the awful news. Gabe hadn't come back.

"Good morning," said the priest, as Alinor reached the top of the short flight. He smiled. "All ready?"

"Is Gabe here?" she whispered.

"Your fiancé is waiting for you at the altar," the priest assured her quietly, as if this last-minute fear of being stood up was the most natural thing in the world. The ambassador offered his arm, and Alinor shook her head at herself: Of course, Bertram would be giving her away. His being here was perfectly natural. She smiled and placed her trembling hand on the grey sleeve. Margaret meanwhile was taking pictures with a little camera she had produced from her bag.

The priest turned, pushed open the door, and then they were inside the cool air of the church vestibule, and there was music in her ears.

There were two men standing at the inner doors. At a signal from the priest the doors were pulled open, and the music changed to the wedding march. Alinor breathed deeply, sent up a short prayer, and followed the priest into the body of the church.

Gabe stood at the altar in front of the rose window, waiting for her, a handsome stranger with blue eyes darker than she remembered, and it was only then that she learned how much her fear of Kavian had overshadowed her wedding day. Without that fear, she might have had another—the fear of marrying a man whom she scarcely knew. For in this church of strangers, Gabe was the one face she knew, and surely the sight of him now should have calmed her.

But instead she was thinking, *My God, who is he? I'm marrying a stranger!*

Her heart beat in suffocating time to the music. She lifted her gaze from Gabe's warm smile and found the rose window behind his head. She remembered the promise of yesterday, that whisper to her heart that what happened to her in front of this window must and would be right; and this, at last, was what calmed her. She would trust the promise she had been given.

The church was small, the aisle short. In no time she was at Gabriel's side. "You're very beautiful," he whispered, his smile deep and strong...and an ugly, livid bruise discolouring the right side of his face from temple to chin.

"Gabe!" she whispered, suppressing her shock with effort.

He shook his head, still smiling, although it must hurt him to use those tortured muscles.

"Never mind," he whispered calmly, but there was something in his eyes that told her the truth. He had been captured and taken prisoner, and he had escaped. And the man who had captured him had been Kavian, Prince of Parvān.

The priest turned and faced them as he gravely opened his prayer book, but whether it had taken an hour or a second to make the movement Alinor could not have said. She was too shocked, and shock has its own time scale. She had suspected, but in her heart she had not believed her own suspicions. In her heart she had been telling herself that the idea was too outlandish, too melodramatic, too gothic to really happen. Why should Kavi want to prevent her marriage to another man after so long? That was what a part of her had been whispering to her inner ear. But now she knew that he had. And now a part of her was screaming that if Kavian wanted to prevent this marriage, he would not give up just because the bridegroom had foiled his first attempt.

"We have gathered together today," the priest began, in a surprisingly deep, resonant voice that, in spite of his youth, brought all the power of the words into the little church, "in the sight of God..."

The words were powerful, but she couldn't concentrate, could scarcely hear them. Her whole body was alive now with danger, adrenalin pumping into her system to fuel her urge to flee. That bruise on Gabe's face had electrified her, and now she knew that the only hope was to run, to run far beyond the reach of Kavian Durran.

What a fool she had been to allow herself to come back! What a filthy twist and trick of fate to have Gabe so suddenly assigned to the place she had hoped never to think of again, let alone come to live and be married! She should have insisted that Gabe turn down the assignment, wait for another in some other part of the world. She should…what would he do? How would he stop the wedding? Because she knew Kavian, and she knew that, once he had possessively decided to stop it, stop it he would. He would not be satisfied to wait till the ceremony was over and then kill Gabriel or force a divorce or declare the marriage invalid or herself a bigamist. He had said he would not allow her to marry and he would keep his word.

Of course. *If any man knows any just cause…* Kavi was probably familiar enough with the Western marriage service to know that that moment was coming. He would wait for that, and then he, or one of his men, would stand up and declare Alinor a married woman. She must prepare herself for that moment. She must marshall her arguments.

I was never married to him. The ceremony wasn't binding, though I didn't know it. According to Parvān law we were never married…and even if we were, he has recited the talaaq to me.

Her blood was noisy in her veins, her ears, so that nothing the priest said could get through. Where were they in the service? What was he saying? How much time did she have?

"…not to be entered into unadvisedly or lightly. And therefore, if anyone knows any reason why Gabriel and Alinor should not be joined in matrimony, let him speak now or forever hold his peace."

The quiet that followed was complete. She had never heard such silence before in her life. Her blood stopped roaring in her ears—she thought her heart, even, stopped beating as she waited for the denunciation.

"Now, Gabriel and Alinor…" The priest was going on,

and she let out her breath with an audible sigh. She couldn't believe it! She'd been working herself up for nothing! What a melodramatic fool she had been, with her wild imaginings! Of course he would not do anything so stupid! He didn't want her, never had wanted her or loved her. Why should he come now, after so many years, to disrupt her wedding?

It had been just a different form of bridal nerves, that was all. She was suffering from very natural nerves, marrying Gabe without having seen him for months, never having known him well...but Margaret was right. He was a good man. She was doing the right thing.

"...I charge you, if you know of any reason why you should not be married, that you confess it now..."

There was silence, while she reminded herself that she had nothing to confess. A woman who had been hoodwinked into believing herself married had no obligation to...and yet, now, at this moment, she wished that she *had* declared the quasi-marriage to her vicar back home. If the marriage had been legal, she was a divorced woman, and shouldn't she have declared that possibility on the special licence application form? Had she been right to suppress all mention...?

Why was the silence so long this time? Did he suspect, this eager young priest on his first mission? Why was the whole world waiting, or had her time scale shifted again?

Then she heard the rustle of astonishment and movement amongst the tiny congregation.

"Well, Alinor," demanded a voice behind her. "Do you confess that you cannot marry another while you are my wife? Or do you perjure yourself before God and man?"

Alinor whirled. He stood in the doorway, a figure swathed in desert robes, his hands on his rifle, in the spreadlegged possessive posture she knew so well. And since he was surrounded by half a dozen of his most trusted Companions, she could be in no doubt about what he meant to do. Kavian Mobad Dafauddin Durran, Hajji, Shahzade-ye Parvān, the Crown Prince of Parvān...had come to claim her.

* * *

Beside her, Gabe turned around without haste to face the intruders. The two men gazed at each other for a moment down the length of the aisle, and first Kavian and then Gabe inclined his head in greeting. It was the greeting of men whom circumstance alone had made enemies. The next moment there were two of Kavi's armed men at Gabe's side, holding him.

"You are a brave man, Mr. Horne," said Kavian softly, but the whole place was so silent now that a whisper would have carried weight. Gabe gazed levelly at him, as if for him the two soldiers who held him powerless did not exist. "You even deserve her. But she is already mine."

This bald statement of possession triggered something elemental inside her, and suddenly Alinor was shaking, not with fear, but with the deepest possible rage. "I am not yours!" she shouted, and the congregation turned to stare at her in awe, for her voice was deep and hoarse, like the cry of a wounded jungle animal. "I have never been yours and I will never be yours! Get out of here! Get out of this church!"

For answer Kavi thrust his rifle into the hands of his nearest Companion and strode down the aisle towards her. "Arguing never worked with you, woman. I will not argue again," he said, and with a speed that made the watchers gasp he reached out and wrapped his hand around her upper arm, pulling her to him.

She stumbled on the heavy hem of her dress and lost balance, and in the next moment she was swung up high in his arms and Kavian, protected now by the automatic rifles of his companions, backed towards the altar.

Everything stopped while that moment was recorded in time: the image of the white-robed prince, his skin tanned by the desert sun, his deep green eyes hard, his teeth bared in a smile of triumph and daring; in his arms a woman of pale, delicate beauty, a circlet of flowers on her brow, her ash-coloured hair tangled but flowing over the dark, strong fingers that held her, her white silk skirt and the flowers she held falling in a mingled swathe to the floor, her eyes icy with fury. Behind them, the rose window glowed with complementary colours of white, rose and blue. To the assembled, touched by wonder, they seemed a work of art.

Just for a moment they were frozen there, and imprinted forever on the memory of those who watched. "This woman," Kavian announced to them, "is Alinor Shahbanu of Parvān, and my wife. I take her by right. Let no man follow us."

Alinor found she was still clutching the massive bouquet of flowers she had so carefully brought from England with her, as if they were precious in spite of everything. Now she hurled them from her, not caring where they landed, and slapped the arrogant face above hers as hard as she could. "I am not your wife!" she screamed.

The blow only jerked his head so that his eyes stared directly into hers. "I warned you," he said. "You chose this." He turned then and headed past the altar, with an abrupt nod to his men, two of whom instantly came down the aisle after him, their rifles levelled on the astonished members of the congregation. Three others remained at the back of the church, blocking the exit. Kavian raised a foot and kicked the door to the vestry. It flew open. Two more soldiers were there, and beyond them, a door to the street was already open. A dozen powerful horses waited there, some with men already mounted. Without a pause Kavi strode through the doors, tossed her up on a black stallion whose saddlecloth was red and gold, and leapt up behind her.

Men were running to their mounts from the church. Kavi did not wait for them all, but pulled on the reins and kicked his horse into a gallop. Behind them gunshots and cries rang out as more men ran from the church and leapt on their horses.

The street was a straggling line of houses that marked the edge of the city. In the distance she could see mountains, the mountains of Parvān, and between these two images, desert. Miles of inhospitable desert. She knew that the desert was their destination.

Chapter 4

Behind them the congregation, careless of the danger, spilled out of the church, shouting, gaping, gesticulating. Sitting sidesaddle in front of Kavi, Alinor twisted to watch behind. She had wrestled wildly with him until he kicked the horse into action. But her courage failed at the thought of leaping from the back of a galloping horse to fall under the hooves of a dozen who followed.

A grey-suited figure carrying an automatic rifle ran out of the church, and she stifled a gasp. It was Gabe! How had he managed to overpower—but he had, for there was one horse to be seen left behind without a rider as the others galloped after them. The horse stirred restlessly, and Gabe caught its bridle just as it began to move off, and swung himself up into the saddle. He had the Kalashnikov, or whatever it was, in one hand, the reins in the other, and he was a powerful rider. She had never seen him ride before, but it was not admiration that drew her heart into her mouth. It was fear. One man against twelve or more!

He was not far behind the last of Kavi's men. Behind him,

now, an ancient battered Land Rover screamed into view from the front of the church, and her heart leapt with dread, for all Gabe's chance lay in the horsemen not knowing he was there. They were already at the end of the road, and galloped off into hard scrubland without breaking their stride. Gabe followed, and the Land Rover. The vehicle would be slower than the horses when they reached the real desert, and she saw no evidence that the men in it had guns. If only they could catch up with Kavi's horse before they reached the sand, she would jump down onto it. That was her best chance. If only Kavi's men did not turn to look behind!

But the sound of the motor was too loud. Two men, turning in their saddles, dropping the reins, raised their rifles. Even in such distress, she could not help feeling awe at such horsemanship. Something that had no doubt come down all the way from the ancient Parthians, with their trick of shooting arrows as they retreated. A skill that marked them as brothers to the Apache.

The sight of the Land Rover was not unexpected, but they shouted in surprise to see Gabe riding close behind. "Lord!" they called to Kavi. "The man follows with Sohrab's gun and horse!"

Kavian's gaze flicked down to meet Alinor's. "A brave man, your chosen," he observed. He called out something she did not understand, but even as he spoke two shots were fired. Alinor gasped, and only Kavi's arm prevented her from falling. But Gabe's progress was not checked. It was the Land Rover that stopped, registering a hit in one tire and the windscreen.

"We have disabled the vehicle, Lord! But the man comes on."

Another shot rang out, but not from Kavi's men. Gabe was closer than before. Not having the trick of riding only with his knees, he held the rifle pulled in against his side with his elbow and was shooting with one hand. "Gabe!" she cried, astonished admiration in her voice, and over her head her captor's face tightened into grimness.

The grey tailed formal suit should have looked ridiculous in such a setting, but in fact Gabe only looked determined, his masculinity dominating the elegance of the costume. He rode closer, while Kavi's men held their fire. "Let her go, Durran!" he called. He fired again. One of the Companions far to Kavi's right swore loudly and bent down over his horse's neck.

"His aim improves, Lord," the Companion called dryly. "That bullet had a kiss as sweet as a woman's. Shall we return fire?"

"Shoot the horse!" Kavi commanded, a second too late. Beside him a Companion had turned and fired once, and Alinor screamed. Now she would have leapt from the horse regardless of the danger under the hooves, but Kavi had guessed it. His arm tightened mercilessly around her, and she was powerless to do anything save watch.

Gabe jerked in the saddle. The gun hung motionless in the air for a split second, and then he was lifted backwards off the galloping horse and fell to the ground.

"Gabe!" she screamed. "*Gabe!*" He lay against the pale sandy earth, the gun just beyond his outflung arm, as they galloped away. The riderless horse came after them.

"He's killed him!" she shouted, punching at Kavian. She tried to grab the reins. "Damn you, stop! He's killed Gabe!" Kavi pulled her in flat against his chest, so that she was half-smothered against his thick robes, and her arms could only flail uselessly against his shoulders. His strength was enormous. She had forgotten what endurance and power he had. She was helpless.

"*Koshte?*" enquired Kavian of the Companion as they galloped. "Is he killed?"

"No, Lord, I took care to hit him in the shoulder."

"It is good that he lives," said Kavi. "He is a man who knows what it means, to live."

He felt her subside and loosened his murderous hold. Alinor could move again. She watched the occupants of the disabled Land Rover reach Gabe and bend over him, saw him raise a hand, but the rest was lost in the distance and the swirl of sand.

"I hate you!" she shouted. She had never been so filled with angry hatred in her life. Her blood sang with the violence of her feeling.

"Perhaps," he said. "But you are my wife."

He shifted his reins into one hand, his arm came up and he drew from his shoulders a wide strip of heavy cotton cloth as they galloped on. "Wrap yourself," he said.

She turned to look forward and gasped at the power of what she saw. They had left the last reaches of the city. A broad expanse of desert stretched from horizon to horizon on right and left, rippling in little grey-gold wavelets as far as the eye could see. Ahead was the mountain range she had seen from the aeroplane, overshadowed by great Shīr, the Lion. The Milk.

Only one thing was not as she remembered it. Just to their right as the horsemen plunged ahead without a pause was a large red-on-white sign proclaiming in three languages, DANGER. DO NOT ENTER. LANDMINES.

Behind them in the minarets of the city arose the plaintive cry of the midday call to prayer. Their pace did not slacken as they entered the desert.

The hours that followed were weary. The heat was relentless, the sun at its strongest as they approached mid-afternoon and the centre of the desert. Sand choked her eyes, her throat, her hair. She had wrapped her head, face and shoulders in the oblong of cotton Kavi had given her, against the sand and the ferocity of the sun's rays, and the thick silk and tulle of her wedding dress was adequate protection for her legs, but she had forgotten her arms. After an hour her forearms and hands were bright red under the broad ruffles of the elbow-length sleeves of her wedding dress, and she was parched with thirst.

Every nerve was stretched with fear of the landmines. At first she had dismissed the sign, although she knew that this

desert had seen terrible action during the war, had been almost as stupidly and wastefully contested as the fields of
France eighty years before. Then she saw a mine, lying in
the sand a dozen yards away, round, dark, unmistakably ma-
levolent. After that she watched the way ahead with restless,
eager eyes, though the chances of seeing a mine before you
triggered it were small. The desert sand was so accommo-
dating.

Two men rode ahead of them, and she could not decide
whether she would hate most to see one of their horses trig-
ger a mine, or feel Kavi's horse do so, or hear it happen to
one behind.

Perhaps he meant her to die. The horse thudded powerfully
along under them, and it seemed as though Kavi would never
tire, either. Her endurance was good, but it would not match
his in this climate. Perhaps he didn't intend that it should. If
he flung her down on the sand she would be dead in an hour,
with or without landmines. And when the birds and beasts
of prey were through with her, the desert would hide her
bones just as it hid the mines. The desert was a convenient
place for villains.

She was getting light-headed, and that was a danger signal.
"Kavi," she muttered. "I need water."

Āb lāzem dāram. She spoke in Parvāni, though she didn't
know it till she heard her own voice.

The horse's pace did not slacken. It was as though she had
not spoken. Alinor bit her lip. She would not ask again.
She'd rather die of thirst than beg this man for anything. She
had begged him once, long ago. She would never beg Kavian
Durran again if he kept her prisoner forever.

His left arm moved behind his body, and, feeling the
weight against her thighs, she looked down to see a battered
water canteen in her lap. Absently she saw that it had stained
the skirt of what had been her wedding dress. She noted it
entirely without emotion. That other life was already lost in
the mists. The only realities now were Kavi and the sun.

With a glance up at his face she took the canteen, lifted it and unscrewed the cap.

"Make it last," he ordered. Obediently she took only a couple of short swallows. She had no idea how long they would be in the desert. She passed the canteen to Kavi in a gesture that was familiar in spite of the passage of time, and he flicked her a look that told her he, too, remembered as he took it and drank.

He drank no more than she before passing the canteen back to her. Alinor screwed the lid on and then slung the strap over her head and shoulder.

He understood the gesture. "Life insurance?" he asked dryly. He knew how little she trusted him. How little reason she had to trust him.

She said, "Are there many landmines?"

"Of course," he said. "Kaljukistan has oil, and the free world has many landmine manufacturers greedy for the business of tyrants. We are better horsemen than the Kaljuks, who have forgotten their heritage under Soviet rule. Therefore they have carpeted the desert with their foul weapons."

She shivered. She had seen those who had had the misfortune to encounter landmines, and live. "How do you avoid them?" If he was telling the truth, it was extraordinary that they had come so far without encountering one.

"We have made two paths mine-free. The Kaljuks know it, but they do not know the landmarks by which one travels them. Thus we can travel over the desert that they have poisoned, while they cannot."

Now she noticed for the first time that they rode in peculiar formation, the Companions. They were strung out behind rather than abreast of the leader, the more usual pattern.

"How wide is your path?"

His teeth flashed. "Wide enough, but still not worth the risk. By the time you got back two miles the wind would have obliterated our tracks and then you would be marooned until I came to get you."

He'd always thought he could read her mind.

"Damn you!" Alinor said savagely. "Why are you doing

this? You haven't made any attempt to contact me for three years. What do you care who I marry?''

''This is not true, Alinor. Why do you lie to me, who know the truth?''

Goaded, she said, ''Once! One message!''

''Did you expect me to repeat myself? I had said what there was to say. You did not reply.''

'''No answer is itself an answer,''' she snapped. It was something he had once said to her, though she had forgotten the circumstances. Anyway, why was she complaining about not having got any word from him? She had been glad of it. She hadn't wanted to hear from Kavian Durran, or see him, ever again.

''Your *no answer that was itself an answer* was a challenge, was it not?'' Kavian said. ''I accepted the challenge. This is my answer.''

She exploded with rage. ''Abduction across a mined desert! That's your answer to a woman who made a mistake marrying you and wants out? I thought you prided yourself on being civilized!''

''You must not confuse 'civilized' with 'Westernized,''' Kavi replied gently, with a calm arrogance that infuriated her the more. ''The two are not interchangeable.''

''Well, if this is the Eastern brand of civilized behaviour I'll take Western barbarism any day!'' she snapped.

''In truth, your actions have been barbarous,'' he agreed. ''But you will learn how to act in a more civilized manner with time. Such things rub off.''

''*My* actions have been barbarous?'' she raged.

Then she told herself he was goading her, deliberately setting fire to her temper in the way only he could do. He hoped she would shout and strike out and prove his point for him. Alinor took a deep breath and turned and looked out across the desert towards the protective menace of the mountain called Shīr.

''You are wise,'' he said mockingly. ''If I lost my temper with you I might stray off the path into the minefields. But

I am sure you will still be angry enough to tell me your thoughts when we reach camp.''

Their first camp was a small waterhole surrounded by a few bits of scrub, where the horses and humans drank and Alinor dipped her arms to cool her burning skin. Like the men, she splashed water on her face and neck. The combination of desert sweat and sand had caused her mascara to gum uncomfortably, and she supposed, as she scooped water into her eyes, that she was giving herself black-ringed eyes. Good. She wanted to look ugly. Let the men see what a fool their prince was, chasing after a woman not worth the price of a single camel.

She took the circlet of flowers off her head, amazed it could still be there. They had not so much wilted as dried in the heat. She pressed a tiny pink bud to her lips and thought of all that it represented. Had the man who shot Gabe told the truth or lied when he said the wound was not fatal? Even if he had aimed for the shoulder, how could he be sure of his aim's being true?

He had still been alive after he fell, she reminded herself. He had moved his hand.

She set the small wreath of flowers in a tiny curl of the spring as an offering and sent up a prayer. Anāhita, the ancient Parvān Goddess of the Waters, had a history of answering the prayers of abducted women.

The men began to move towards their horses again before she remembered to fill the canteen. She looped the belt securely across her chest and then arranged the white sheet of cotton over her head and upper body so that the canteen was hidden against her side, stood up and made a business of brushing down her skirts. The water had refreshed her, had made her hope. If Gabe could steal Sohrab's horse, so could she.

Alinor walked awkwardly. Her ride had not been comfortable, she had been sitting sideways for hours on a ridge of the saddle, and now she limped a little from the ache in her buttock and thigh.

The riderless horse that Gabe had ridden was there, looking fresher than all the others. Was Kavi right—could one not be sure the marks of their passing would remain in the sand to mark the safe path? It was still clearly visible as far as the eye could see, a long, almost straight line of hoofprints that disturbed the neat ripples of glinting sand.

She did not let herself look long at that freedom road. A quick glance, and then away. She limped more than before, wincing as she approached Kavi beside the black horse.

"What is it?" he asked.

"I've hurt myself sitting sideways," she said, with blame in her voice. "Did you imagine I had a comfortable seat, or is it a deliberate part of the punishment?"

"Will it be more comfortable for you to ride behind me?" She had done that before, long ago, and found it comfortable enough. Then she had been exhilarated, thrilling to the strength of the body that pressed against her, the power that she enclosed in the circle of her arms, so like that of the horse under her thighs. But his eyes told her that was a memory he courted no more than she did.

"It would be more comfortable for me to ride my own horse," Alinor snapped. "But I don't fool myself my comfort is your first concern."

He looked assessingly at her, one strong black eyebrow raised. "This waterhole was very heavily mined," he observed. "Seven men were crippled or died while we cleared it. We did not clear very far beyond the immediate circle of what was necessity, because we could not afford more casualties."

She stared insolently at him, pretending utter ignorance. "What does that mean?"

"If I let you ride Sohrab's horse, which I well understand your reasons for wishing to do, Alinor, you would be so much a fool to try to escape *here* that it is an insult to your intelligence to suggest that you would try it. But I want to hear you say that you understand what I am telling you. Sohrab's horse is strong, and does not know you. It will mean certain maiming or death for someone if you try to flee. How much of a fool are you, Alinor?''

She stripped off her tights and shoes and put on the pair of cloth boots Kavi gave her, tying them below her knees, preparing to mount Sohrab's horse, while the men waited. Then Kavi lifted her and flung her up astride. The saddle was a thick blanket with stirrups, more comfortable on her bare thighs than leather would have been. The skirt of her wedding dress covered her knees and flowed out over the horse's rump, not unlike Kavi's own riding robes. In spite of everything she felt excited to be riding over the desert again, towards the mountains. She had always enjoyed the freedom of the desert, except on that last, dreadful journey, where hell had been equally before and behind, where she could see no future whether she stayed or went....

She rode beside Kavi, spurring her mount into a slow canter as he did, loving the feel of the horse, the dryness of the air, even the scorching sun. Suddenly she felt strong, as if she could ride forever. She glanced back over her shoulder. Beyond the line of men who followed in twos and threes, there was the path. Kavi's horse was tired. It had carried double weight for hours. Sohrab's horse was fresh, and she was light. She could almost certainly outstrip him. But she did not dare to gallop off into the desert to avoid the men, and if she tried to ride through the middle of them they would prevent her.

If he were lying about the landmines...

"Why are there no signs?" she asked suddenly.

Kavi looked over at her.

"No warning signs about landmines," she elaborated. "There aren't any here."

He laughed, but not with mirth. "Anyone who has got to this place either knows all about the landmines and the pathway, or they are operating under divine guidance. Either

way, they do not need painted signs." He looked sternly at
her. "If you ignore my warnings, it will not go well with
you, my wife. If you lose a leg, a hand, or your face, your
punishment will be immediate and permanent. If I lose a
man, or even a horse, your punishment will be delayed and
temporary. But you will be punished, whatever happens. You
will not escape."

Suddenly she knew that he was telling her the truth about
the landmines. It was in the tone of his voice as he spoke of
losing a man. She knew that he was sick of seeing his father's people torn apart in this way, that he would never get
used to such wantonness of destruction and loss.

Now, for the first time, she looked into his face and saw
how the past three and a half years had changed him. War
had taken its toll of the youth and vitality she remembered.

"Were you—in the fighting?" she asked.

"Every citizen of Parvān was in the fighting," he said
coldly. It cut her off, just as he had used to do in the old
days. *I'm your wife!* she had cried then. *Why won't you talk
to me?* But the words had never affected him. He was a man
who bore trouble and tragedy alone. She had scarcely been
aware war was threatening when the first casualties arrived
in the hospitals.

I didn't ask about every citizen of Parvān, she might have
said now. *I asked about you.* But what was the point? She
was no longer interested in the impossible task of establish-
ing lines of communication with Kavian Durran. She was
engaged to marry Gabriel Horne, and that was what she was
going to do. If he was still alive.

"I want to ride," she said impatiently to Kavi, shrugging
off the weight of the old irritation, the frustrated failure that
her attempt at marriage had been. "What's the landmark
from here?"

"I will ride with you," was all he said, and spurred the
black horse into a gallop. There was a wind now, coming
off the mountains, cooling and invigorating. As her horse
reached its stride, her dress lifted from her knees and

streamed out behind, leaving her thighs naked to the fierce caress of sun and wind. The heavy cotton wrapping her head remained obediently in place. Suddenly her anger melted. She felt like one of them, like a desert warrior, riding for victory and freedom across the sands. They rode side by side, knee to knee, Kavi and Alinor, and she remembered with something like pain that it was in such moments as this that she had felt closest to him. Not arguing in the bedroom, but riding over the plains together.

The closeness had been a lie. Kavian was close to no one. Nevertheless, for the first time in years, the memory of the loss hurt.

In another hour they reached the mountains, and began the climb up through the rugged rocks towards the green of the valleys. The sun would be setting soon, and she knew they were still hours from the capital. There were no roads through the mountains on this side, only the donkey tracks that had been there for generations. She was tired, though she would rather die than say that she was incapable of more.

They reached the top of a valley where it was already night, and dismounted to make the descent. In daylight one might ride down the slope, but not with the sun already below the ridge. "We'll reach camp soon," Kavi said, as they paused. She saw trees far below, and smelled the unmistakable scent of water and green growth.

This was the Parvān she remembered best, the Parvān of the high valleys. Not the ferocious land of the lion, but the generous land of flowing milk.

Chapter 5

They had met at university. Alinor's father was a career diplomat, and from the age of six Alinor, born and raised in Canada, had travelled and lived in many countries of the world. So it wasn't unnatural that she should dream of a career in diplomacy for herself. Her father had advised her to choose an area and make herself an expert on it, as the best way of getting work with a Department of External Affairs being cut to the bone.

She decided on Central Asia. Her father had had two prolonged tours of duty there while she was growing up, and she felt as much at home in that part of the world as anywhere on the globe. Political events were moving fast there, and one thing seemed certain: expertise would be needed. Kaljuki was a useful language, being closely related to several in the area, and Kaljukistan was one of the new independent republics. She chose Kaljukistan and Kaljuki as her special field of study.

Her father had been temporarily posted to London, although the posting would probably be confirmed, and he and

the family be there for at least four years. Rather than go all
the way to Canada away from them, Alinor applied to uni-
versities in England. But almost immediately after the school
year had started, her father was transferred to a post in the
United States. It seemed merely an ironic twist at the time,
no more than was to be expected from the Department of
External Affairs. Later she thought of it as a dreadful coin-
cidence: if they had had advance warning of the move, she
would have gone to university in Toronto. And none of what
followed would ever have happened.

She was lucky to get a room in a university residence for
overseas students halfway through first term when someone
abruptly left. Alinor moved before her family did, and it was
a foretaste of what was to come: she knew she would miss
them dreadfully. Her first term was divided between her studies and helping her mother organize the family move, so that
she felt she hardly knew she was at university.

In late November, they left. And Alinor discovered that
while going away from your family might be considered an
adventure, having your family go away from you was nothing but heartbreak. She was very unhappy. She did not particularly like England, or feel at home there. She was suddenly, for the first time, aware that to travel so extensively
in childhood, living in half a dozen different cultures, had
cut her off from feeling any connection to her own. What
was her culture? Who were her people? Where was her
home? She had links with half a dozen cultures, but she had
none to yearn for.

The winter rains depressed her. And she hated the poky
shared room and the bad food at Gateau Hall for Overseas
Students, which everybody called the Ghetto.

In her alienation it was a huge relief to make friends with
Lana Brooks, an American student from her history class for
whom she felt a real affinity. Lana, a beautiful, pearly-
skinned redhead, was bright, laughing and sure of herself, all
the things that Alinor just then was not. Lana had come to

London by choice, to get away from a too-protective family and to see something of the world. She had never before been out of the U.S.A., and this was her great foreign adventure. Alinor liked her the first time they met, and Lana's vitality and optimism were just what she needed to help her break out of the mild depression that had settled around her.

There was another student she noticed, too, but not with any feeling of instant affinity. She noticed him because he was the kind of man everybody noticed, but she didn't like him.

Kavian Durran was a postgraduate student from Parvān. Although the School of Asian and Eastern Studies was full of students from abroad, he was one of only three Parvānis there. His area of study was Kaljukistan also, though as an undergraduate, Alinor had otherwise nothing in common with him. He spoke very good English, but Parvāni was his native language.

Kavian Durran only ever got angry when he heard someone say that Parvāni was a dialect of Kaljuki. He considered the Kaljuki dialect, which he also spoke fluently, a crude deviant language, mispronounced and corrupted by the Turkic peoples who had swept across Asia with Genghis Khan, conquering everywhere, and destroying, en route, the tiny mountain kingdom of Parvān.

Parvān had been an enlightened monarchy when Europe was still being overrun by the Visigoths. So said Kavian Durran, whose name, if you had sense, was pronounced in the Parvāni, not the Kaljuki accent: *Kah*-vi-yan Durr-*ahn*.

He neither confirmed nor denied the rumour making the rounds, that he was Crown Prince of Parvān, and no one knew whether to believe it or not. Parvān was a small, inaccessible country that had always discouraged tourism, and not much was known about it. It had been virtually surrounded by the Soviet Union for decades, its only non-Soviet border sealed by inhospitable mountains. The Kaljuks at the university, newly released to study in the West, all said that the place was full of goat-herders living in the Middle Ages, and that was why history had passed it by: it could hardly be called a sovereign state. Parvān had been a "province" of Kaljukistan, they said, for centuries before the Soviet revolution in 1935. It had only been left alone since then because it was valueless and inaccessible. And in those decades since, little Parvān had got ideas above itself. The idea of a hereditary "Crown Prince" of Parvān was laughable. Now that Kaljukistan itself was free of Soviet rule, they would soon bring Parvān back into line.

It was difficult to know which story to believe. Whoever he was, Kavian Durran certainly *looked* like a Crown Prince—tall, lithe, and fiercely handsome, with the blackest of black hair, the greenest of piercing eyes, a thickly curling beard that gave him the air of being from another era, and a central massif of a nose that was by itself more arrogant than anything Alinor had ever met with. There was always a buzz of awareness among the women present whenever he entered the university cafeteria or common room or library.

Alinor felt the buzz in her own system, but it was not the buzz of attraction. If anything, he antagonized her, even at a distance. She hadn't exchanged two words with him, but there was something about him that she knew she didn't like. He was never rude to anyone, but he strode around the place as if he owned the university and half the city as well. Once, in an argument with a Kaljuk, he had delivered a retort that had stopped everything: "Your father bent his neck to the Soviet yoke. Mine did not. It has poisoned your independence of thought, and your manhood."

It left everyone without a thing to say. He didn't seem to understand that the college was a hotbed of left-wing intellectualism, or if he did, he didn't care. He tore through conventional thinking and ideas as he strode through the corridors of the school: with a high-handed air of having the right.

He had a recognizable group of followers amongst the students. Whether he sat in the students' common room or the cafeteria, or outside on the steps, half a dozen or a dozen people would always collect around him. From his two fellow Parvānis this was perhaps natural, but it was a mystery what the others got out of it. It was not that he held forth to them, or even acted as if he thought himself their leader. Often he sat in silence while discussion raged around him. And yet he unmistakably *was* their leader. When he got up to leave, the group lost its centre. Discussion would fade away, people would begin to read, or smoke, or simply drift off.

It irritated Alinor to see that these people often sat actually, as well as metaphorically, at his feet. It was not consciously done—there was a chronic shortage of chairs in the common room and students quite often flung themselves down on the floor beside seated friends—and yet there was a difference between those students and the ones who sat on the floor around Kavian Durran. It wasn't long before she pinpointed this difference: it came from Kavian himself. There was something in his air that seemed to indicate that it was natural for his followers to sit below him. It was as though he was used to a throne, too used to it to notice.

He began to be her pet hate. She only rarely attended a seminar where he was present—he was working on graduate research and she was a mere undergraduate—but she saw him often enough, with his loyal little clique in attendance. She saw, too, how a gesture from one autocratic hand could shut up someone in full flow, how a raised eyebrow could make another voice his thoughts.

"He's got them all hypnotized," she would say irritably, watching from across the room. "He'll be declaring himself the Messiah next!"

"He really gets your goat, doesn't he?" Lana said at last. Lana had quickly become a close friend.

"You have to admit he looks dangerous!" Alinor said.

"Does he?" Lana turned and looked at the man, willing to see what Alinor saw in him. "Dangerous to whom?"

"Anyone who gets involved with him." Alinor was gazing across the room to where Kavian Durran was listening to one of the members of his court, his green eyes fixed on the boy's face. "Look at that kid who's talking, he's hypnotized! He's mesmerized them all, you can see that by looking! Next he'll be ordering them to commit group suicide or something."

Lana had no trouble sorting out the different *he*'s in this diatribe, and she was laughing before it was over. "You're jealous!" she accused merrily.

It stopped Alinor like a cold hand on the back of her neck. "Jealous of what?" she demanded breathlessly.

"I'm not sure. Maybe you want a court of your own. Or maybe you want to be part of his. Maybe you wish Kavian would look at *you* like that."

And just then, he did. Perhaps he was only drawn by their fixed concentration, and yet she had the curious conviction, as that deep green gaze unerringly found hers across the room, that he looked at her as a matter of pre-determined choice, and not because her gaze had drawn his.

It was quick, a count of three and then he turned his head away, but Alinor was shaking. It was as if in those few seconds he had commanded her to come to him.

What was worse was her inner desire to obey.

She became frightened. There *were* people who had uncanny powers of mind that gave them control over others. That wasn't a fantasy. And one thing you could be sure of was that once you submitted your will to such people, you had no control anymore. That look had told her how vulnerable she would be to Kavian Durran's will, and she reminded herself constantly after that how dangerous it might be to put herself within range again.

"Are you happy where you are?" Lana said to her one day as the two women sauntered along Tottenham Court Road towards a sandwich bar, in search of lunch. "Where you're living, I mean?"

"Happy? In the *Ghetto?*" Alinor laughed. Unlike some of the other residences, the Ghetto had a reputation for noise and loud parties and a less than total devotion to studies.

Most overseas students, at university on minimal grants and determined to succeed, worked hard. But not those who collected at the Ghetto. They didn't give a damn about daddy's money or the future.

"I've got a spare bedroom in my flat," Lana said now. "I'm a bit lonely there, on my own. Would you be interested in moving in?"

"I'd love it," Alinor exclaimed at once. "But I'm on a pretty tight budget. How much is the rent?"

"Could you afford sixty pounds a week?" Lana asked anxiously.

"You've got a two-bedroom place for one-twenty a week? Wow!" Alinor said. "Has it got cockroaches? Does it leak? Never mind, I don't care if it has rats! I'll take it!"

"Oh, great! Let's move you in this afternoon!"

At that, Alinor shook her head. "I've got to give two weeks' notice at the Ghetto."

"I won't charge you for the two weeks. It would take me that long to find someone else anyway, and I'd rather have you than anyone else, so what's the point in waiting? Come on, let's do it!"

After classes that afternoon the two women went to pack up Alinor's things and then stuffed them into the back of a black cab and Lana gave her address. And that was the very first inkling Alinor had that things were not quite usual about her friend Lana.

"Regent's Park?" She repeated the name faintly. "You have a two-bedroom flat in Regent's Park for one hundred and twenty per week? Don't you mean per day?"

But Lana only smiled and shook her head. Alinor pressed her, but she would say nothing. A few minutes later the taxi drew up in front of the massive, pillared, cream-coloured sweep of the famous Nash terraces, an address of fabulous wealth and connections. Alinor looked at her friend in amazement. Lana's face was alight with a kind of conspiratorial glee as she helped the driver unload Alinor's things. And then it dawned on Alinor: her friend had somehow happened onto one of those impossible strokes of luck that did sometimes happen in London. She was illegally subletting some flat that had been ridiculously rent-controlled for the past thirty or forty years and hadn't been repaired or redecorated since the war, but would still be considered the find of a lifetime.

The communal areas, of course, breathed wealth. Alinor was pretty used to luxurious ambassadorial homes, but this was really the top of the line. The beautifully designed buildings were two centuries old, and perfectly, lovingly restored. The uniformed porter called Lana by name and helped them load all the cases into the wrought-iron lift, and a minute later she was unlocking a wide door and ushering Alinor inside.

Well, it was no forty-year-old sublet. It had been re-done yesterday. Huge rooms, wonderful, sweeping windows with views over the Park, unbelievable carpets, floors and furniture, and a kitchen from the future. And best of all, complete and utter silence. Alinor began to laugh.

"Lana," she said, "what on earth—!"

"It's ridiculous, isn't it?" Lana agreed, giggling. "I told Dad it was ridiculous, but he thinks I'll be safe here." And then the two girls burst into uncontrollable laughter, as if they had broken the bank at Monte Carlo.

When they had calmed down, Lana said, "Look, I want to tell you the truth, but I have to swear you to secrecy. Do you mind?" And then she confessed that she was the daughter of Jonathan Holding, the computer multi-millionaire. She had taken her mother's name to hide behind, because her father was worried about kidnap attempts if people knew who she was.

"We haven't always been rich. I grew up in Silicon Valley in a totally ordinary house, and we never saw Dad, he was working so hard. And then one day—you know—" Lana looked at the gilt mouldings and the rich carpets around her and shrugged. "This."

The secret drew them even closer together, and they became each other's best friend. Alinor's loneliness and longing for her family, her sense of perpetually not belonging that a lifetime of movement among different countries induced, eased. She was by birth a North American, like Lana. That open-hearted self-confidence, the heritage of the citizens of young countries, was by rights her own heritage. Not that Alinor put it in quite those terms to herself.

Alinor found she felt the pull even when she saw Kavian Durran's head in a crowd, for he was tall enough to be visible even in a packed room. She began to feel threatened, even though he never looked at her again in that same way. She became careful of letting herself look at him, in case her gaze should draw his. She would find an excuse to leave the common room when he arrived. If he was in the library's Central Asia room when she went in to work, she would find a desk elsewhere, though it wasted time to be constantly going back and forth with the books she needed. In the cafeteria she generally led her friends to a table at a distance from Kavian Durran's.

One day, standing in a cafeteria line chatting to Lana, Alinor turned to discover that Kavian Durran had come in with half a dozen of his "disciples," as Alinor now sarcastically called them, and was standing right behind her.

He glanced at her only briefly, but she felt the embrace of his aura over her whole body, felt the inner conviction that if he now ordered her to do something—anything!—she would be powerless to refuse. She began to shiver.

"You've gone white, Alinor!" Lana said, in sudden alarm. "What's the matter? Bend down, quick! Get your head down!"

Alinor waved a hand. "No, it's all right, I'm not going to faint or anything. I just—" She pressed her hands against her eyes in something like panic. What was wrong with her? Why was she thinking such crazy thoughts?

And yet, even then, with her eyes pressed shut, she could feel Kavian Durran's presence.

"I think she's cold," she heard a voice say calmly. Then she was enveloped in warmth. She opened her eyes to discover that Kavian Durran had taken off his thick black jacket and placed it over her shoulders, and was calmly fitting the zipper together.

In another second, with a little *bzzzp!* she was Kavian Durran's prisoner.

Her arms were folded against her chest, and he closed the zipper to her neck. She felt cocooned and helpless, like a child, warm and cherished, like a child. In that moment, she suddenly almost felt that she loved Kavian Durran. What a fool she had been to be afraid of him. Of course she could trust him. Anyone could.

The green eyes were watching her, friendly but impassive. He had taken away his hands from the collar of the jacket and stood with them held loosely at his sides.

"You've stopped shivering," he said, and smiled the most seductive smile in the world.

The panic set in again. She could feel how she was being drawn to him. Was this what he did to people, was this the beginning of that hypnotic effect?

She looked at him, unblinking, feeling it impossible to smile, though she should have, to cover her panic. "Thank you," she said. She swallowed. "I'm fine now. You can have your jacket back."

"Why don't you keep it?" he said. His voice was deep and attractive, and his manner an unconscious *noblesse oblige.* He was like the king in some fairy tale she had read, giving his cloak to a beggar. "You can return it to me another time."

"No," said Alinor. "I can't move. Please unzip me." If she sounded panicked or angry she didn't care. She wanted out of this jacket, she didn't want anything of his in her possession, making her seek him out to give it back.

He nodded lightly, but there was a look in his green eyes that was not light. His fingers brushed her chin as he found the zipper's tab again, and then she was turning and slipping the jacket from her shoulders.

"Next, please!" said the woman behind the hot food counter. The line-up had moved forward, and as Alinor gave her order, Kavian Durran turned back to his friends and the world was normal again.

Much later, she remembered that moment of perfection in his presence, that feeling that she loved him. After that she avoided him with something like desperation. She was frightened of what power he might have over her, if she let him. Now she absolutely left the room if he entered it. Or she put pillars between where he sat and herself.

It wasn't easy. There were few places for students to congregate in the college building, and now, perversely, it seemed that wherever she went, Kavian Durran was either there already, or would turn up. In the cafeteria she would suddenly find him at the table immediately behind hers. In the common room, tucked in a corner behind a pillar, for sure someone immediately opposite her would call and wave, and Kavian Durran would come over to talk to them. If she sat on the steps outside the main doors, he would be there in front of her, blocking out the sun as he talked to her neighbour.

One day in early spring, sitting by herself under a tree on the university lawn, she almost screamed when Kavian Durran dropped down at her feet from a branch above.

"*Beh Khoda tokel,*" he said softly, dusting his hands as he looked down at her. *Trust in God.* It was the traditional Parvāni greeting, short for *May you trust in God,* and she automatically responded, "*Beh Khoda.*"

He was wearing an ordinary tan leather bomber jacket and black jeans and boots, and yet somehow he still managed to look exotically attractive, like a sixteenth-century Venetian pirate in modern dress. His black hair was so thick, his eyes just faintly slanted under thick, level eyebrows, his mouth so strongly defined behind the free-flowing black beard, and that nose...

"What were you doing up the tree?" Alinor asked, before she could stop herself.

He shrugged. "Trying to feel at home."

At first she didn't follow his meaning.

"We don't have such big cities in Parvān. It is hard to be always surrounded by London."

To her mingled dismay and delight—for he was a man with powerful charisma, and whatever her brain told her, her *self* thrilled to his nearness—he flung himself down by her, stretched out and plucked a blade of grass. Putting it in his mouth, he gnawed on it thoughtfully, his eyes screwed up as he stared into the distance at nothing.

"Cities are an evolutionary task for humanity," he observed. "Suddenly, in one century we have to learn to live with millions of other people in a confined space."

She frowned. "London's been a city for a lot longer than a hundred years."

"But what did we mean by *city* a hundred years ago? In eighteen hundred this place where we sit now was a farmer's field. The edge of London was just over there."

He pointed a lazy, graceful hand to indicate an area that was a street or so distant from where they sat. Alinor sat up. "Really?" The college was in the very heart of London. The city now stretched for twenty or thirty miles in any direction from where she sat.

"There are records and diaries that mention this place in the nineteenth century as being countryside. Not far away there were summer cottages for the rich. So you see it is no surprise if as a species we have not adapted yet to our new environment."

"Or even as individuals." She smiled. It was the first time she had smiled at Kavian Durran, but she didn't think of that then. "How big are the cities of Parvān?"

"Not big. Shahr-i Bozorg has no more than three hundred and fifty thousand people. It is our capital."

In the road there was a sudden cacophony of horns as several drivers simultaneously objected to the presence of others on the road. Unconsciously Alinor sighed. London was a very exciting place to be, but...

"I've never been there." Her parents had not taken her with them on the trip they had once made there. "Is it nice?"

"Very beautiful. You will come and visit one day."

It was just in the way of conversation, but he was closer than he knew to the facts. She would spend the next academic year as required abroad in the university in Kaljukistan. If she was allowed, she would certainly visit Parvān.

"You are studying Kaljukistan," he observed after a moment. He turned and focused on her. So he did know. She shivered as her fear of him abruptly returned. She wanted to deny it, as if she superstitiously felt that to give this man any piece of information about herself was to give him power over her. She stared at him unblinking for a moment while he looked at her. If it was a contest of wills, she discovered, he won. She lacked the strength to refuse to confirm his statement, and anyway, of course he knew. Finally she nodded.

He nodded, too, and played with the strand of grass in his mouth. "Why?"

Alinor babbled something about hoping to find work in the Embassy there, or with a trade association. Again he nodded, taking the information in, then looked into the distance.

"They want war with my country," he observed.

She was shocked. There was talk, of course; but he spoke with a curious emphasis that made it seem immediate, brought it home to her. If there *was* a war, her career would probably go on hold for as long as it lasted. Her grey eyes darkened as she watched him.

"Are they going to get what they want?"

"Those who want war have one way to get what they want. If they attempt to invade the sovereign territory of Parvān they will get what they want. They will be at war. But they will not win such a war." He paused. "It is foolish to begin a fight unless one is certain of winning," said Kavian. Then he looked at her, and it was as if the words had special meaning between them.

"I don't know what you think you're talking about," she said rudely.

He looked at her with an eyebrow raised, and now she felt that his initial easy manner had been a mask, and that he had dropped it. In the dark, intent eyes now was the real man. "Why are you afraid of me?"

She'd have denied it under torture. "I'm not afraid of you!" Then she had to cough to clear the frog in her throat.

"What, then?"

She felt she would lose any argument, that he would tie her in knots. She parried, knowing it was feeble, "What do you mean?" The only hope was to get away, but his long body was so easy and relaxed she would look a fool if she suddenly jumped up and ran.

"Even now, you are nervous of me. If it is not fear, what is it?"

"It's not anything at all! Why should I have any feelings for you? I don't even know you!"

He held out his hand, and after a moment, feeling compelled, she put her own in it. "I am Kavian Durran," he said, shaking her hand briefly. "Now you know who I am."

Dark, lithe and powerful, with those deep green eyes, he had always reminded her of a panther. But she could not have said why the simple words seemed so threatening, so loaded with dangerous intent. She tore her hand out of his light hold and scrambled to her feet.

"Now I know you," she agreed flatly. "But I still have no interest in you whatsoever, and never will have." She dragged the strap of her heavy book bag over her shoulder and walked away.

He made no answer and no move, and when she turned and looked back at him from the steps of the college, he was still there, lazily chewing the blade of grass, his eyes on her. At a distance, his resemblance to the easy grace of a big cat was even stronger.

She shivered with the superstitious dread of one who has tempted the gods. Her heart began to beat harder as the conviction stole over her that, intrigued by her behaviour, the panther had begun to hunt her.

Chapter 6

After that she could not avoid him. She thought he took delight in tormenting her. In the library, he sat beside or opposite her. He showed up at lectures that were too far beneath his academic level to interest him, lectures he must know she'd be attending. If she arrived early, Kavian Durran would come in and sit beside her. If she arrived late, the only seat available would be the one beside him. And somehow he could always manage to get her into conversation, however brief. He had a fascination, there was no doubt about that. A fascination that drew her and made her uncomfortable at the same time, like an addict constantly being tempted by what she knows it will be death to touch. Once, entering the Central Asia room where she worked in the library to find it crammed with no chair available, she was certain she saw him signal the student beside him to leave. Then he gestured to her with an imperious charm that made her simultaneously want to slap him and obey. She stubbornly went out to another room.

But it wasn't always so easy. Especially when he began

to invade her dreams. In her dreams, he pursued her, and she ran and ran, but she never got away from him. If she ran upstairs, the stairs went nowhere. If she slammed a door, he was there before she could shoot the lock. She would wake sweating, her heart racing, just as he caught her.

Once she awoke with a start to find someone bending over her in the darkness, and the scream that had been in her throat in the dream ripped out of her, scaring her into real consciousness. "It's all right, it's all right, it's just a dream, honey," her roommate whispered in soft concern, and Alinor drew a deep, shaky breath.

"What is it?" Lana asked gently. "Want to talk about what's troubling you?"

"Oh, that man! that damned—! Why doesn't he leave me *alone?*" Alinor gasped, sitting up and starting to shiver. Lana didn't have to ask who. She knew, or had guessed a certain amount about Alinor's paranoia around Kavian Durran. What she hadn't realized was that Alinor was having regular nightmares about him.

"He's in your dreams now?" Lana asked.

"He's like…he comes through doors, I can't stop him, I can't get away!"

"Well, you gotta stop running, that's all. Turn around and face him," Lana said firmly.

"What?" Alinor demanded.

"Yeah, what's he going to do to you? It's only a dream. You aren't going to die, are you?"

"Sometimes it feels like it!" Alinor muttered. Turn around and face Kavian Durran? It would take more strength of mind than she had. "He's really frightening, Lana."

"He won't frighten you anymore if you stop running."

"Famous last words," Alinor said. "Don't people die when they dream about being hit by a train?"

Lana shrugged. "Who'd know?"

Both girls laughed, and under the brisk breeze of her roommate's common sense, Alinor felt her worry ease. Lana went back to her own bed, and never mentioned her theory again.

But the idea of "facing" Kavian Durran—in life if not in her dreams—began to haunt Alinor. She found she wanted to face him out. Turn on him one day, and demand...but what was there to challenge? He sat beside her sometimes in the library and the lecture hall. He chatted to her, if anything Kavian Durran said could possibly come under the heading "chat." What did that prove? She knew, and he knew, but if he denied it, what could she say?

She began to be frightened by the devil in her that wanted to challenge him. She had flung down the gauntlet once, and he had immediately begun to prove his power to her. She knew she would lose any real duel with him...he had said it himself. "It is foolish to begin a fight unless one is certain of winning."

She knew that part of her did not care whether she won or lost. That part only wanted the battle. She began to be afraid of herself, too.

It had been a beautiful spring day, the brilliant sunshine after several days of solid rain calling everyone out. The library was much less crowded than usual, but Alinor had an essay due. By evening she had the Central Asia room all to herself, three big tables surrounded by chairs all empty. She worked on as the sun set, and the world beyond the big windows grew black. The darkness seemed to enhance the silence, shrouding it in cotton wool. She heard no noise except the *scritch* of her own felt-tip against her notepad, the *whrup! whrup!* of thick pages as she turned them, the *chunk* as she replaced a book on the shelves.

And then suddenly there was another sound, the high hum of tension. She was standing at a shelf just then, flipping through a book to see if it was what she wanted, her back to the door. When she heard the sound that was no sound, except along her spine, she cautiously did not turn to the doorway, but glanced towards the windows. The whole room was reflected there against the night.

Behind her, in the doorway of the room, she saw a figure that she knew at once was Kavian Durran. *This room is a goldfish bowl at night,* she told herself. *Of course he saw me from the path.*

She set the book down and turned; and now, suddenly, when for the first time since that moment under the tree there was no one else around, the tension between them—something—hit her like a blow in the chest.

He was just inside the door. With his thickly waving black hair, his neat, full beard, those exotic, emerald green eyes, he really was like someone from another world, another era. It struck her suddenly how unconventionally handsome he was. No wonder she was always so knocked out by him— he was as beautiful as a medieval portrait of Christ.

He hadn't moved, it was only that looking at him directly was more difficult. They stared at each other. *What are you doing here?* she almost demanded, and bit back the words just in time. Was she crazy? He had as much right as she did to be in the room.

"I was just leaving," she muttered stupidly instead. Then they stood in silence, motionless, staring. A hair was tickling her cheek, but she couldn't even lift a hand to brush it back, because he was watching her. It was the moment she had been waiting for, she realized: her chance to challenge him. But she was afraid to speak. She could remember nothing of all the words she had rehearsed.

"Why do you avoid me?" he asked at last.

She felt a shiver of what felt like pure fear freeze her spine. "I don't avoid you. I hardly know you." How dry her mouth felt. She licked her lips.

"If you did not avoid me, you would know me better," he pointed out, and she shivered again, without knowing why.

"Why do you chase me?" she countered. Still they had not moved, like two statues in a museum. Well, he was, anyway. Marble. They said marble was always warm, that it pulsed with life. Kavian Durran was still, but she could feel his heartbeat from yards away. Her hands were cold with nerves. She supposed his hands, his chest would be warm. Hot. Burning her if she touched him.

He laughed lightly, throwing his head back just a little, and then drew in his breath between his white teeth. "And what shall I answer to this?" He looked at her levelly, half-smiling. "Why do I chase you? Why does the stag chase the deer? Why does the nightingale mourn the rose? Why does the moth seek the flame?"

She lost her breath, as though he had punched her. All she could do was gape at him. This was worse, far worse than she'd imagined. He wasn't just tormenting her. He was *after* her. The thought made her light-headed with shock. Her brain refused to consider what this meant.

Now he moved towards her, slowly, while fear kept her frozen, a rabbit fixed by the headlights of doom. There was nothing to put between them, she had put down the book and had nothing. Her back pressed into the shelves, and her skin ran with shivers like a pond blown into wavelets by a gust of wind.

"Why?" she said helplessly.

He was close now. "The stag seeks the deer for her grace," he said. "The nightingale yearns for the beauty and perfume of the rose. The moth—" He lifted one hand and drew a strand of hair from her shoulder. Although she was staring mesmerized at his face she somehow saw, too, how the tip curled in his palm, how he cradled it like something precious. "The moth dies for the sake of union with the light." His voice died to a murmur. "Your hair is like light."

His eyes fixed hers, green, but the centres black, hypnotic. He drew the strand of hair to his lips and kissed it on his fingers, his gaze still holding hers.

"My light."

Her heart was killing her. It kicked against the wall of her

chest as if it must escape. She had no idea what she felt, or
what she knew. Every certainty seemed turned on its head.

The kiss she felt in her flesh, as if she knew now how his
mouth felt against her breast, as if the curl had measured the
exact degree of the heat of his lips.

Of its own accord, her hand lifted and drew the lock of
her hair out of his grasp, reclaiming it. Her whole body went
cold, her skin shivering into goosebumps. As the curl moved
across his palm he clenched his hand unconsciously, to keep
it, and then, by a clear effort of will, let it go.

Face him, she ordered herself. *He's made it clear. Now's
your chance to tell him. Confront him.*

"Leave me alone," Alinor said. Her voice was hoarse.

He flinched imperceptibly, as if she had struck him and
found his cheek a rock. But he made no move to speak.

"I don't want you following me anymore."

His eyes were still on her, watching her reaction like one
who could not grasp its meaning. "You have been working
a long time," he said then. "Come to dinner with me. I am
sure you are hungry."

As if on cue, the gong went, signifying five minutes to
library closing. The synchronicity of it got to her on some
primitive level, telling her nervous animal brain that his control extended even to this, that the library closed at his command. She choked for air, and then her lungs gasped open
as she remembered to breathe again.

Alinor stepped sideways along the shelves away from him,
and then turned and walked back to the table where she was
working. At a safe distance, her back to him, she said, "No,
thank you. I have a meal waiting for me at home."

It was a lie, but she needed a lie against him.

"Of course you are afraid," he said from behind her. His
voice was calm, he hadn't moved to pursue her, as though
now that he had established the facts, he could be easy. "It
frightened me, also. You will feel better when you accept
what is inevitable."

She should have challenged it. She should have said something like, "nothing is inevitable between us, so get out of my way," but, as if a hand had closed on her throat, speech was impossible. She stood with her back to him, her head bent, and by the time she had produced sufficient courage to lift her head, she saw the empty room reflected in the window. He had gone as silently as a lion, having delivered the last word.

Accept what is inevitable. It rang in her ears as she hastily stuck a grubby note to the pile of books she had removed from the shelves, asking the library staff not to re-shelve them, grabbed up her own books, slung her bag over her shoulder, and left the room.

She half expected him to be lurking somewhere, to be waiting on the front steps, even to be at her bus stop. He was nowhere to be seen, but she didn't breathe easily again until she was inside the apartment and had shot the bolt.

"Hi! Are you all right?"

She turned. Lana stood in the doorway of the kitchen, wrapped in her all-encompassing, multi-stained apron. She stood with one hip slung forward, her left arm across her chest, her right hand, holding a wooden spoon, propped against her chin. She was watching Alinor quizzically.

"Sure. Why?"

"I don't know, honey. You kind of look like a rabbit who's just barely made it back to the warren. Who's the fox?"

She should tell Lana. Lana was her best friend, after all. But somehow she couldn't get it out. She just couldn't say the words "Kavian Durran." Not if they were going to be followed by "has just promised me that getting involved with him is inevitable."

"Oh," her roommate said, after a short, obvious silence in which the name had apparently written itself on the air in letters of fire and she had read it. "I'm making spaghetti. Want some?" So she hadn't lied to Kavian Durran after all, Alinor reflected stupidly, as if it mattered. Lana was a great cook, and even better at not pressing for secrets. The ideal friend.

Alinor nodded, more grateful than she could have said that her roommate wasn't going to try to force a confidence. Her brain was a whirl of feelings that she didn't understand and couldn't control. She never found it easy to talk about feelings, and right now it would be impossible.

That night of course she dreamt about him. She ran and ran through dark streets—but without running himself, he was always there, just behind her, close enough to touch her if he reached for her. But he didn't. She ran, and he was there. Her brain grew puzzled by how it could be that he was always there, without making an effort, without running, and at last it crept upon her that this was a dream.

She stopped running. *It's a dream. I'm safe,* she told herself, and turned and faced Kavian Durran. They looked at each other, while her heartbeat stifled and fear choked her.

You see, said the dream Kavian, reaching for her, and then she was in his embrace, and the fear wasn't fear anymore, it was something else—and now her heartbeat was like a backing of jungle drums, and she was still choking with emotion—but the emotion was no longer fear. He held her and smiled as nameless, unfamiliar sensations and feelings hammered through her system, and his eyes fixed her as his mouth came close to hers.

A rush of sensation and expectation exploded through her. *But it's not a dream. It's real!* Alinor said, and all that feeling was transformed into fear again, a fear so powerfully overwhelming that she had never experienced anything like a tenth of such impact before in her life, waking or sleeping. *No!* she cried. *No!* With every inch of strength she possessed, she pushed Kavian Durran violently away, and awoke to find herself sitting bolt upright in her bed, her heartbeat bouncing off the walls of the room with a clamour that deafened her.

She lay shivering in her bed for an hour afterwards, irrationally convinced that Kavian Durran knew that she had dreamt about him, until Morning had broken like the first morning. The dawn danced against the thick drapes till it found an opening. She watched as sunlight reached for her bed with a long, slow arm. The light fell across her bed because it must, she thought, it was the nature of light. Somehow it reminded her of Kavian Durran, as if he, too, might be a force of nature merely obeying his own innate laws.

But Lana had been right. Whether because of the real life or the dream confrontation, Kavian Durran stopped pursuing her after that night. She saw him at a distance as often as before; she never again caught him staring at her. She glanced his way often, but he seemed to have forgotten her existence. Sometimes she awoke feeling sure she had dreamt of him, but unable to remember the dream.

What she could always remember was a sense of loss.

The dance was billed as "Pre-Exam Sixties Blowout." The roommates told each other they were each working very hard, and exams would soon be upon them, and that they needed the break badly. A night of beer and loud music and dancing would set them up for the long haul through the exams.

It was warm weather for spring, and Alinor and Lana dressed in similar flower-patterned ankle-length dresses and platform boots, and parted their hair in the middle and let it hang straight over their shoulders, then set off together to meet other friends at the party.

Alinor danced wildly, letting the music thunder through her, not resisting it. It was like a shower of sound, washing away tension and worries and exam nerves, deadening thought. She danced, with no one in particular, until she was covered in a fine sweat and had worked all the kinks of long hours bent over a desk out of her body.

It was a beautiful, summery night. The party was on two floors of the college, the bar in the basement and the common room just above. The doors of the bar opened outdoors onto a small patio, with a broad flight of steps leading up to the central lawn. Above, there was a paved terrace around two

sides of the common room, with high French windows leading in.

The party wasn't well attended. It had been badly timed
for those students who had exams early in the schedule, and
when Alinor emerged for air after an hour, there no was no
one on the terrace or within the circle of light that was
thrown onto the grass of the central courtyard. She lifted her
hair off the back of her neck as she stepped into the gentle
wind, and then onto grass.

For once she was not thinking of Kavian Durran. She
wasn't thinking of anything, the music had blanked her mind
and she wandered gratefully at ease, taking in the stars, the
night, the thudding of the bass beat, the way the sweat was
drying on her face and back and arms, leaving her shiverily
cool. That was all.

There were trees sprinkled across the lawn, and she wandered lazily towards a huge oak tree at the far end that was
reputed to be centuries old. It had been saved from the de-
veloper's axe by student protest once in the sixties and then
again in the eighties. It was thick with new leaves, casting a
dark image against the full moon, and she felt the strength
of its embrace as she stepped under the shadow of its
branches and reached her arms around its black trunk.

"If the light comes to the moth at last, can the moth be
blamed for what follows?" said a voice just in front of her,
and for one moment of almost terrifying chaos, it was as
though the tree came to life under her touch. Then she knew
that it was not the tree's trunk she embraced, but Kavian
Durran. Alinor gasped and stepped back, too late. His arms
were tight around her body, her hands resting on his shoulders, nearly around his neck.

She held them up, away from his flesh, as though to rest
her arms on his, to let her hands fall against his shoulders,
were supreme danger.

In spite of her resistance, he drew her to him, so that her
chest was against his, her lower body between his legs.
"What do you think you're doing?" she demanded. Shock

was making her blood whirr and pound through her system, made her muscles weak.

She saw his face, pale in the moonlight, that she should have seen before. "I swore I would not make love to you unless you came to me yourself," he said softly.

Alinor's mouth fell open and she gasped for air.

"What are you talking about? I didn't come to you, I didn't know you were here!"

"You knew," he contradicted her urgently. "You knew. I called to you, and you came." And then one hand slipped up to the back of her head, and the other pressed against her back, and he bent over her and held her and made her meet his kiss.

Chapter 7

His lips touched hers, and something within her broke apart—a shell around a golden, glowing centre of light that now poured out into her system, and she was hungry, starving—for his mouth, for his breath, for his scent, for his touch...for his passion. She clung to him, body, heart and soul, and opened her mouth under the yearning, wild seeking of his. She felt like someone else, someone not herself—or perhaps someone more like herself than she had ever dared to be. She was confused by the crazy, conflicting sensations from her body and her mind. Her skin was alternately hot and cold, the touch of his long, lean fingers sometimes warming, sometimes chilling her. She sweated with inner heat, and was cooled by the summer breeze; she froze with inner confusion, and was warmed by an invisible fire that scorched her skin. Her ears were deafened by the thunder of her own blood, unable to hear and yet knowing what words he whispered and muttered to her in his own tongue, that most beautiful, most poetic, most enchanting of languages. The wild poetry took her soul on a swooping, arcing flight to a region she had read about but not believed, nor even dared to yearn for.

She sobbed, and clung to him. She did not come to herself, but knew, somehow, dimly, that they lay on the grass under the great oak. Its black, sheltering branches must be above her somewhere, but she was filled with dazzling, sheltering light and could not see them.

He was not making sexual love to her. She understood that, too, and why. In that moment of all-seeing, all-knowing, it was not sex that they wanted, not yet; it was the mating of souls now, and he understood somehow that she must have that before the body. Or perhaps he too needed it that way.

He held her head, he enclosed her, he kissed her, they clung. He spoke of love, telling her what his love of her meant, a fiery, passionate speech that would have made a man sound a fool in English, but somehow not in Parvāni, not in the language that was still called "the language of poets." Not in the language that had declared, centuries ago, that "a king must be a poet, and if he is not, a poet must be king."

She lay enchanted in the night, her hair spread out on his arm and the grass, her eyes shimmering with distant moonlight, smiling at the perfection of things while he spoke. She answered him softly, accepting everything, for everything was simple now, and everything changed forever.

He would telephone his father in the morning. She would write her exams, nothing must interfere with that. Then they would fly out to Parvān and be married there, "at his father's door," Kavian said. It was an expression that did not register with her, though it should have.

They would return together to England, where both would finish their work. Afterwards, there was work she could do among his people: education, or diplomacy, or trade, whatever she liked.

Two days later, the meaning of that expression "my father's door" dawned on her: it was the ancient word for "royal court"—the Door, the Sublime Port, where the Sheikhs of old had listened to the entreaties of their subjects. If it were not for the rumour that had always circulated at the college, she wouldn't have given it a second thought, but—

"Who is your father?" she asked, seeking him out as a new young plant seeks the sun, hungry for sustenance, straining towards him. Now that her resistance against it was wiped out, she felt all the naked power of his magnetism, and her heart ached.

"My father is Kavād Panj," he said simply. Kavād the Fifth. It was her area of study, of course she recognized the name. King of Parvān. If she had thought it old-fashioned that he should seek his father's permission for his engagement, here was reason enough. Especially if—

"And you—are you—?" She hesitated, suddenly not wanting to hear the answer.

He looked at her for a long, silent moment, understanding more than she could have expressed, his face expressing more than she could take in—fear, uncertainty. His hand came up and gripped her arm, high, at the shoulder. She felt urgency, possessiveness in the hold, as if he wished he had married her already. As if afraid that his next words might mean he lost her forever, and he could not bear to think what that meant.

"I am my father's heir," he confessed roughly. "One day you will be queen of my people." He did not say *if you marry me,* but she heard it in the harshness of his voice. He wasn't sure of her. He was afraid.

Her skin broke out in shivering, the reaction of one who consciously confronts the vision of a difficult, painful destiny. Well for those who are led blindly to the point of no return, but she had the power of choice. She could turn back now, and no one could blame her. Even his eyes, although they showed black fear, promised not to judge her if she quailed. He waited in silence for her decision, knowing that what she said now would be the truth of the future for both of them. She might change her mind later, but he knew that the truth she stated now would be the one they returned to in the end.

"Oh, God, Kavi, am I strong enough?" she whispered at last, and he sighed with relief, for to measure oneself against a task is no bad beginning.

"You are steel," he said firmly. "If you do not know it, this is because you have not so far been tested to the height of your strength."

"Won't your people—your father—expect you to marry a Parvāni woman?"

"My father and my people expect me to marry a woman who is worthy of them," he answered. "I shall do so."

And after that it seemed easy, as though she suddenly awakened to the fact that her life had been a training ground designed for the future Queen of Parvān. She knew so much about his country's neighbours, had contacts there now, from her father's time in that area—those who had been her playmates were now being groomed to take seats of power and influence. She understood the language, the culture, the ancient, noble history. And she loved it. She had spent formative years in that part of the world—there, as much as anywhere, felt like home to her.

His father sent his permission quickly, and looked forward to welcoming his son's bride as soon as they could make the journey.

Alinor's degree required her to spend her second year abroad, in Kaljukistan at the university of Shahriallah. Only Lana knew she was not simply going out early to that part of the world to have a summer of practice with the language before starting at the university there. Only Lana knew that she was flying directly to Parvān, and that she and Kavian planned to marry almost as soon as she arrived—and it had taken her a month to confide this news to her friend. Alinor was not naturally communicative, not easily trusting. In a lifetime of moving from country to country she had learned to keep what was closest to her heart private. In fact, only Lana knew that Kavian and Alinor were serious. Although they had never explicitly spoken of it, they had somehow tacitly agreed that the fewer people who knew about their engagement, the better. They spent what brief moments they had together away from the college.

There was more to it than sensible caution, perhaps. Was she afraid of the reaction she might get? Maybe she feared the cold shower of common sense, which might force her to look dispassionately at the massive step she was taking. Possibly even then she had been planning for a future in which she returned to England with her life in tatters and no one the wiser. If she failed in the course she was embarking on, Lana at least would never say, *I told you so.*

Perhaps even then, even in the first flush of joy, delight and hope, she had sensed some threat of future pain.

She had not immediately told her mother about Kavian, putting it off later and later, instinctively shrinking from the necessity to spring on her family the full truth at once. Envying the easy openness some people—like Lana—seemed to have with their parents, Alinor wondered how to handle the totally unexpected disclosure that she was about to marry the Crown Prince of Parvān.

First she asked Lana's advice.

"Just tell them you love him and are going to take the plunge," her friend advised cheerfully. "They'll understand."

"Yes, but—how'll I break it to them who he is?"

"You mean they don't know who it is you've been dating?"

Alinor bit her lip, feeling socially dysfunctional. "They don't know I'm dating anyone...seriously."

"What are you telling me? They don't know anything about anything and now you have to spring it on them, not just that you're in love, not just that it's serious, not just that you plan to get married, but that the guy in question is going to be King of Parvān someday?"

"That's the picture," Alinor said unhappily.

"Well, call me a potato and bake me," Lana said helplessly. "Why? I mean, why didn't you tell them before?"

"It might not have—worked out."

"Honey, mothers like to hear the details even if it doesn't work out. Don't you know that?"

"My mother's not like that," Alinor said, and Lana gave up with a shrug.

In the end, Alinor wrote a short letter first. She said that she had fallen in love with a Parvāni, she said that they hoped to get married eventually, that while she was out in Shahriallah she expected to travel to Parvān and meet his family…and that she would call soon.

To her surprise her mother telephoned immediately from the States, worried, anxious, and yet willing to be happy. "Is he a student at the university?" her mother demanded almost at once.

"Yes, he is."

"Your father says Crown Prince Kavian of Parvān is studying at your college. Have you met him?" her mother went on quickly, and Alinor, her heart pounding, hid her hysteria behind a giggle.

"Yes," she said. She ought to have known her father would be on top of things. That part of the world had been his area of interest for years.

Her mother sailed on. "You do realize that war is almost certain, don't you? The college really oughtn't to be sending anyone out there this year, your father says."

"We're still hoping there won't be war."

"Well, good luck, but you know your father is always right, and he says no one's going to lift a finger to prevent it because of Kaljukistan's oil. Darling, you will come straight back if things start looking bad, won't you?"

She didn't answer. She would not come back, not if Kavian were fighting a war. Impossible.

"Anyway, what I really want to know is—your father says the scuttlebutt is that two of the Companions are there with

Prince Kavian, and it hit me—you know, there can't be that many Parvānis at the college—if it's one of them, be careful, Alinor! Don't go marrying into a noble Eastern family without giving it a lot of thought. You'll be expected to be useless and decorative, won't you?''

"I'm not going to do that, Mother. I'm going to get a job in education. Teach women, or something.''

"What? I mean, you are? Alinor, this sounds a lot more decided than what you wrote. What's going on?''

"Um, Mom—''

"You've already made up your mind, is that it? This visit isn't a test at all.''

She sighed nervously. "Well, yeah. I was trying to break it to you gently.''

Her mother sighed, accepting it. "So far away. Oh, well, with any luck we'll be out that way again in a few years. I do get so tired of shopping malls and twenty-four-hour news. What's his name? Is it one of the Companions of the Throne? It is, isn't it?''

"No. Not exactly.''

"Alinor, what does that mean, 'not exactly'? He either is or he…'' Alinor almost saw the light go on. "Oh no! oh no!'' There followed a long moment of breathless surprise, during which Alinor could think of nothing to say. "Prince Kavian? It's Prince Kavian himself?'' her mother breathed, and then, "Oh, *Alinor!* Where's your father? Alan! *Aaaalaaaannnnn!*''

He called her *Nuri,* which meant "my light.'' Not in his own language, but in Arabic, the language of the Koran. "Alinor,'' he breathed once. "*Nur ala Nur.* Your name is in the Koran, do you hear it? *'Nur ala Nur'*—Light upon Light.'' He elongated the vowels, and rolled the *r*'s on his tongue like liquid honey, so that the sounds thrilled her.

Those few weeks passed in an electric high tension of work, study and snatched moments when, even then, they were scarcely ever alone. Alinor was studying hard and writing exams; Kavian, too, seemed devoted to putting in impossible amounts of work before their departure. She didn't remember eating or sleeping, there seemed no time, no need for such ordinary things.

But it began even before they left. Kavian was increasingly withdrawn, uncommunicative. She had thought that once her exams were finished they would spend time together, getting to know each other. But she scarcely saw him. He was always surrounded by people she didn't know, and in particular the two Parvānis, who now accompanied him everywhere. Her visa came through, their flight dates were confirmed, he showed her another kindly written message from his father...and still he had no time for her at all. If she had stopped then, if she had troubled to think...but she was besotted, full of yearning and optimism, believing that love meant she could share herself at last, soon if not immediately, could set down her heart whose weight she had carried alone for too long.

She accepted that he had business he must complete on his father's behalf before leaving London. She accepted everything, the waiting, the anticipation, the renewed loneliness, a loneliness that was deeper than what she had felt before she knew him, because before there had simply been no one, but now *he* was not there.

Later, of course, she learned that her father had been right, that he was not deliberately avoiding her—that what preoccupied Kavian was the looming possibility of a Kaljuk invasion of Parvān and his father's desperate attempts to convince the international community to prevent it. But she never learned to understand why he had not told her so.

Her heart soared with hope on the morning they finally left Heathrow Airport on the first leg of their flight to Samarkand and then to Shahr-i Bozorg. Now she would be alone with him, now their relationship could begin. There was so much to tell him, so much to learn....

His two Companions, Arash and Jamshid, the two students who had formed part of his court at university, sat immediately behind them in the plane, and her heart seemed to sink and grow cold with what she suddenly felt was inevitable—her own continuing isolation. Kavian did turn to her then, but she could not relax, not with those two just behind. They were travelling first class, there was plenty of room for privacy between the rows, but when he reached for her, taking her hand between both of his, she shrank just a little, as if he had tried to kiss her in a public place.

Kavian seemed not to notice. He lifted her hand to his mouth, kissing it and then setting it free. He smiled at her, and she half-smiled in return before dropping her eyes and turning to the window. And that little exchange seemed to set the seal on what the trip would be.

It was a long, tedious journey. Alinor hated flying. They never let you alone. There was always something to engage your attention, as if you were a three-year-old, incapable of entertaining yourself or enjoying your own thoughts for five minutes together. The constant supply of mints, drinks, appetizers, food, snacks, movies, music, captain's announcements and the aerial map with the white line marking their trip slowly drove her crazy. What made it worse was the admixture of Kavian's presence, his smiles, the words he whispered from time to time, the promise in his eyes that was making her nervous, her sudden, gnawing fear, now that it was too late, that she had trusted him too far, too soon.

At Samarkand they got into a small burgundy-and-white plane with a green lion and "Royal Air Parvān" painted on the tail. It flew low over desert and foothills, and Kavian leaned over to point out the great mountain, Shīr, and to recite the old benediction of his nation: *Shīr belongs to us, and we to Shīr.* She was a jumble of nerves and anticipation by then, seeing in the phrase—in the mountain itself—half threat, half promise.

The plane came in for a landing at a city set between the mountains. As it descended, Kavian leaned over her again to point out a towered, turreted, rugged building set on an eminence over the city against the mountain.

"My father's palace," he said simply.

Alinor rested a trembling hand against the plane's window and stared down. Palace? This was where she was going to live? This domed and turreted structure looked like a medieval fortress, it looked like the Tower of London, like an ancient prison! *Palace?* A current of anticipatory dread ran through her, replacing her happy excitement entirely.

"It looks—so old," she whispered.

"Mmm," Kavian agreed, and she was sure she didn't imagine the tinge of pride in his voice. "It's built on the foundations of a fourth-century Sassanian palace that was destroyed by Genghis Khan, and with some of the same bricks. The site is probably even older than that."

Anything could happen in a place like that. She might disappear and never be heard of again. It struck her how little she knew of the man whose wife she had promised to become, whose religion she had promised to accept, of whose country she knew only from books. And in her fear, she cried, foolishly, "I can't live there!"

She turned, watching him frown at the abruptness of it. "What did you say?" Kavian asked, as though he thought his ears had misled him. He spoke in his own tongue now. *Chi gofti?*

"I—can't we live somewhere else?"

There was disapproval in his eyes now, the first time she had ever seen it directed at her. "Do you expect me to take an apartment for you down in the city? I am Crown Prince, and my father is old," he reminded her. "I must be with him. Especially now."

She flinched under the lash of his disapproval and said no more. Perhaps if she had asked what she could so easily have asked: *Why especially now?* and if he had confided in her, things might have turned out differently. But she only turned to the window and watched the palace with growing dread, as long as the angle of the plane's approach allowed, and that first step towards lack of openness between them had perhaps paved the way.

On the ground there was no doubt that Kavian Durran was the heir apparent returned to his own land at a moment of crisis. It was not that the airport officials kowtowed, they did not. Kavian had told her that his grandfather had dispensed with the ancient royal customs decades ago—it was in the air of respect, gratitude, even relief—the small nod of satisfaction, as if they had told themselves he would come but were nonetheless grateful to be proven right.

At last, very belatedly, Alinor began to put the pieces together, to hear again certain things he had said, to which she had previously attached no significance...to wonder what crisis was impending at his father's palace. Was his father ill, dying? And perhaps for the first time she was really looking at what it meant to marry a man who would be king of a country—not on some distant day, but soon, while she was still young.

They were picked up by an antique, polished Rolls Royce in mint condition and driven through ancient bazaars and streets of modern housing, past the magnificent mirrored dome of the Central Mosque, always climbing, until the road was above the city, snaking around a precipitous hillside, then leading through gates in a turreted stone wall of unguessable antiquity and into a cobbled area, full of small buildings, laneways, cars, people, animals, that made up what amounted to a village clustered around the skirts of the palace.

It wasn't like anything she'd experienced before, and she had plenty of experience of the unusual and the antique. It wasn't even like a movie—the noise, the people, the horses and camels were too real for that. It was simply...another world.

Yet for all the strangeness, there was a troublingly elusive familiarity. The high stone walls casting their protective shadows onto the folk below, the leaded casements, the mosaic tile, the fountains...all had a storybook flavour, and at last Alinor pinpointed her recognition. It reminded her of stories she had read in *The Arabian Nights*. "Arabian," of course, was a misnomer: the stories came originally from the ancient Persian empire, an empire which, two millennia ago, had included even this tiny kingdom. But now for the first time she saw the reality that the book described.

A Thousand Nights and a Night was the proper title. And Alinor thought of how, during those thousand and one nights, the clever Scheherezade had saved her own life through telling her Sultan husband intriguing stories, always unfinished at dawn. Something a little like dread whispered over her skin and Alinor looked at Kavian, sitting beside her in the car, and she wondered what she could do to save herself if her life were threatened in this alien environment. She doubted whether telling stories would do the trick a second time.

Chapter 8

They came slowly down the track—an arrival very different from that first arrival in his land, four years ago that seemed an age—and night fell on them like a presentiment of doom as they descended. High on the other wall of the valley the sun still shone, but here all was dusk.

The feel of grass underfoot was a well-remembered luxury after the heat and dust of the desert and the stony passes, and the horses snorted gratefully and shook themselves at having been relieved of their human burdens.

It was a long way down. Long before they reached the bottom, she saw the camp where they were headed, a camp of typical Parvāni tents, the one in the middle flying the royal standard, a green lion emblazoned against a white mountain on a burgundy field. She wondered why they were here. When they first entered the valley, she had expected that they would billet in a village overnight; it was too far to the capital for one afternoon's ride. The encampment surprised her. She could think of no reason for it.

"What are you doing in the camp?" she asked, with the

curious return of an old intimacy, betraying her understanding of him and his ways.

"Hunting," he said briefly. She was silent with surprise. She had followed the news of the war, compulsively if unwillingly. She knew what a beating Parvān had taken at the hands of their well-supplied enemies, knew that in the end they had only gained the victory through mountain doggedness and determination. And now, within months of the war's end, the Crown Prince was out with a hunting party? She could think of no explanation for it—unless perhaps that the capital was starved for meat and this was how it was supplied.

But even that did not account for Kavi's presence in the camp. He must have better things to do than kill meat.

It was hard going, leading the horse with one hand while she held up her heavy silk skirts with the other, and tried to avoid holes and loose stones. Kavian did not offer to take Sohrab's horse's rein from her, a fact that surprised her until she lost her footing in the gloom and was saved from a fall by her grip on the horse.

She noticed that Kavian was carrying an assault rifle in his free hand. He, too, was encumbered by the loose folds of his desert costume, and she knew from experience that he would dispense with it now that they were in the high country. He borrowed the Arab outfit through necessity. It was desert wear; he was a mountain man.

There were boys waiting to take the horses when they reached the valley floor, and Kavi sent his horse off with an encouraging pat on the rump, then strode towards the tent that flew the standard. He did not look to see if she followed, but of course she had to. There was nowhere else for her to go. If he had assigned her her own tent, he would have said so before now.

The tent was less luxuriously appointed than in the times she remembered, which meant this was a working, not a pleasure camp. In the old days a hunting party had been for pleasure, but that meant nothing now. There were two larg-

ish, square rooms, as always, the inner one spread with carpets, blankets and the cushions that made up the bed, a high-
sided bathtub behind some drapery. In the outer room there
was a desk and chair in one corner, a low broad table surrounded by cushions in the centre. Carpets covered the grass,
and the inner hangings hid the cloth walls and gave the tent
an air of permanence that was quite false. Within half an
hour of the order to strike camp, she knew, the tent would
have disappeared into neat rolls on the backs of the mules.

Now that the necessity for movement was past, she was
exhausted. She stood watching as Kavian stripped the desert
robes from himself and then was revealed in the much more
familiar flowing white cotton trousers and long, loose shirt.
He picked up a dark waistcoat from the back of a chair and
pushed his arms into it as she watched.

Now she recognized him. Now he was Kavian Durran, the
man who had been her husband, the mountain man, the man
of the desert—the same man, though harder, and her heart
began to beat in painful, hard thuds. ''Kavian,'' she whispered involuntarily.

His face as he glanced at her was impassive. His eyebrow
went up in inquiry, but the movement did not give his face
the cast it had once done. He looked impatient, arrogant. She
lost the courage for whatever she had been going to say, or
confess.

''You've taken off your beard,'' she said instead. Somehow this was the first moment she had had the luxury of
realizing it.

''I have had to go disguised as a Kaljuk,'' he said briefly.

''To—to get me, you mean?'' She regretted the lost beard.
His jaw was strong, and there was nothing now to soften its
lines, to raise a false hope of tenderness.

''And other times.'' To her surprise, he picked up a rolled
wool hat and put it on his head, then reached down and lifted
a band of bullets.

''Kavian!'' she cried again in surprise, and he stood

poised, enquiring, waiting, the bullet belt dangling from one hand.

He *had* changed. His cheeks were thinner, gaunt almost. Without the protective cover of the white cotton robe, the cast of his face was harsh, his eyes dark with a past which she had not shared.

"Yes?" he prompted impassively.

"But—where are you going?"

He moved again then, slinging the bullets over his chest, reaching down with one rough hand for the rifle that leaned against the desk.

"On reconnaissance," he said, answering the words but not the emotion behind them. "We have been away two days. That is too long. There is a woman about who has been asked to take care of you. Find her. She will supply you with a bath, and clothes. Then I suggest you rest. We ride again tomorrow."

The tent flap moved, and she was alone.

Curiously, it was the meeting with his father that had calmed her wild panic when she'd first arrived in Parvān four years ago. Sheikh Kavād Panj was a man of such clear and unimpeachable integrity, such kindness, goodness and generosity, so upright, so firm, so true, that he made the reflection of those qualities in his son instantly recognizable.

Alinor liked him at once, if liking could be held to describe the mixture of respect and regard she felt. He had a rich sense of humour, and a high intelligence, and he charmed her as well. He welcomed her as a daughter, as his heir's rightful and well-chosen bride, and he seemed to like her on sight. In his presence, Alinor felt the return of her calmer, more accepting state of mind, felt a resurgence of the courage she needed to meet a difficult but rightly chosen future.

Kavian had another close relative in the palace, whom she also wanted to love: his Aunt Puran, the sister of his mother—who had died when Kavian was thirteen. There were also cousins of various ages, one of them the daughter of Puran, a fifteen-year-old who clearly "worshipped Kavian's shadow," as the Parvāni saying had it, and was at first wary of Kavian's chosen bride. But Nargis admired Alinor so much, and so much wanted her approval and affection, that she ceased to resent her presence in Kavi's life within a week.

Alinor declared her acceptance of the One God in the Sheikh's presence, in a quiet, informal meeting, and the next day the wedding ceremony began. She was dressed in draped, green silk trousers and a beautifully made gold lamé tunic, with a floating, gold-embroidered green silk scarf to cover her hair. Her forehead, nose, wrists, hands and feet were decorated with delicate, ravishingly exotic, fabulously rich jewellery. The colours she wore made her normally greyish eyes seem a gold-flecked green, and the rich jewels gave her face an exotic, mysterious cast, so that the women who dressed her said she looked like one of the inhabitants of Kamrang, a province in the south of the country where the people were fair-haired and remote.

She sat beside Kavian under a tiny canopy of cloth of gold, held up by four symbolic pillars. It was a rite left over from the old religion, with Muslim trimmings added. Kavian was dressed in cloth of gold with burgundy, and wore a burgundy turban trimmed with gold, whose two gold-encrusted ends lay against his shoulder. *He* looked like an engraving from *A Thousand Nights and a Night* now, and the sheer power of his masculinity, in its dazzling peacock display, took her breath away.

Sacred food and drink was placed before them, which she fed him and he fed her, and they recited words so ancient that their meaning was lost to living memory, but their power nonetheless held the listeners silent.

The food seemed all honey and crushed nuts, stirring her senses to a peak, and all had to be eaten, so that when a drop spilled her husband—handsome, powerful, strong, passionate, like a sleek-pelted animal—licked it from her finger. She closed her eyes briefly, breathed and recovered; and under whispered instruction from the pretty handmaiden beside her, opened her lips and allowed Kavian to place a sugared sweetmeat between them. One strong forefinger he held there, and she licked at the crumb that resolutely adhered to it. When it did not release, her lips sucked at the firm pad, and then she gently nibbled, and the grain came away on her tongue.

The cheering and laughter of the assembled brought her from the trance she had not known she was in, and she looked quickly to Kavian for the explanation. He leaned down sideways and whispered, "When a bride shows her teeth at such a moment, it is said the marriage will be tempestuous, but the love life…rewarding," and she lowered her eyes and head, abashed in this roomful of approving strangers, while a smile tugged irrepressibly at her lips and a blush stained her cheeks and forehead.

His father's people loved it. They said it was a good omen for the marriage, and for the country.

Afterwards, they were led by a torch-bearing crowd through a labyrinth of halls and rooms till Alinor had lost her bearings entirely, and they had entered a very old part of the palace. Then the tumult convinced her that at last they were nearing their goal. Ahead was a massive pair of elaborately carved and decorated wooden doors of great age. The ancient Parvān Royal Bridal Chamber. Every royal bride for hundreds of years had spent her first night with her husband in this room. Two of Kavian's Companions stepped forward, carrying their torches high, and opened the doors.

She had only a second to wonder. Her ever-present handmaiden and instructress whispered with gay solemnity, "Now, Mistress, the coins!" and Alinor remembered the little gold bag that had been pressed into her hand with the injunction, "Spill them when I tell thee!"—for the handmaiden by ancient right spoke to her mistress in the familiar. Awkwardly, her fingers trembling, Alinor spilled the coins from the purse into her hand, and flung them so that they splanked and tinkled on the stone floor, as they had done for countless generations of brides before her.

Immediately all were on their knees, eager, for to capture one of the coins meant good luck for the bearer for the life-time of the marriage. Then, when all eyes were thus averted, Kavian bent and swung her up high in his arms. Laughing with shock and excitement, her hands catching in her delicate scarf, Alinor tossed more coins out behind, until the little bag was empty. Ahead of her, the two Companions, the only ones not to chase the lucky coins, stood with averted eyes, and Kavian strode across the threshold with his laughing, slender burden. Then the doors closed behind them, shutting out the laughter and the voices, and they were alone together almost for the first time since that moment under the oak tree, in a distant life that she had already forgotten.

The passionate desire to possess her had been growing in his eyes for hours, nakedly, burning, for he had made no attempt to disguise it. Now as he set her on her feet she felt his hands tremble, and she swallowed convulsively and looked anywhere but at him.

The room was softly lighted, deeply shadowed, the low broad bed at its centre thick with pillows, cushions, rugs, and pelts, and draped with silk and silk carpets. Carpets were spread everywhere about the room, floor and walls, in wild, luxurious abandon, the finest, most delicate of silk carpets she had ever seen. Birds, trees, flowers, roses, mandalas and a hundred other designs, some old, some new, some priceless antiques. Behind them, hiding the ancient stone, the walls were lined in ornately, exotically sculpted and carved wood, shaped into flowers and birds and trees, full of tiny doors and drawers and inset mirrors.

On a low table surrounded by cushions there was laid a tray with a meal keeping warm over small, golden-flamed candles. Behind it, a charcoal brazier glowed in a massive hearth, taking the chill out of the air, for even in mid-summer the ancient stone walls deep in the heart of the palace retained their native coolness.

She looked anywhere but at him, her nerves high and tensed, but the casual words that she wanted to utter, to calm herself and him, would not form in her throat. Her lips parted only to take in the lightly perfumed air of the room: the scent of rose, and musk, and fragrant wood.

And then he was before her, his masculine magnificence blocking out sight, and smell, and thought, and he was both the unknown country, and her husband.

"What is your name?" Alinor asked.

"Golnesah, my Lady."

She spoke with the mountain dialect; that would be unusual for a servant from the palace, which drew mainly on the population of the city. Mountain people did not understand the concept of personal service as a way of life, as employment. The tribes had their leaders, of course, but such leaders were given obedience as a functional necessity and from choice, and they both respected and were respected by the members of their clans as equals.

"Do you come from the palace?" Alinor asked anyway.

"From the palace! No, Lady, my people summer here in the valley again, now that the war is over."

The woman gestured out the tent door as she spoke, and in the gathering gloom Alinor saw the lights of distant fires far down the valley. Not a servant at all, then. Someone had ridden down the valley to beg the favour of a woman's assistance for the Crown Princess, and Golnesah had offered. She had come as a favour to her Prince, not as one seeking payment.

"The bath is warm, Lady," said Golnesah. Her accent was difficult for Alinor, whose ears had been attuned first to "court" Parvāni, and more recently to Kaljuki, but although the endings and the pronunciation were different, the actual words could be discerned.

"Thank you," she said. "I shall be grateful for it."

"Shall I help you disrobe?"

"I would take it as a kindness." How much more quickly the old forms returned to her lips than she would have guessed, as though she had slept heavily and was groggy, but not as one who has been away for long years and expected never to return.

Golnesah stared curiously at the tight bodice of the heavy silk dress, until Alinor belatedly understood her problem. "It opens at the back," she said, turning and presenting the long, sweeping back closed with a hundred tiny, round, silk-covered buttons.

"Ahhh," breathed Golnesah, in the tones of one taking in a curious fact about a distant and probably mad people. A dress that buttoned at the back! How to get into it quickly if bad weather threatened the tent, or a predator threatened the livestock when the men were absent? And how to get out of it except with the help of a husband who had returned exhausted from his labours and would have no patience for such buttons?

But they were beautifully made, the buttons, as fine as those on the royal robe that had been given to her own great-grandfather by the king many decades ago, though of course those had been covered with cloth of gold. Golnesah herself had never seen that robe, but the story of it was still told. A man who had performed a signal service for the king and was rewarded with the gift of a robe was a man of repute in his tribe, the honour cherished by his family for generations.

"A beautiful robe, my Lady," Golnesah said, beginning to undo the buttons at the neck. The lacy white strapless body stocking the Princess wore underneath was another source of surprise. "How cunning!" Golnesah said admiringly. "To give the skin itself the impression of being embroidered with silk! I have heard that in India women paint the palms in henna with such designs, my Lady, but such takes many hours of work. You take this off and put it on again in the blink of an eye." She helped her Lady out of the pretty underwear and into the tub of warm water that awaited her behind the screen of a hanging carpet.

When she had put it on, Alinor thought, she had expected Gabe to help take it off, and remembered with distant surprise that this was her wedding day.

"Aiee, Mistress! What is this?"

She had awakened on that long-ago morning to find Kavian gone, and the pretty handmaiden of the night before standing in the middle of the room, the gauzy scarf in her hand, staring at the floor. Sun came through a row of tiny windows bordering the dome high in the ceiling to cast patterns of coloured light all over the room.

"What is it?" Alinor had struggled sleepily to one elbow, and then blushed as the silk sheet slipped down her body to expose her breast. There was nothing there, and yet the marks of Kavian's hands and mouth were so strong on her memory she half felt the girl must be able to see them.

"From where did it come?" The girl was still staring at the floor. On the carpet near her feet the sun glinted on something round.

She remembered the coin falling to the floor as Kavian pulled the scarf from her hair, in that brief instant before his kiss had wiped out everything but the knowledge of his presence. "It got caught in my scarf," she said. "It fell out later."

"Aiee, Mistress! Aiee!" She'd never actually believed before that a woman could make that sound, but she was hearing it now. And the meaning was clear—it was the keening of disaster.

Her skin was suddenly sharply on end with nerves and fear. "What is it?" she demanded, sitting up and reaching for the robe of last night. "Dallia, what is it?" She stood and crossed to the girl, whose black eyes, opaque with horror, were now so different from the dark laughing jewels of last night.

"Did not you hear me say, Mistress, that you must throw

every coin?'' Her eyes focused abruptly and she began to comb the floor with her gaze. ''How many fell, Lady? How many coins? No, my Lady!'' she cried, as Alinor stooped to the gold coin. ''Do not touch it!''

Suddenly Alinor understood. She had violated some tradition. The presence of the coin in this room meant bad luck or worse. In spite of herself she could not prevent the girl's horror from shivering her own skin, lifting her own hair with fear of the future.

''What does it mean?'' she asked quietly.

''It was one coin? There was no other?''

''I only noticed one.''

Dallia's breath was released on a sigh and a muttered word of thanks. ''One is an Enemy, my Lady.'' She broke off.

''An enemy?'' prompted Alinor.

''An enemy coming between you and your husband.'' She tried to smile. ''But please God none here shall come between you!''

She went out, and returned in a few minutes with a child she had found somewhere in the palace. The child, a bright-eyed, sturdy creature, went straight to the glinting coin and picked it up.

''There!'' said Dallia triumphantly, as if what had passed had positive significance, and whisked the child out of the room. Yet Alinor had the feeling that there was more that she had not been told, and that it was not good.

When her bare foot trod on something cold and she looked down to see a second coin hidden in the soft fringe of a carpet, she couldn't stop her heart's superstitious leap of dread. As the door handle moved, she lifted the edge of the carpet and kicked the coin underneath.

Dallia came back into the room, all smiles. ''What would two coins mean?'' Alinor asked calmly later, as the girl combed her hair.

The long steady stroking stopped. ''Was there a second coin, Mistress?'' she asked breathlessly.

Alinor smiled and shook her head reassuringly. "I wonder, that's all. And is there a meaning for three coins?"

Dallia made a little motion of the head, like a shrug. "Three coins is bad luck for the husband," she said, "for it means a wife who is inattentive to her duty."

She was going to leave it there, but Alinor had to know. "And two?" she prompted.

Her eyes became hooded with discomfort. "Two is Death, my Lady," she said. "But death shall not come between you and my Lord for many years, please God."

But she was wrong. The wedding was celebrated for five days. Within two months, the first Kaljuk troops began to invade the desert.

When she got out of the bath and dried herself, Golnesah shyly offered the Shahbanu her own *shalwar kamees,* one that she had brought with her from the nomad summer camp. Alinor was relieved. She had been wondering for some time what she could wear. The costume was sturdy and well-made, but the tiniest trace of gold thread in the fine embroidery at neck and cuffs of the tunic told Alinor that this was Golnesah's best and prettiest outfit.

She could not refuse the gift. She was, in effect, a guest in Golnesah's valley, and the tradition of hospitality was very strong among the Parvān mountain tribes. So she admired the fine workmanship of the embroidery and the turquoise colour, and received the gift as graciously as she knew how. She knew she fell short in this particular Parvān social skill, and that Golnesah would consider her foreign, awkward, and a little rude. But with Parvānis it was better to fail on the side of rudeness than to risk sounding condescending through over-flattery. Parvānis despised oiliness in human relations, whether from king to subject or from subject to king.

Golnesah served her a meal as she half-sat, half-lay on the cushions at the low table. Alinor recognized the table and some of the plates, but the other times she had sat at this table in this tent had been very different. Kavian had sat beside her then, and fed her delicacies at night, and in the day rode with her—wild, mad rides over the desert and in the forests, and wild, delirious nights, when Kavian loved her with a passion so fierce it was almost desperation—that she only later understood was born of his knowledge of what was coming.

A place was set for Kavian now, but he did not appear.

Chapter 9

She awoke with the dawn chorus. She turned to look at the pillow beside her head: she was alone. In the night she had imagined that Kavi came and slept beside her. In her sleep, she had been inhabiting an earlier year, when it had been natural for him to be there, and so she had not awakened fully. She could not be sure now whether it had been dream or reality. The covers on that side of the bed were disturbed, but she might have done that herself in sleep.

The background of chirps and warbles from the waking birds was overlaid suddenly with a new voice of pure-throated melody piercing the clear mountain air. A *bulbul*, the Eastern nightingale. It was a song of heart-stopping, almost painful perfection; a song she had not heard for years, rich, fluid, bursting, water tumbling over rock. She lay for a moment unmoving, not even breathing in the attempt to absorb every pure, high, thrilling note.

Unexpectedly, and with terrible immediacy, she remembered that morning three and a half years ago...the last time she heard the *bulbul*. And between one breath and the next her heart ripped in two in her breast. She jerked upright, holding herself and gasping against the stabbing memory. How beautiful the *bulbul*'s song had been that morning! A song of breathless joy, like a celebration, going on and on, as if the bird would sing forever. In her pain and nightmare anguish then she had felt it as mockery. It *had* been mockery. The song had promised happiness, but that morning was the destruction of all happiness....

Her eyes burned painfully now, and her cheeks were wet all at once, as if the tears came out of the skin of her cheeks, out of her pores, as well as her eyes. Sweat broke out over her whole body. Her flesh itself wept.

The bird passed on; a *bulbul* rarely stops long, although on that long-ago morning it had stayed forever, killing her with its message of love and joy. Alinor breathed and willed herself to calm. It had not hurt like this for months now; she was learning to cope. Coming here had broken down the wall she had been building, that was all.

With a sudden upsurge of anger that blotted out the hurt, she cursed Kavian in her heart. Damn him! What had he brought her back for? To prove something? To restore some point of masculine honour? He didn't want her. Why should he care who she married? *I divorce thee, I divorce thee...*

The violence of her feelings drove her up out of bed. Snatching up a square of cloth, she pulled it around her naked body and strode into the next room. Golnesah lay amongst the cushions, wrapped in a blanket, sleeping deeply. Alinor stopped short, then continued across the room silently, slipped through the tent door and drew the fresh mountain air deep into her lungs.

It was a fine summer morning in the making. Above the mountain ridge the sun breathed light onto the darkness of the sky, but night still lay over the valley. She heard a horse stir and whicker in the pen under a clump of trees, heard the wind lazily drag a flap of canvas against itself; above it all, the birdsong.

Far along the valley she saw lights that said the nomad

camp was already awake. Here in Kavian's camp no one
moved, there were no fires yet, and as quickly as that her
decision was made. Quietly she stepped back inside the tent
to the bedroom, pulled on the turquoise *shalwar kamees,* and
the cotton moccasins Kavi had given her yesterday, snatched
up the white scarf and, walking as softly as she knew how,
slipped out again. In two minutes she had left the camp behind and was headed down the valley.

They had had a month, a little month, of joy. At the time
she had felt as though it would go on forever, but afterwards
she had seen it as a moment whose death was inherent in its
very intensity. Like the petrol-fed fire that flares up with brief
brightness and then dies, like the burst of creative genius
which overtakes artists who are destined to die young, it had
no future except ashes. She saw that now.

They had been wrapped in a cocoon of love. The rest of
the world did not exist for her. After his marriage it was
traditional for the Crown Prince to be relieved of all state
and other responsibilities for a month, and in that month, as
tradition dictated, they lived in the Bridal Chamber. They
had spent their time in a haze of emotional, sensual, physical
and intellectual delight. He would take her riding over the
desert, and at the end of the journey there would be a tent
between the trees of an oasis, silk cushions to lie on, dates
and nectar to eat from Kavian's fingers. He would take her
to the high valleys, and there would be a series of nomad
villages, and a warm welcome with goat's milk and cheese
and fresh green herbs and the flat, delicious bread called
naan to eat.

They would sit on spread carpets on the ground, eating
and talking with the men of the village while the women
served them. This division did not interfere with the convivi-
ality of the moment: the nomad women were not silent in
the presence of men, laughing and contributing to the general
conversation as they moved to and fro serving the simple,

delicious meal, and it was a custom too ingrained for the participants to notice it.

Alinor noticed, but she was too happy for it to mar her own pleasure in the moment. She laughed and joked with the women as they served her, and accepted what she found without wishing to change it.

They admired her pale hair, and said she was like the tribes in the south of the country, Kamrang, and in nearby Nuristan, the Land of Light. There, too, the people had yellow hair and blue eyes, a memento of the great Iskandar, who two thousand three hundred years ago had come to conquer and had left some of his Greek and Macedonian soldiers behind. Was she, too, descended from Alexander the Great?

Well, it was always possible. There was a theory afoot that a tribe of Greek pioneers had sailed to the British Isles and were the original Britons or Celts or something. Alinor was certainly descended from the British, so it was possible that there was a blood link in the remote past. She only laughed, shaking her head, and said she didn't know, but the women must have caught the fleeting thought in her tone or her eyes. And the word spread among the nomadic tribes that the new Crown Princess had the blood of Iskandar in her veins.

It was not just the countryside that he showed her. There were mosques and the temples of older religions—fire temples and Buddhist shrines—there were museums, there was the palace itself, with its treasures from twenty-five centuries of Parvān history. There were the ancient sites—an old Greek theatre on a hillside, the rows of seating still intact, the actors' entrances, the stage, the pillars easily discoverable amongst the fallen stones, the acoustics remarkable even after two millennia. There were ancient temples, too, some so broken they were only lines of stone in the earth.

His country had a rich heritage, and he was proud of it. The cultures of the whole world had met here, and his people had reaped the benefit. There was beauty everywhere, natural and man-made, ancient and modern. He told her stories of his country's past and present as they moved among the monuments and treasures, making her, too, proud of her adopted country's past.

And then, at the end of it all, there would be a return to the Bridal Chamber at the palace, the world shut out, and only each other to occupy their attention. Then he introduced her to the joy of sharing all that she thought, felt, and was with another. For Alinor, whose life had been marked by constantly recurring separation from friends, and who had early learned to keep herself back from real dependence on another, it was a flooding relief to love and believe herself loved forever. She gave herself up to it completely.

Physically, too, he gave her total pleasure, and she responded by giving him total trust. It seemed to her, in those heady days, that each day, each moment, brought them closer together, and she wondered dimly what would happen when they became each other. For the logical end of this togetherness was that they should literally become one.

He said, Who knocks for entry?
I replied, It is Thou.

They were the words of one of the many poets of the country, whose work Kavian recited to her as they lay eating peaches and pomegranates, dates and figs in their apartment, or rode the desert, or climbed the heights. She was approaching closer and closer to the moment when it would be true, she thought, when to go further forward would mean to become not only one flesh, but also one Self.

It was all unreal. It was false. Later she would marvel at how deluded she had been during her thirty days of perfection.

He sat on the slope above the encampment, in an outcrop of rock that hid him from casual view. There was no real need for a night watch, but he had been a fool to think he could lie beside her and sleep; he watched instead.

The voice of the *bulbul* danced on the air, lifting his heart from the void, and he breathed deeply. He saw the bird dart along the river and settle on a branch overhanging the water.

It sang again, and he knew suddenly that she was awake and hearing the music with him. A lifetime ago it was one of the things they had shared, the mysterious power of that song that bound the heart with a silken thread and drew it from the bosom.

She had always reminded him of the song of the *bulbul*. He lost himself in her: his cares, his heart, his self lifted in her presence....

But she had been as impossible to hold as the song, as the rippling water the song resembled. He had yearned for her at first, but then he had banished her face from his thoughts. At first, too, he had believed that she would surely return to help him combat the nightmare destruction of his life, his home, his people. He had not believed, in spite of what he had been told, that her heart was as cold as the last three years had finally proved it. And still, he had gone after her, claiming what had been his own...without understanding the future of his actions, or even his own hopes.

There was movement in the shadows near the tent, and he became still with watching. Had some madman managed after all to cross the desert to rescue her? His hand moved, and familiarly clasped the smooth wood and cold metal of the rifle across his lap. With practised speed he raised it to his shoulder, his eyes fixed on the distant shadow.

A river ran along the valley, with a well-worn path beside it showing the prints of humans as well as animals. About halfway along there was a small woods spreading out to the hillside. If she reached that before any alarm was raised at least she would not be instantly visible. Alinor hurried. The leather-soled moccasins gave her a secure footing on the dirt path. The sun was climbing up over the ridge, bathing the higher reaches of the valley behind her with light. She was in gloom still, but how long before the first bright rays illuminated the valley floor?

When would the alarm be raised? Golnesah's people were already up and about, and did that mean that habit would bring the nomad woman awake? Alinor had wrapped the white cotton headscarf around her head. In her trousers and tunic, with the telltale pale hair covered, there was nothing about her mere presence to arouse suspicion. She might be a woman from the village on an errand.

So long as Golnesah slept. Alinor glanced behind again. Daylight pursued her along the valley floor, making her heart beat in fright, but the forest was close now. She could make its protection before the sun caught up with her. She walked faster.

When had it all gone wrong? She had known that when the month was over he must return to his work, she had known the honeymoon would not last forever. But she was unprepared for the abruptness of the change. They moved into new apartments, leaving the cocoon of the Bridal Chamber for the bustle of the more modern part of the palace. From being in his company twenty-four hours a day, she now scarcely saw her husband. Kavian came and went without explanation, and sometimes was away for days on end. He would come in tired, silent, and uncommunicative, and would be gone again even before she could send for a meal. Or she would send, but he would have gone by the time it arrived, leaving her to eat in lonely magnificence the dishes she had chosen to tempt him.

At first she had plied him with questions, with wanting to help, but he did not want to discuss his work with her. She decided in her own mind that there must be secrets of state that he could not tell her, and instead of questions she tried to ease the burden she knew he was carrying with little stories, anecdotes about her day or comments about what little she heard of world affairs. These, too, he rebuffed. "My *bulbul*," he would call her, watching her with a tolerant smile, and she understood that her chatter disturbed his train of thought.

His silence and preoccupation soon called up her old feelings of isolation, and eventually she became as silent as he.

What was there to say, after all? He was a man of the East, to whom women were of secondary importance, whose role was defined and limited by a man's needs. He had ceased to need her for companionship. She began to resent not only her unthinking haste in marrying him, but his arrogance in bringing her to a place where, as a Western woman, he must have known she would be completely out of place.

She had long since given up asking him about the work he had once said she could do among his people. "Not now, Nuri, you must await events," he had said, and she felt it as contempt.

Soon sex was their only ground of communication. And as her resentment increased, as she felt less and less valued for herself, even that gave way.

It was a long, hot summer. The ultimate disillusionment came when she learned what was the trouble that had plagued him, and that he had not been able to discuss with his own wife. She found it out on the day when he was actually there for a meal with her.

"I suppose I'd better think about getting over to Shahriallah and finding accommodation soon," she had said.

His eyes were dark with fatigue, but she had long since learned to express no concern, to ask nothing. Her concern meant nothing to him.

He had looked at her with tired astonishment.

"Chi miguyeed?" he asked. *What are you saying?*

She smiled irritably. "If it's escaped your notice, it hasn't escaped mine that the academic year is about to begin, and I've got a fair bit of preparation to do for it."

And that was how she learned that Parvān and Kaljukistan were already technically at war. There were Kaljuk military encampments on the edge of the Parvān desert even now. The border was closed, and even if it were not, the Parvān Crown Princess was not going anywhere where she would be likely to be taken hostage.

It shocked her out of her resentment and bitterness. She stared at him in horror. "Oh, Kavi!" For a few moments there seemed nothing she could say. "Oh, God, Kavi, what's going to happen?" For she knew from her studies what might and money there was behind the newly-formed Islamic Republic of Kaljukistan, and that Parvān had only its people's determination and its own resources.

"They will not win this war," he said. "But it will cost us dearly." And then she saw the anguish behind his shadowed eyes, and her heart wrung for him. She moved around the low table and knelt by him, feeling helpless and yet determined to help.

"There must be something I can do," she whispered, and reached to touch his cheek. It was the first time she had offered to touch him for days, but he caught her hand in his before it reached its destination, dropped a kiss on the palm, and set it back in her lap.

"There is nothing you can do at the moment. Stay here in the safety of the palace," he said, as though decorative women were a much-needed rarity in times of war and she was no more than decorative. Then he got to his feet. "I must go."

She made no protest at the rejection, merely bowed her head where she knelt and listened as the door opened and closed and he exchanged a word with the courtier who stood guard outside.

It never occurred to her to return to England to continue her education. Not then. If the country was at war, Kavi would need her. In spite of everything, her place was beside him.

He had kept to the shadows of the rocks as he descended the mountain behind her, had moved quickly to the place where the horses were quartered and pressed the soft-mouthed black's nose in the signal for silence. The other horses moved restlessly but made no sound as he bridled the black; he did not waste time for a saddle.

He waited till she was under the protection of the trees, then spurred the horse to a canter. She would hear him soon—would sense the pounding of the hooves through the earth—but without knowing what direction he came from.

She might run, but she could not escape him.

She had had two companions in the palace. The King had been struck with illness early in the fall and was confined to his bed, though no one said what the trouble was. His doctor came and went and looked more unhappy with every visit. One day the King sent for Alinor. She was happy to go— she liked the old man.

"We are both frustrated with having nothing to do," he said kindly. "We must entertain each other."

Of course, he did not have "nothing" to do, he had simply changed his venue of operations to his own private apartments. Advisors and ministers still came and spent long hours with him there, but it was true he could not work as hard as formerly. Alinor realized that it would be her task to take his mind off the events that were causing him stress, for an hour or two each day.

They became close. In those early days, she still believed that this would be her country. And the King was an experienced story-teller. She sat by his bed listening to his tales, and felt, although he never stated it, as though he was passing on a treasure to her, one that it would be her duty to guard and pass on in her turn.

Her other companion was Kavian's niece, Nargis, who began to hero-worship Alinor. From the perspective of an age of fifteen years, her cousin's wife seemed the embodiment of exotic elegance, style, and modern female wisdom. And she was so perfectly beautiful, with her long pale hair.

Between them, Alinor felt comforted. She was content to wait for events.

Her heart was beating hard with fear, not exertion, when she finally reached the cover of the trees. She did not know the valley, or at least could not recall ever having visited it before, but common sense dictated that the nomad camp further along must be by the shores of the river which she saw here. So if she followed the bank, she would get through the forest and down the valley. It was a fast, rushing river: probably it would not meander too much in its journey. The birds were loud now, hundreds of them sat in the branches singing, and between their song and that of the water all else would be drowned out. She would not hear any sound of pursuit. She did not rest, therefore, but hurried faster. Under the cover of the forest there would be no one to see and wonder why a woman was running so wildly.

She was in the unpleasant state of knowing nothing at all of what she ran to, and very little of what she ran from. Kavian, of course. She was running from him. From the past.

There was one other companion she had, with whom she spent more and more time. Nargis's mother and Kavi's aunt, Puran. A sister of the King's wife, widow of his cousin, she was already sixty years old. Nargis had been the child of her middle age, born unexpectedly not long before her husband died. She cherished her beautiful Nargis, and although at first she had been hostile to Alinor's presence, Puran said, her heart could not keep from loving whomever Nargis and Kavi loved.

It was to Puran that Alinor's royal and religious education was entrusted, to Puran she turned for expertise on the labyrinth of palace protocol. Puran had come to the palace only after her husband died, but that gave her fifteen years more experience than Alinor. There were so many things that a future queen had to know about the customs of the palace and its inhabitants. It was Puran who explained the day-to-day running of the palace, what Alinor's duties were and would be, now and when peace was restored, and later, when the Sheikh died and Kavi was crowned. From Puran, too, she learned to recite the daily prayers, learned to keep an ear open for the Call to Prayer wherever she was.

Alinor increasingly came to depend on Puran for all information: what clothes were appropriate on which occasions, how to address servants, what the Parvān people expected of their Crown Princess, what was the correct Parvāni pronunciation of the language. Nothing would alienate the Parvāni people faster than a princess who spoke with the Kaljuk dialect, no matter how few words of it she spoke.

Alinor had been right in that first, curious dread upon seeing the palace—it was a fortress. For a crown princess, anyway. She quickly learned that, whatever she did in Kavi's company, the Sheikh's people would not expect to see their Crown Prince's wife wandering in their fascinating city and markets by herself, or even accompanied by Nargis. Puran was careful to send a man with them whenever they went out, and chided Alinor lightly on expecting Western freedom here.

"Kavi said this wouldn't be necessary. He said I'd be a free woman here."

Puran sighed. She understood how the restrictions must chafe Alinor, but these were difficult times. The Sheikh could not afford to lose the good opinion of his people when a war might be looming. Alinor understood, but it upset her, all the same. She wished Kavi had been less optimistic and more honest about what her life would be. She wouldn't have made a different choice, but she'd have preferred to be prepared.

"They won't recognize me, if I cover my hair," she protested once.

Puran merely said, "There are few tourists in Shahr-i Bozorg. Of course people will know who you are." Then she shrugged. "Of course, if you must go, if this is more important to you than anything else, than this country, then you should go. Of course Westerners are very individualistic." She meant selfish. Faced with an invitation worded like that, Alinor had given in.

After the war began, it grew even worse. Now a man had to be taken off some more important duty to accompany her, and she could not be so selfish as to demand it. Gradually, the narrow world of the palace became Alinor's life.

She began to feel deep anxiety about the future. When Kavi had been promising her that she could work at whatever work she chose with his people, he seemed to have overlooked what her duties would be when she was Queen. When she had believed the prospect of his coming to the throne was a long way off, she had been content not to question too deeply. But now the Sheikh was in bed with an illness no one had explained to her, and she did not know what the prognosis was.

But all that was nothing compared with what was to come.

She felt the unmistakable thunder of a galloping horse in the soles of her feet, and suddenly a black fear invaded her heart: she knew without looking that it was Kavian behind her, in full, angry pursuit, and she understood with a thrill of fear how little she knew him, especially now. What had nearly four years of war made him? Once he had let her go. How would he react to her attempt to escape now?

The hoofbeats grew louder, and all the birds stopped singing. Even the river had softened its headlong rush, here where there were no rocks to challenge its progress, and it opened into a deep, clear pool. There was nothing now to soften the sound of determined pursuit and the spectre of his retribution.

She recognized the spot, not in itself, but in the kind of place it was: such waters as this—still pools under the protection of trees—had in the old days been places of worship to the goddess Anāhita. Anāhita, the special protectress of women, was probably still acknowledged by most mountain women in some form. They would not consider it "religion" to cast a flower into such a pool and ask for the lady's help, any more than did those who tossed money into a well back home, but they were repeating with their actions the ancient rites of worship. And of course, some of the tribes were still of the old religion. They worshipped Anāhita as a duty, kept her place of abode sacred, never polluting it.

And gods who are acknowledged retain their powers. Alinor rushed to the pool's edge and stared down into the smooth-surfaced pool, swirling and eddying a little from obstructions on the bank. Would the water goddess offer her a way out? There were legends about Anāhita's rescue of women who committed their lives to her keeping; stories of women who were carried away from danger to a place of safety. But the water looked deep and dangerous.

The thunder increased, and now, almost panic-stricken, she turned her head, and saw him, mounted on a snorting black horse, riding straight at her. He looked fierce, wild, murderously angry, his eyes flashing, his hair and clothes flowing in the wind of his speed, his teeth white against the desert-tanned skin. She wondered how many men had seen this sight as their last view of the world, and then, with a little prayer, Alinor turned and gave herself into Anāhita's keeping.

It was the King who first told her about the ancient religion, for Puran only shuddered and claimed to know nothing about it. Alinor was fascinated by it, and in particular by the presence of goddesses among the ranks of the deities.

Anāhita, Goddess of Waters. Dallia, secret expert on the old rituals, taught Alinor to place a flower or a small bouquet on water as an offering every morning, and whenever she came upon a river. Anāhita was particularly present in those small, still-seeming pools that sometimes form in rivers or falls.

If Puran had known that just after the dawn prayer most mornings, the new Crown Princess of Parvān slipped invisibly out of the palace and up the mountain path to the narrow river that ran there, crisp and cold; that every morning she set a new flower on the tiny pool that Dallia had pointed out to her, that once a month on Anāhita's day Alinor went further upstream to the dangerous, bigger pool that formed where the water was trapped by rock and bathed there naked, she would have been aghast.

But Puran never found out. It was a secret between Alinor, Dallia, and whatever women of the tribes she met also performing the ritual…and, she suspected, King Kavād, who never failed to remark on her pink cheeks and damp hair, or remind her that it was Anāhita's day.

It was the King who told her the ancient legends, too. How the great Iskandar had fallen in love with a Parvān warrior princess, and how she had refused to marry him because of a vow to Anāhita, to whose service she was dedicated. Kavākeb became his mistress instead—her vow apparently placing no embargo on sex, only marriage—and fought many battles by his side.

One day, after a losing battle in which she was separated from her lover on the battlefield, and pursued by soldiers, Kavākeb had leapt into a river, which at last carried her to a cave. There the warrior princess had called upon her patron goddess, Anāhita, and a door in the rock opened and then closed behind her, admitting her into a garden. From the garden, Kavākeb followed the path of the river through the mountain to safety.

The water was ice-cold, and she came up gasping from the shock. The quilted fabric of her tunic felt as heavy as armour, and the stream was moving faster than she had thought. She felt the power of the current underneath the deceptive surface, which dragged her out of the pool and along the river, and she had no control over her speed, or direction. All she could do was guide her progress somewhat with swimming strokes. If the current got no stronger she might be able to keep herself from dashing against rocks.

Another eddy caught her and she was swung around. Now she could not see what rocks might loom ahead, but she could see Kavian on the bank far behind her, his horse pulled to a snorting stop as he stared at her in furious amazement.

Then he spurred the horse again, and galloped along the bank till he passed her.

The river turned her helplessly again, so she only heard the splash of his own leap into the water beside her. Then his hands were on her, strong, hard, angry hands in a merciless grip, and his voice cursed her once.

"Leave me alone!" she cried, though between the cold and her fear she was hoarse.

"Don't be a fool!" he shouted. "Are you trying to kill yourself?" His grip on her tightened, one arm only. He began to use the other in powerful strokes to draw them by degrees in towards the bank as the river dragged them along. She could not resist, clamped against his side as she was, but she tried. Then she heard the noisy roar from ahead of them, and understood that it was the roar of water meeting rocks.

"If you fight me I will knock you out," he said, and he meant it. But she had spent childhood summers in Canada; she knew the sound of rapids. She began to kick, not to get free, but to lend her efforts to his.

He reached the edge at last, dragged her out, shoved her bodily and untenderly up onto the bank, climbed up himself, and then, headlong, without a pause, flung himself full length on top of her. And before she knew anything, his mouth was savage on hers in a kiss so wild and merciless it stunned her.

Chapter 10

The kiss was powerful, punishing, thorough, and it knocked whatever breath she had left out of her. He held her head, his body imprisoning her, and his lips devoured hers with a pent-up force that might have been passion, or only anger.

After the first shock, she became aware of herself, of her chilled body, of the grass under her, and of the heat where their bodies met. Of the heat and pressure of his lips, the powerful length of the hard warrior's body along hers, the strength of arms and thighs, the hunger in him. And then, the stirring of her own hunger, the fatal melting, like that first melting so long ago, under the oak tree in London, that had sealed her terrible fate.

It was a long time since she had been kissed. It was as though one kiss could wipe out the past, could make her as hungry as she had been in the days when she had loved him so desperately and unreservedly. The urgency of his arms, his body, the power of feeling his chest, his legs covering her like a protection against the world, made her sob and part her lips under the fierce pressure of his. His hands clenched in her hair, against her scalp, and her arms stole up around his back.

His mouth lifted a little, and tenderness took hold of him. Feeling it move through him, pushing at the clinging roots of the anger in his heart, Kavian let her go abruptly and rolled away.

She stifled the cry of protest that rose to her hungry lips and turned her head away. "What do you think you're doing?" she demanded in a cold, small voice.

"I would like to shake you," Kavian said, and, getting to his feet, dragged her up after him. She looked up at him, all her hatred returned. They stood in the green forest, with all the rich fertile sensuality of nature surrounding them, gazing at each other in open hostility.

"That's nothing compared to what I'd like to do to you!" Alinor said. "Why have you brought me here? What do you want from me?"

They were both dripping with water, but neither took any notice of the fact, so gripped were they by the moment.

"From you *I* want nothing." He spoke dismissively, but the anger was there in his eyes, anger and something else, so that she missed the curious stress on the word *I*.

"Then why am I here?" she demanded, outraged protest making her voice almost a shriek. "What the hell is going on?"

"If you had a soul, you would know," he returned. "I should not have to tell you why I have gone after you like a stray dog that does not know where it belongs."

She started to speak, but he carried on over her words. "What did you think? That I would allow you to marry another man while you are married to me? That I would stand aside and let *my wife* commit the crime of bigamy?"

"You *divorced* me!" she shouted in fury. "Are you trying to pretend—"

"I did not divorce you," he said flatly, his eyes glinting like chipped stones. "Don't talk such tripe. And you did not divorce me. Do you think I am unaware of such things? You are my wife and you remain my wife.''

It was just as it had been before, her screaming like a fishwife, him impassive. They hadn't been in each other's company a day, but he had always had the power to reduce her to the kind of insane behaviour that otherwise appalled her.

"You didn't divorce me? Are you forgetting something, or did I imagine that little moment when you said *I divorce thee, I divorce thee!* to me? Maybe it was the *bulbul* I heard, is that it?''

He stared at her for a moment, an expression in his eyes that silenced her mockery. "Don't talk like a fool," he said. "Do you ask me to explain the rules of marriage and divorce to you? You know them as well as I do.''

"Thank you, I preferred not to wait for the other shoe to drop!" A Muslim divorce was not complete without a third repetition, but he knew as well as she did the particular laws applicable to the Parvān royal family.

"You preferred not to wait for anything," he said with cold contempt. "Not for my father to recover, not for me to return from war, not for your—" He broke off, and she saw that he was fighting for control of his anger. He turned away. "I will not argue with you here. Get on the horse.''

Kavian whistled, and the black horse sidled over, blowing a little in affectionate response. He patted the magnificent beast's neck and muttered a word.

"Get up," he said again.

She stood with her arms folded over her breasts. "I don't intend to go with you. I am not your wife, and I am engaged to be married, and as soon as I can find transport I'm going to—"

He bent to pick her up and threw her up on the horse's back, then climbed up behind her. Before she could move, he had spurred the horse to a gallop.

"I will tell you a story of our country's past," said the old King one day. In spite of her troubles, her increasing feeling of having been betrayed by his son, she still visited his sickroom; in spite of everything, his conversation and kindness comforted her. "One day, if God wills it, you will have a son, and you will tell it to him."

"Only my son?" she had teased gently.

He was in bed; it was one of his bad days. His face showed the serenity of those who accept suffering. But the suffering he accepted now was not that of physical pain, but what he saw in the future.

"There may be others," he said. "It is not possible to see just at the moment," and she realized with a little shock that he had not been referring to an old man's romantic ideal of his son's son, but to an actual child whose future he saw.

When she was with the King it always seemed right that she had come here. Whatever was happening between her and Kavi, the King's calm approval made her feel that she had chosen the future which had been chosen for her. "Tell me the story" she begged softly, for not quite yet could she say "our country" as he had done. That would take time.

And so the King told his tales while Alinor listened, enthralled.

Most of the stories he told her of the history of Parvān would never make their way into history books, but had been told in the family for generations. Alinor found she loved listening, and, not trusting her own memory, would return to her apartments in the palace and write them down.

Kavi was by that time in the thick of war, and she thought she saw what fear prompted the Sheikh's impulse to pass on the oral tradition to her. But it didn't really make sense: if Kavi died in the fighting, who could benefit?

It was some time before she understood the totality of the King's vision: he must have known, even before she did, that Alinor was already pregnant with his grandson.

It was clear even from a distance that something was up in the camp. Men were running from their tents, their guns in their hands, and someone was calling out indistinguishably. Kavi spurred his horse to a gallop, and as they approached, one of his Companions, Nima, ran up with the news.

"A prisoner, Lord!" he said. If he noticed that Kavian and Alinor were streaming wet, he made no sign. "Rostam has brought him in."

In the centre of the encampment there was a small crowd of men standing around another man who was on his knees with his hands tied behind his back. His head was bent and he stared at the ground. Without a word Kavi swung off the horse. "A Kaljuk," Nima added unnecessarily.

Kavi turned back to Alinor, still astride the horse. "Go into the tent," he ordered softly in English. "Even if you rode to the other end of the valley, you will not escape me." Then, accompanied by Nima, he strode over to where the prisoner cowered.

The sun was already hot, her clothes were beginning to dry on her body. Alinor dismounted and left the horse with the boy who ran up to take it. There was nothing else to do, nowhere to go. Inside the tent, she was immediately embraced by a flow of concern from Golnesah.

"I was at the Sacred Pool in the forest," she said in explanation. "I fell in. Kavian rescued me."

"We need weapons," Puran had said one day. "Why does your father not act for us? What does he wait for? Was it not all agreed at the beginning?"

Nothing at all had been agreed, but Alinor merely shrugged.

"My father doesn't have much influence, you know. He's not in this area anymore. I've written him, but his voice won't have much impact on Western policy."

"His voice!" snorted Puran. "Why does he not send money, as was agreed? Kavi has performed his part of it, and you do not do yours. Where is the money that was promised?"

"Money?" Alinor repeated blankly.

"What does he have money for, except to save the country of his daughter's husband? Kavi has made you princess. In time you will be queen. But only if we have money for arms now! Tell your father to send money for arms. Tell him how much we need it! Does he not love you? Are not you his only daughter?"

"I'm his only daughter, but my father is not rich, if that's what you mean."

"Don't be a fool, girl! I know it, my brother-in-law knows it, why do you think this marriage with a *farangi*—a foreigner—was approved? He does not understand why your father waits."

She stared at the older woman. "Kavian thinks my father is rich?"

Puran put down her work. "You did not know? But I believed that there was a clear agreement—perhaps it was between Kavian and your father, and not you? You kept your background a secret. The name you use is not your father's name. Your father is a very rich man. Kavian knows it all. Do you tell me that there was no pre-arrangement?" She clucked her tongue, while Alinor stared speechlessly at her. "Holy God preserve us! What a fool Kavian has been!"

"Kavi has never said a word of this to me!" Alinor protested.

Puran fixed her with a black, compelling stare. "But you must give the money anyway. If Kavian does not ask, it is because he waits for you to offer. It will be dangerous to wait longer. The mountain tribes are armed with sticks, with axes, the Kaljuks with mortars. We must have guns. Tell your father. Please, Alinor."

She could hardly breathe for pain. "Kavian knew about...?" She tried again. "Kavian thought I was the daughter of..." Alinor covered her face with her hands. Behind her eyes she could feel a headache tearing its way in. She had never been subject to headaches before her pregnancy; now any kind of strain went immediately behind her eyes.

"Um…what did he…" She started again. "Who does he think—oh, God—who does he think my father is, Puran?"

"I do not remember the name, only that you do **not** use it. He is rich in California."

Rich in California. Alinor almost laughed. It sounded like the title of a film. "Jonathan Holding," she said evenly. "Is that who Kavian thinks my father is?"

Puran looked at her in slowly dawning horror. "It is not so?" she whispered. "Is this man not your father?"

"My roommate's father," she said, with ironic false brightness, while her head seemed torn apart by pain. "The girl I lived with at university. I guess Kavian married the wrong girl."

They took the prisoner to a cave high up the hillside, Kavian and a number of his men, and then did not appear again. At lunchtime a boy came down to request that food and water be sent up to the cave. It became apparent that whatever plans Kavian had had for moving camp today had been shelved.

Alinor helped Golnesah to prepare and pack the food for those in the cave, while the others in the camp prepared their own. In daylight it was obvious that the camp was a war camp. The men were constantly armed, and went out and came back on regular forays. If they brought back food in the shape of small animals they had hunted, it was half-absently: they had not gone out for that reason, but had killed their meat as opportunity arose.

If at first she had imagined that they were waiting to see what pursuit there would be after the kidnap of herself, Alinor soon learned otherwise. It was Golnesah who told her, as she kneaded the dough for the *naan,* that they were looking for Kaljuks who had crossed the border illegally. She did not know why.

Now they had caught one.

Kavian returned to the tent that night looking grey, exhausted and grim, and in spite of herself, Alinor's heart went out to him. "You look like death!" she said.

"I feel like death," he said, dropping his rifle to lean against a chair. He sank down on a pile of cushions. "Nuri, is there any food?" he asked wearily, and she knew that she was seeing a man who had come back to camp many times in the past few years, weary of war and killing, to find there was no food to sustain him. She felt a stabbing guilt for the fact that she had left him to such a fate instead of sharing it with him. In that moment she felt, too, the first understanding of how terrible his three and a half years had been.

"Yes," she said, for what else had there been to do all day, save prepare simple food against her man's return, like any mountain woman? "Yes, there's food."

The large low table was laid with a meal at one side of the room, but she brought a small carved wooden table and unfolded it beside him, then set one of the plates on it, and poured him the herbal infusion that Golnesah had made. He grunted appreciatively and reached out to take one of the attractive little morsels she had laid on the plate and tossed it into his mouth. He ate three in a row and then sighed deeply, as if the food had the power to dispel the experiences of the day. Meanwhile she described learning how to make the mountain dish from Golnesah, from the limited ingredients that were at hand.

"Thank you," he said, and smiled at her, the old smile, the smile of tolerant amusement. Next he would be calling her his *bulbul,* she thought, and stopped talking. "You always brought comfort," he went on softly. "No matter how evil was the day, to be in your presence at the end of it was enough to make me forget."

She glanced at him in quick confusion. "Really? I—I never knew that." She looked away, and his voice fell on her bent head.

"No? I thought I had said it many times. Your voice is

like the song of the *bulbul*. It draws out one's cares and gives them to the wind. Even now. Even after so much."

She stared at him. "I never knew," she said again.

"You have talked for another since," he reminded himself. "Gabriel. What does Gabriel compare your voice to, my wife?"

"Nothing at all," Alinor said, in another tone entirely, as the little bubble of potential understanding between them burst. "There's a hot bath ready. Will you have that before you eat the rest of your dinner, or do you want to eat first?"

"All the duties of a dutiful wife," he said. "Perhaps it is as well for me that you kept in practice." He stood up and began to strip off his waistcoat and shirt as he moved into the adjoining room. Alinor went outside, to get the last bucket of water from where it sat simmering on the fire.

When she returned with it, he was standing in lamplight, stripped naked, reaching for the soap and cloth that she had laid out on a stool. She stopped and unconsciously stood looking at him.

He was like a painting, but by no artist whose hand she knew. Standing in the gloom against a backdrop of beautifully woven hangings, with the lamplight bathing his pale skin, shadow nesting in the hollows of his hard body...he was thinner, much thinner than he had been, and there were scars she had never seen on his flesh before. One high on the right arm, a purling of the flesh as though a tiny finger had pushed it into a little mound, one on his breast, and one, fresher than the others, that looked like a bayonet or sword thrust, low across his hip and thigh. She wondered how close that blow, whatever it was, had come to destroying his manhood, and was abruptly, desperately glad for his sake that no such evil had befallen him. How could he have survived the loss of that masculine power? He had been a fierce, proud lover with her. Even now the memories stirred her, and she felt the skin of her cheeks and across her chest prickle with the increased heat of the blood that fed them.

He was standing unashamed, watching her watch his body,

his posture strong but easy, soap and cloth in one hand, his eyes dark. "You will have no chance for further comparisons of me and another man," he said, as though she had spoken. "I do not bring you back in order to make you my wife again."

If he lied, it was to himself also, and Kavian did not bother to turn away to hide from her eyes the way that his flesh gave the lie to his words. It was not that he desired her, but only that a woman's eyes on a man's naked flesh must always cause it to stir.

He stepped towards her and reached for the pail of water in her hand. Alinor swallowed, her eyes fixed by the dark nest of hair and strong flesh that arose from it. Three years, three long years. And he had kissed her this morning, a kiss so...and he was naked, her animal brain kept on noticing, naked and with desire causing his flesh to make itself ready for her, turning itself into marble in order to give her the pleasure she remembered...

But she heard his words then, as they filtered up through the layers of her preoccupation to consciousness at last. She tore her gaze away from his nakedness and looked up into his eyes.

He had been more and more stirred by the hunger in her eyes. Against his will the hand that reached for the bucket of water shifted, and would have reached for her arm, her face, her hair...

"Well, I'm glad to hear that," Alinor said, her voice and eyes suddenly cold. "Because you aren't going to get a chance at making me your wife again!"

She bent and set the pail on the ground, a movement that brought her mouth so close to his loins that the air crackled. Then she whirled and was gone.

Chapter 11

"I'm going to leave you," she had said baldly.

Kavian had come home that same evening, after her disastrous conversation with Puran, for the first time in a long time. Until then she had told no one about being pregnant, wanting to tell him first. The timing wasn't good, of course, but she had thought he would be pleased...

Now she knew that he would not be pleased. He would not want to be tied in this way to a mistaken marriage. Of course, if she had been the woman he thought she was, if she'd been Lana, he'd have been delighted to have this to hold over Jonathan Holding's head: one day your grandson will be the Sheikh of Parvān if only you use your money to save it now...now it was all clear. The determined pursuit, everything, from the beginning.

He had come in that night to consult his father, dirty, battle-torn, deeply fatigued, grateful for the prospect of an hour snatched with her before going back to his men. The bath and the meal had been waiting for him, but like a child she had not been able to wait for misery.

"I'm going to leave you," she had said.

He had stood by the steaming bath, too tired to speak as he silently stripped off his battle dress. He was Commander in Chief of his father's forces, the Royal Parvān Armed Forces. He had got his shirt half unbuttoned when she spoke.

He smiled. "Come back soon," he commanded. "I can bathe alone, but I will not eat alone. I need my wife beside me."

"Kavi, I want to go home."

He frowned, and she hated herself for adding to the cares, the fatigue he carried. Then she reminded herself that the comfort he sought from her was money.

"Home? What do you mean? Your home is here."

"I want to go back to London. Or—" since she really hadn't thought it over "—to my parents in the States."

He stopped undressing. "Why? For how long?"

"For good, Kavi. I'm going to leave you."

He went completely still. She had never seen any living thing, even a tree, so still. It was like watching death, she thought.

"You are afraid of the war?"

"No."

"What is it, Nuri?" *My light.* "What troubles you?"

She could not tell him. She couldn't say, *I just found out you married me for money I haven't got.* Her throat hurt and her head hurt and she felt battered. Now she wished she had let Puran tell him what mistake he had made before she said anything. "I think we made a mistake, marrying each other. I think we should give up now. Anyway, I don't think I'm really cut out to be Queen of Parvān."

He stopped unbuttoning his shirt and grabbed her by the arm. "What are you talking about?" he demanded. "What is wrong with you? Are you angry because I brought you here and now there is war? But I could not know for certain. We hoped it would be averted. What should I have done? Left you in England until I was certain what would happen?

You are a strong, brave woman, you are not afraid of war! You said you would fight beside me!''

He tried to kiss her, but she avoided his mouth. She felt as though some demon had got hold of her brain, was driving her in a way she would not have chosen to go. Why hadn't she let him have his bath and his dinner? She was being goaded by pain, by the renewal of that old sense of isolation, and it was making her do terrible things.

But she could not stop. ''Please don't kiss me. I'm trying to explain.''

He shouted at her then, angry and cheated and understanding her not at all. He shouted, telling her that she betrayed him, and turned to snatch up his gun, and then he was gone. Then she snapped out of it, then she tried to stop him, but it was too late.

He left the palace immediately, and went back to the war. The next day there was a battle in the desert, with heavy casualties. But Kavian did not return to the palace afterwards.

There was blood on his shirt. Alinor picked up his clothes as he bathed, and saw the dried blood first on the knee of his trousers. There was more on his shirt cuff, and the front of the shirt was spattered with flecks of it.

''Have you hurt yourself?'' she asked, when he came out of the bedroom bathed and changed.

''No,'' he said.

They held each other's gaze for a long moment. ''Is he still alive?'' she asked grimly.

He shrugged at her ignorance. ''The Kaljuks are not such brave men. The first sight of their own blood is usually enough. Other people's blood does not trouble them, even that of women and children, but their own is precious enough.''

''How do you expect to preserve Parvān civilisation if you act like a barbarian?''

''I do not act like a barbarian,'' he said mildly. ''I protect my people in whatever way is required. This is not barba-

rism.'' He was angry, but not because her jibe reached him.
Something was simmering deep in him, and if she stirred it,
would she bring his anger on her own head? She stood staring at his face for a moment. It was a hard, cruel face now,
a face that had suffered too much, lost too much, made too
many hard decisions, done too many necessary things. He
had won a war against all the odds, and how could she judge
him?

"Did he tell you anything?" she asked after a long moment.

His face closed down. "He told us what he knew."

His tone said that was all she would hear from him. This
much at least had not changed, Alinor told herself in sudden
irritation. She sighed explosively and went and sat down on
the cushions by the table without a word. If he was hungry,
let him join her. If not, let him leave, or go to bed, or whatever he damned well wanted.

"This looks delicious. Did you learn all this from Golnesah today?" Kavi said appreciatively, sinking down beside
her.

She said deliberately, "She told me what she knew."

Kavian looked at her. "Why do you want to hear the details? They are unpleasant."

"Oh, and women should be spared all mention of what's
unpleasant," she returned dryly.

He smiled a little, and took the food she ungraciously
shoved towards him, as gently as if she had knelt at his feet
to offer it. "Why should they not?" he asked quietly. *"Bis-
mullah."* He began to eat.

"Correct me if I'm wrong," she began, still ironic, but
somewhat abashed by his politeness. It was Parvān custom
that harsh words should not be taken in at the same time as
food. *When food is being eaten,* Puran had explained, *the
heart is open. The tip of a hard word will pierce the open
heart like a spear. That is what we believe.* "But the kind
of warfare where women were the safe haven went out with
the invention of aerial bombardment, didn't it?"

"What do you mean?"

She had seen the pictures. She had read the news reports till her eyes had seemed to weep blood. She knew what she knew. "Women suffer the tortures of hell. They carry on planting, and harvesting, and milking goats and preparing food through a hideous war waged against civilians. How does not talking about it spare them?"

He understood what she was saying. "You were not in this position, however. Why should I have brought the war to you?"

"Didn't you ever hear of shared suffering, Kavi?"

"There is some suffering that cannot be shared," he said, his voice flat and distant.

"I know you think so," she returned dryly; and suddenly, as though goaded to it, he erupted.

"Truly, can you not understand this? War is not a day at the office! Do you think a man can fight a battle with his feet soaked in the lifeblood of his friends and be himself? And come home and relieve his feelings by talking about it to his wife? Such a man *has* no feelings, Nuri! If he did, he would be mad!"

"So what happens, then?" she demanded. "Everybody pretends it's not happening? What good is that? When a woman has just lost her hand, or her eye, or her baby to a landmine, or her village or her fields or her well or all three to carpet bombing, she's supposed to talk to her husband about the weather?"

Kavian eyed her for a long, measuring moment. "Do you think it hurts a woman to lose her baby, Alinor?" he asked.

She jerked upright as the shaft pierced her open heart. "Yes, I do!" she said, through her teeth. What did he mean, *think?* How dare he put it that way? How dare he suggest that she had not suffered? "Yes, I *think* so!"

"How long does it hurt her?"

She could not believe the edge in his voice. As though he wanted to punish, not comfort her. As though he blamed her

for what had happened. How could he speak to her like that?
"I don't want to talk about it," she said stonily. "It's over."

"You have put the child out of your mind?"

"Shut up about it!"

"You put him out of your mind?"

She had told no one about it, and she could not tell him now. To no one had she confessed the terrible, punishing compulsion of grieving mothers the world over, to count the days, the months, to say to oneself, "Today he would have been such and such an age..." She had believed Kavi grieved, too, when he heard—had believed it must touch him, in spite of everything. There had been times when she had wanted so much to be with him, to share the grief with the only other person capable of understanding. Not in her lowest moments had she ever imagined that Kavi would *blame* her. Like any Middle Eastern chauvinist, thinking women only good for one thing, and angry when they fail.

"How dare you talk to me like this! You have no reason and no right to blame me!"

"I have no right? A woman runs away like a coward, like a thief in the night, and her husband has no right to blame her?"

"You weren't my husband. You aren't now."

"What are you talking about?" he demanded furiously.

"'I divorce thee, I divorce thee,' Kavi, remember?" she shouted. She couldn't bear this. Abruptly she dropped her head. "Oh, hell, let's stop this! Let's eat."

There was a terrible silence from him for a moment, and without lifting her head, she reached out and took some food from a plate and put it in her mouth.

They did eat, in silence, for a few minutes. But for once, Kavi could not contain his feelings.

"You knew very well why I said this. Why do you mention it? You knew I did not mean it," he said.

"Did I?" she responded without emphasis. She lifted food to her mouth.

"Of course! You were so unreasonable, so many arguments, every time I saw you. Of course I only said this to wake you up, to make you think what you were doing. A man says these words not when he means divorce, but when he wishes a woman to look at what she is doing!''

She wasn't really listening, but that got through to her. She turned and looked him full in the face. ''Really? Have you ever heard of hormones, Kavi?'' she demanded.

''What do you mean?''

''For God's sake, I was pregnant! I was seven months pregnant with a very difficult, horrible, disastrous pregnancy and you were away most of the time getting yourself killed, for all I knew. Do you have any idea how vulnerable a woman's feelings are when she's pregnant?''

He stared at her. ''I see,'' he said slowly.

''It was as if you'd carved it in stone and hammered the stone to my heart. To me it was a terrible betrayal. That you could say that to me when I was pregnant with your—''

She broke off, pushing back the sudden eruption of feeling that threatened. He was not interested. All he was interested in was blame. She would not expose herself to his anger. ''Forget it,'' she said coldly.

He ignored that. ''You believed me, then? You thought I intended to divorce you?''

''Oh, yes,'' she said dryly.

''But no Parvān man divorces his wife in such a manner. Even if it is allowed under religious law, have you forgotten we are a secular state? In any case, it is impossible to divorce when a wife is pregnant. It is not legal. You know this.''

''But the royal family is above the law,'' she pointed out.

''Historically, yes. But my great-grandfather renounced such privileges many years ago.''

''Well, good for him!'' she said brightly. ''Have you finished your meal, or can I get you something more?''

After that night, the terrible night when she had threatened to leave him, the fights started in earnest. She never told Kavian what Puran had told her, but although he never mentioned the subject to her—how could he?—she believed Puran told him about his mistake. She saw him less and less. Whenever she did see him, they fought.

She always ended up shouting that she wanted to leave him, but it was not true, and she could not understand why she felt so driven to say it. She loved him, he was her husband, she was pregnant with his child. Perhaps all she wanted was to hear him say he would not let her go.

In any case, the war made her leaving nearly impossible. The airport was closed to civilian traffic, the desert full of soldiers, the entire border with Kaljukistan closed, the other borders mountainous and impassable in winter. There was little mail going outside the country, none coming in.

If he had wished he could have done it, of course. He could have put her on a military flight, or asked for diplomatic safe passage for her. But he did not do so. She never understood why. She was always waiting for the blow to fall. Maybe that was why she threatened to leave—so that when he finally said it, she would have said it first.

She was safe in the palace. His ancient forebears could not have known it, but they had chosen a site safe from aerial bombardment as well as most other kinds of attack: the mountains were so close, a plane would have to pass along one narrow and dangerous flight path, with an impossibly sharp climb at the end of the run. Any pilot foolish enough to risk it would run a great risk of immolation against a wall of mountain. It would not be worth the attempt. The city was an easier target.

She had been nervous of his reaction if she told him she was pregnant, and so she told no one. It became harder to keep it a secret as time went on, because she was ill. She could no longer drink tea or coffee, and many foods turned her stomach. She began to have cravings for ridiculous things, foods from her Canadian childhood that she had not eaten in years, like hot dogs and butter tarts. Food that would have been impossible to obtain even were the country not at war.

Dallia knew—it was impossible to keep it from her personal maid—but she swore Dallia to secrecy. She hardly knew why she did so—what could she gain? She knew she was confused and thinking disjointedly, but once she had learned to mistrust Kavian she could feel safe nowhere.

From his sickbed, the Sheikh, with the help of his advisors, was handling the negotiations with foreign countries, the offers of aid and the price demanded. One day Kavian came in from the front for discussions with his father. He sent Alinor word that he would see her that night.

He was determined that this night should see no fighting. He would not argue with her. He would court her instead, he would remove her fears. At heart, he was sure, she had courage. He would call it up in her.

He bathed in another part of the palace and went to her in civilian clothes. It was late, but he had ordered a meal to be sent to their apartments.

She was pacing the floor when he arrived. He didn't let her speak a word; he kissed her—tenderly, at first, and then, as he tasted the hunger on her lips, with increasing passion, his intentions already half forgotten. "My love," he said, "my light," and she sobbed and clung to him like a starveling. Then he was sure he could win. He kissed her and held her, and reminded her how much he loved her, and when he felt her tremble his hungry passion for her soared.

He made love to her until she wept with joy, and then he wept also. She lay across his naked chest afterwards, her hair splayed out around them, her skin slippery with their mutual sweat, and it seemed as though no words were necessary. They had perfect understanding. He heard the servant bring the food into the next room, and he rose and brought it into the bedroom and set it beside their bed. And then he offered her food from his own hands, which she tried to resist.

"Eat, Nuri," he whispered, and she could not refuse such a loving command. But within a few minutes, she stood up and moved to the bathroom, and only when the sound of her vomiting reached him did he understand.

* * *

Alinor learned what information they had extracted from the Kaljuk captive through Golnesah. It was not good, but as Kavian had said, they had been half expecting it. The man was a member of a group of terrorists. Their plan was a campaign of bombing—the House of Parliament and other buildings—meant to foment revolution, overthrow the monarchy, and bring Parvān to the rule of Islamic law.

What was news was the unwelcome information that the rest of the group was already within Parvān's borders, and on the way to the capital.

They would break camp at noon and go back to Shahr-i Bozorg. That much she had learned from Kavi's own mouth, before he went off in the early morning. Golnesah also knew it; she would return to her people's village that day.

Alinor had come with nothing, and so she had nothing to give the nomad woman in recognition of her service. At last she remembered the wedding dress, which Golnesah had lovingly cleaned and folded and wrapped with white cheesecloth. Alinor brought it out and asked Golnesah to accept it.

It was a very ancient tradition, the giving of a "robe of honour" between a sovereign and a subject who had performed some signal service. Alinor knew even that Golnesah's great-grandfather had been given such a robe by Kavi's ancestor. Golnesah accepted the token with the gratitude of one who felt herself honoured. Alinor was relieved.

"Perhaps, as it is difficult to put on as it is, you will cut it up and make something more useful of the cloth," she suggested. Golnesah opened her eyes wide.

"Not to offend thee, Lady," she said, in the proud but polite manner that mountain folk used to their sovereign, "but I shall wear it as you do yourself, for the riding of horses. I am, God be thanked, a good horsewoman. During the war, the Sheikh required all our horses, but now already we have two again, and I often ride. This robe I shall wear upon such occasions."

Torn between admiration, tender amusement and pain, Alinor inclined her head. "May you ride all your days." It was a traditional farewell.

"May your own days be long, Lady."

Chapter 12

"Alinor, are you pregnant?" he had asked in soft amazement, when she returned to the room where he sat.

She knew he would guess. She steeled herself to look at him. "I don't think so," she said stupidly.

"But you are sick! What else can it be?"

"Yes, I mean yes, I am."

He gazed at her. "Is this why you are so afraid, why you wish to leave me? You fear not for yourself, but for the child?"

She took a deep breath and saw where it would lead if she said no. She was not strong enough now for what would ensue. She was too emotional now to listen to his explanations of his reasons for their marriage. She knew she would cry and plead, adding humiliation to everything else. So she let him believe the answer was yes.

I can't face it, she whispered to the fates. *I feel so weak and ill. If he can pretend he loves me, I need the pretence now.*

He seemed delighted—not just by the pregnancy, but by

the excuse it provided for all her confusing behaviour. He put out his hand and when she put her own into it, he drew her down on top of him and kissed her gently, smiling. "Why have you not told me before, Nuri?"

"I wasn't sure you'd be—I didn't know how you'd feel. It's not the best time, is it?"

"If God has chosen it, it must be best," he said simply. "Is it a boy or a girl?"

She laughed. "Kavi, how am I to know that here? We're miles from an ultrasound machine or a doctor capable of giving an amniocentesis!"

He frowned amusedly. "Women know. What can a machine say that your own heart does not already know?"

She was more used to people mocking women's understanding of their own bodies. "Well, then, it's a boy."

He smiled. "Good, this is very good. This will please my father." She was instantly nervous.

"But Kavi, what if I'm wrong?"

"Then it will please me. I hope she will have *kamrang* hair, and eyes just the colour of her mother's." He paused then, as if understanding something. "Is this another reason that you fear to stay? For the sake of the ultrasound machine? Are you afraid our medicine is not good enough, Nuri?"

She saw the frown in his eyes, as though the same fear had suddenly occurred to him. And suddenly it all seemed real. They were husband and wife, delighted by the prospect of their child's birth, worrying about the future, sharing feelings for the first time in weeks. "No," she said. "I'm young, and my mother always said the women of our family have easy births."

He kissed her hand in gratitude. "We have not the latest equipment in the hospital, but my father has sent many skilled doctors to the West for medical training in the past twenty years. You do not have to worry about this."

"Anyway, I always said I'd have natural childbirth and a midwife. Can't I have a midwife, too?"

"Ah, what a diplomat the Shahbanu Alinor is! I will say

to the tribes that you have asked for a midwife from among
them. The mountain women are excellent midwives—they
have so much practice. They have seen everything.''

"I didn't know the tribes were so prolific. Do they have
lots of babies?''

Kavian smiled. "The mountain midwives deliver all the
animals, as well as babies. Cows, horses, sheep, goats, even
dogs where there is a problem.''

"Oh, well, I'll be in good hands, then!'' she said giggling,
for Kavian's obvious happiness and lightheartedness at the
news had grounded her. "Anybody who can deliver a sheep,
after all!''

But the happy pleasure they found in each other's company did not last.

"You have been wise," said Puran, with a warm smile.
"This was well done. Almost I suggested it, but then I
thought better of it.''

"Suggested what?'' Alinor was in bed, for now she could
admit to feeling sick and needing sleep. She rarely truly enjoyed the older woman's company, but she was so desperate
for human companionship that she was pathetically grateful
to her for her visits.

"It was not merely for money, you know, that my brother-
in-law wished Kavian to marry when he did. I am sorry if I
made you think so. It came of my impatience because you
were not offering the money. But of course this was not
Kavian's only reason for marrying you. Of course he has not
married a woman he does not love for the sake of money.''

"Oh,'' said Alinor quietly, for she could hear the insin-
cerity that Puran tried to hide. She wondered who had ordered her to try to fix what she had broken—Kavi, or his
father?

"And now, the baby, of course— There is no wisdom like
a woman's wisdom! We say that.''

She felt very stupid. Her head was clogged with cotton
wool and there was no reality except the baby that was grow-

ing inside her. She smiled, wishing her own mother were here instead of this strong-featured, powerful old woman who didn't look as if she'd ever had a head stuffed with cotton wool. She tried to imagine Puran pregnant and stupid, and failed. "I don't feel very wise."

"My brother-in-law has always feared that a war would end his line. There is only Kavian to carry it on. My sister had no more children. Of course, we planned that Kavian and Nargis would marry when she turned seventeen. They have always loved each other, you know she worships his shadow. But when war became inevitable, and Kavian was going to fight, we knew that—she is so young, she is still growing, not like myself at her age. It would be wrong for her to bear a child so young, her hips still so slender... When Kavād learned what his son intended, to marry a wealthy American's daughter, he said to me that God had answered our question. He sent his approval and urged Kavi's immediate return, so that the line could be assured. I thought him wrong, I thought to wait one year for Nargis could be no bad thing. But the King said that war would come sooner than that, and you see that he was right."

Alinor lay in a cocoon of cotton wool, letting the words wash over her. "What's the war got to do with it?" she asked. It was only afterwards that the words would become a torment to her.

"If Kavian dies, there will be trouble with the tribes. Not now, but when the war is over. But if he has a son, even though it is an infant when he dies, the tribes can be kept in line. Of course he will not send you away when you hold the future of the kingdom in your womb. It was very shrewd of him to tell his father it would be a boy. There will be time enough to disappoint him if it is not the case."

"But I really do feel it's a boy," Alinor said, disliking Puran's admiration without really knowing why. "I didn't just make it up."

"Of course," said Puran at once. "Many women feel that it is a boy at the beginning, so anxious are they to please

their husbands. Later you will feel more confident." She
smiled and shook her head. "I said, too, that foreign women
did not like to have children, that you would refuse to do so.
That is why I did not advise this course of action." She
raised her hands in a self-deprecating shrug. "But again, see
how wrong I was.

A long procession of horses, mules and men climbed up
the hillside towards the northern pass. Kavi rode beside Alinor, though anything like escape would be impossible now.
Halfway along the procession one man rode with a blindfold,
his hands tied behind his back, one of the Companions leading the mule he was mounted on. Unable to see or anticipate
the struggling movement of his mount, Alinor reflected, he
must find it an uncomfortable ride. Under the blindfold, the
flesh of the man's face was bruised black.

She watched the prisoner wordlessly while he was in view
at a bend in their way, and then turned her head to find Kavi
watching her. "Is that how you treated Gabe?" she asked
with biting reproach.

"Your fiancé is not a sneaking coward who wars against
unarmed women and children, he is a man. Therefore I
treated him as a man," Kavi replied, with a haughty masculine pride almost unknown in the West.

Until this moment she had been half-doubtful, but this
confirmed her wildest suspicions. "You really kidnapped
him?" she demanded incredulously.

"I wished to avoid embarrassment for you in the church,"
Kavi said silkily.

"Oh, give me a break! You didn't want to spare me anything!" she said contemptuously, and then she was caught
by a dangerous look in his eyes, and quailed. "Sorry," she
muttered, for the look reminded her that, while he would put
up with many things from her, he would never accept that
tone in her voice. She could scream like a fishwife, she could
blame and berate him, but if she let contempt thread her
tone... *Do not speak to me with this in your voice, Alinor,*

he would say, for he had never called her Nuri in such moments. *This is not a voice to use to your husband. I am a man, a warrior, I come from a tribe of warriors.* He never said 'prince,' or based his demand for respect on the royal blood, but only on the fighting spirit of his mountain and desert ancestors.

He accepted the apology with an arrogant nod that half annoyed and half awed her, and then went on as though the moment had not happened, as befits a monarch with a subject who has erred through ignorance, "I informed him of how things stood between us, that you were not free to marry him. I asked him to renounce his claim to you in return for his life and his freedom. He refused."

She gasped. "He did?"

"He said that you had assured him that our marriage had never been legal and that in any case I had divorced you. He said he naturally accepted your version of events." He turned to gaze at her. "Did you indeed tell him these things?"

"Of course I did. It's the truth. What did you do then? Have your flunkies beat him up? They seem pretty practised." She threw a glance in the direction of the Kaljuk prisoner.

"I am not accompanied by flunkies at the moment," he informed her graciously. "I told him that I would keep him prisoner in order to prevent the marriage."

"But you thought better of it later. No doubt because you remembered you had no legal claim, after all."

"Alinor, you are very much a citizen of the West, holding in contempt all rituals save your own. But I assure you, a Parvān marriage is legally as well as morally binding, and is recognized in all the countries of the world."

She stared at him, for his voice carried conviction. "But—" She fell silent in confusion and dismay.

His eyebrows were up, inviting more, but she only challenged, "Why did you let him go, then?"

"I did not let him go. He escaped. He attacked his guard barehanded—"

Alinor smiled smugly. "Gabe is a seventh Dan black belt."

Kavi's eyes glinted with danger. "Do not sing to me the praises of another man, my wife," he said softly.

She turned away, furious with herself for being unable to answer.

After the announcement of her pregnancy Alinor had one more visit with the Sheikh, who smiled and told her how pleased he was, and told her another legend to tell her son. But after that, his condition grew suddenly worse, and there were no more meetings. He was too tired, she was informed, and had to save his limited energy for visits from his advisors and his son.

She was often desperately lonely. Winter set in, and there was more snow than she had seen in her life. She never visited Anāhita's Sacred Pool now, and realized how much she had needed those laughing morning bathes with the tribal women. Kavi hardly got to the palace, rarely had time to spend more than an hour or two with her. Their truce did not last. They argued often. It always ended up with him demanding to know what she wanted. "What do you *want*, Nuri? What do you want from me?"

What she wanted was to believe that he loved her.

"I love you! Of course I love you! What else can I do? What can I say? Believe me!"

But she could not believe him, and it would start all over again.

"How is your father?" The Sheikh's health was one thing that had never seemed to make it into Western news broadcasts. They had ridden in silence for an hour, a silence punctuated by the cries of the uncomfortable Kaljuk, whose feet were tied under the mule, and who fell half off from time to time.

"My father is in hospital," Kavi said briefly.

"I'm sorry." Ridiculously inadequate words. "Will I be able to visit him?"

"You would, if he were here. He has gone to Germany. Our hospitals are too understaffed to cope with twenty-four-hour nursing, and the kind of drugs he needs are the last on our list of requests to the Red Cross."

She knew how much he loved and revered his father. She searched for words, but found none. "I'm sorry," she said again. "Has he been there all this time?"

"He has been there for some months. He lasted until the peace, and then gave way."

"So he recovered a little after that second attack?"

"What second attack?"

"When I was pregnant. I used to visit him every day in his room, and then, just after…then he had—I don't know, I always thought it was another heart attack, or whatever it was. And I wasn't allowed to see him again."

The horses jogged along under them, while Kavian gazed at her. "You've forgotten. It was not he, but you, who were too sick. You were in bed. You would not come to him, and it was thought best that he did not try to visit you."

She frowned in amazement. "No, Kavi, I'm sure—no, I was all right, I was tired, but not that tired! I'm sure I was told…" She trailed off. "Puran said he was too sick to see me, I'm sure of it!"

Kavi only shrugged and looked withdrawn, which effectively dried up her interest in asking about anyone else in the palace.

At the last her only regular companions were Puran, Nargis, and Dallia. With Dallia, Alinor's limited grasp of Parvāni meant her conversations were generally restricted to the physical world—what food or drink she wanted, how she felt this morning, what a cold day it was, how much it had snowed in the night.

Nargis was determined to improve her own limited English through practice, something Alinor now found mentally exhausting. Only Puran understood what Alinor was going through, could comfort her in a reasonable English with the promise of future well-being, could relate Alinor's experience to that of a thousand other women. Only she understood her fears and worries, and could sympathize with her anguish at the way she had been used. When Alinor began to long for her own mother, for a doctor who spoke her own language—because the doctor who came up from the hospital to treat her had taken his training in Germany—for childhood foods and familiar places, Puran understood. Kavi had been selfish, she said, although she well understood why. He should have sent her abroad to have the baby in peace. Suppose a plane were to get through and bomb the palace?—then all would have been in vain.

But there was no way out now. Alinor must stay and have the baby here, unfair as that was. There might be a way out over the mountains with a proper guide, but not in midwinter, and not for a pregnant woman. If only Puran had known before winter set in how desperately Alinor would long for her own home at this time, she would have done something. If only Alinor had confided her pregnancy to Puran earlier. But it was all too late now.

"Mistress," Dallia whispered to her once, flustered and anxious and looking over her shoulder, "remember the coin! Remember the coin!"

She watched him covertly, whenever the demands of the terrain drew his horse slightly ahead of her own. It was over three years since she had last seen him, except in news photographs, but there was more than three years of change in him. He still rode tall in the saddle, but now there was a different quality to the line of his back, as though his endurance had been tested to the last degree, and he had overcome.

His beard had always given the handsome young prince an enormous presence and charisma, but the newly-revealed chin bespoke a man's decision and firm resolution.

With a pang she remembered the high-spirited young man she had once known, bright, courageous, optimistic, but above all, young. The man before her now was not old, it wasn't that, but he was... *seasoned.* He looked like a man who has experienced most of the surprises life has to offer, and expects to be able to deal with anything that comes his way.

He looked like a man who has learned that most of the surprises life has to offer involve suffering.

Unaccountably, her heart wrung for him. Her sufferings over the past few years had been hard, but they must have been small in comparison with the constant daily hardship, destruction and grief Kavi had met. She had one precious little life to mourn. He had an entire nation's.

It was some time before she did remember the coin that Dallia was referring to—the gold coin that she had fatally carried into the bridal chamber with her and which meant an enemy. She frowned over Dallia's meaning for a while, until she remembered something else—the second coin. The coin that Dallia knew nothing about.

She began to worry compulsively over which meaning the coins held. If the jinx had been removed on the first coin, did that mean the second coin now had the meaning of one coin—therefore an enemy—or did it still have the meaning of two coins?

Suddenly she grew terrified for her baby. She was having such a hard pregnancy, and she did not know what that meant. Did women who had hard pregnancies lose their babies more often than others? Was there any connection?

She was pathetically dependent on Puran now, had come to love her almost as a mother. Puran was her expert on the great business of childbearing, as she had been on the House of Durran and palace life. When the superstitious dread of the coins overtook her she at last consulted her mentor.

"You dropped two," Puran repeated carefully, "and the child picked up only one." Alinor's heart sank. She had been hoping that a strong, sensible woman like Puran—a woman, moreover, who rejected all truck with the old religion as being a pollution of Islam—would have no patience with ancient superstitions, but although the older woman was doing her best to hide it, she clearly felt appalled. She smiled a cheerful smile that did not reach her eyes.

"But you yourself did not touch either coin," she said bracingly, as if that made it all right.

"No, I said, I stepped on one of them."

Puran's eyes were instantly hooded. "Ah—ah well!" She shrugged and smiled again. "This is only superstition, my dear, it is best not to worry about it! In any case, we are surrounded by death. The war gets daily worse."

But there was a pitying light in Puran's eyes that terrified Alinor, and when she bowed her head and muttered a quick prayer, Alinor quailed. "Tell me! Tell me!" she begged again, as Puran gazed mutely at her, and her friend sighed and shook her head sadly.

"My child, a woman who has seen two coins—forgive me, I should have asked about this! Then I could have advised…"

Alinor waited with her heart between her teeth.

"A bride who has—two coins—she is best advised not to become pregnant for one entire year after the marriage has taken place."

The adrenalin of fear pumped through her body, making her weak, and the baby within kicked in response. It was foolish, stupid, nothing but an ancient superstition, as little connected to reality as black cats and ladders. So Alinor tried to tell herself, but the fear went deeper than logic. It was a threat to her baby, and it went deeper than anything had gone before. She felt it pierce the marrow of her bones.

The journey up to the capital took many hours, and they were among the saddest of her life. The valley they had camped in seemed to be one of the few that had escaped the devastation, perhaps because it had no permanent sites. Now she saw exactly what it was that had changed Kavian. The destruction had been wholesale. Villages which once had thrived, surrounded with flocks and crops, lay bleakly empty, grey and unpopulated, shattered structures of brick and stone standing without roof, window or door, barren and comfortless under the bright sun. Whole hillsides that had once been green terraced fields were burnt and grey. Mosques and schools were piles of rubble, wells and conduits that had been constructed centuries ago to bring water from neighbouring valleys or from deep reservoirs had been smashed beyond repair. The rivers themselves were polluted with death and poison.

Shahr-i Bozorg looked like nothing on earth. The Street of the Silversmiths, where once she had wandered for hours in silent fascination, the Street of the Potters, the Leather Workers…all were starkly empty, mounds of brick where stray dogs foraged and starved. A once-beautiful modern residential district looked like a piece of footage from a black-and-white war film. No flowers, no brightly painted doors and windows, no greenery remained. Children wandered here and there, as thin and hungry as the stray dogs. Where once there had been modern kitchens with electric stoves and ovens, she saw smoke rising from open fires amid the ruins.

Somehow the shining mirrored dome of the Central Mosque had escaped.

A few trees were putting out shoots of green as the faintest bud of promise.

Long before they reached the ascent to the palace she was in tears. They were her husband's people, and now she saw, with the clarity of hindsight, how she had betrayed them and him, leaving them in their hour of darkness. What could they understand of her reasons? She felt a shame so deep nothing could wash it away.

Her last meeting with Kavi had been terrible—she could no longer remember why. They had fought like cats, she had screamed at him, she had threatened to leave him...then he had said it. "Alinor! I divorce thee, I divorce thee!" The words had been ice bullets in her heart; she had gone cold all over, head and heart and flesh. And before she could speak, he had turned on his heel and left her.

She went into labour nearly two months before her time. The German-trained doctor was busy with a huge influx of war casualties at the hospital and would come as soon as he could get away. The midwife simply did not respond to the message they sent.

There were only Puran, and Dallia, and another midwife whom Puran found somewhere. Alinor was terrified, sick, and suffering a pain she would not have believed it was possible for a human body to experience. There was no pain-killer to be had, except some concoction of herbs on a piece of sponge that they placed in her mouth. It did not take away the pain, merely made her too light-headed to resist it.

She had never been so afraid in her life. The fear was, if possible, worse than the pain. Her baby, Kavian's son...she kept almost fainting with the pain, but she knew she must stay awake to help them, to help him push his way into the world. She spat out the cloth soaked with herbs, and screamed and screamed with an agony that she knew she would remember all her life long.

"Water!" she cried to Dallia once. *"Āb! Āb!"* And after that whenever she seemed to lose consciousness the little servant would throw water in her face to wake her.

She had trusted Puran for months, but now, suddenly, startlingly, she did not trust her anymore. Puran had lived sheltered in the palace all her adult life, from the age of sixteen. What did she know about managing childbirth?

After that, fear and pain simply consumed her. From bouts of mindless agony she awoke only to terror. There was no respite. She called for Kavi then, and when he did not come she learned to believe that he lay dead on some battlefield. Surely, surely, if he were alive, he would have come to her?

It was the depths of hell and agony and it lasted thirty-six hours.

"He's dead! Where is he? Where's my husband? I need him! Why isn't he here? He divorced me. Did he mean it? Isn't he coming?"

"Push, Alinor!"

"Push, Mistress, you must push now, for your baby's sake! *Push!*"

"Kavi, Kavi! Oh, God, he's dead, isn't he? Why doesn't he come? Why did he divorce me? Is he dead? Oh, my baby, my baby!"

"Push! Push!"

"Push, push!" she chanted, reminding herself. "Push him out, oh, my baby, come out now! Come, come…" She began to scream again, as the pain hit a pitch that must count among the finer torments of hell. "Oh, where is he? Where is he? Is he dead? Somebody tell me the truth! Is he dead?"

She cried it over and over. She meant Kavi, it was Kavi she feared for. Outside, in the early spring morning, the *bulbul* was singing a promise of joy and celebration, but her heart was black with fear, and it could not follow him. She pushed the baby out at last, crying her fear for her husband, but when Puran bent over her and whispered, "Yes, my darling, it is God's will. He is dead," somehow she knew that it was not Kavi Puran meant, but her darling, her beloved son.

Then she welcomed the blackness that came down, shutting out the *bulbul*'s lies.

She knew there had been a siege of the capital in a first, early push in the war. It had been beaten back, but the Kaljuks must have got close enough to the palace to use mortars, because the road up was all but impassable. Or perhaps the bombers who had assailed the city later had after all got closer than had been thought possible. There were goats wandering along it, and the horses could pick their way between the holes, but in several places the edge of the cliff had given way, reducing the road to a path scarcely five feet wide. No car could pass now.

Alinor heaved a sigh of relief as they passed through the gates. The palace itself was untouched. Its ancient turrets still stood, still with their roofs and windows intact. Tears burned her eyes again, this time in gratitude that something should have been saved from the horror, even if it were only one building.

But the beautiful playing fountains that had once charmed her were dry. There were many more people in the courtyard than formerly. It was crammed now with tiny lean-tos, with children and animals.

She looked at Kavi. "This was the only refuge for the city during the siege, and now, for some of those who have lost their homes, it is temporary accommodation. Many work in the city to rebuild their homes during the day, and at night they return here. There are fewer now that summer is here and it is possible to sleep in the open."

He opened the door of the palace and stepped into the Great Hall, and Alinor looked around her and cried, "Oh, Kavi, no!"

Nothing remained, save the bare stone walls. The tapestries, the carpets, the wonderful, centuries-old works of art, the miraculously painted miniatures, the frames of ivory and lapis lazuli, the carved marble bowls—all the treasures of the royal house of Durran were gone. Somehow this possibility had never occurred to her. She had been in some way prepared for the destruction of the palace by bombs, but she had not thought of this.

"We needed weapons," he said.

She followed him from room to room, and the story was everywhere the same. Lamps, tables, stools—all the best of the old treasures had been replaced with the crudest of practical pieces. In one room a miniature remained in painful beauty on an otherwise empty wall, in another a carved wooden screen, a carpet too worn to interest collectors in a third. Even the little charcoal braziers had been replaced with ugly modern substitutes.

"I thought I knew," she said, facing him with sorrow and regret in her eyes for all that she had seen today. "I never understood how bad it was." Almost, in that moment, she could forgive him for wanting to marry a rich woman. He must have foreseen this, after all. And to foresee it must have meant to wish to prevent it.

He took her to their old apartments, but nothing was recognizable there. The walls were bare, the stone floor cold. A modern, Western sofa sat in the sitting room, ugly and out of place, but offering at least some comfort in an otherwise comfortless room. There were a desk and chair, a few cushions, a low carved table that she remembered from before. She had served meals to him on that table: it was at the same time a symbol of the happiest and the most wretched meals of her life.

She looked at him, but there were no more words.

"Wait here," Kavi said, after a moment, and left her.

She was hideously, horribly ill after the birth. She had nightmares in which her baby cried for her and she could not go to him. She saw Kavi and her mother, too, but though she reached for them, she could never touch them.

It was short. Within a day or two she had recovered. Her body still ached, her mind reeled with pain, but she was herself. And with all of that self, she yearned now for her husband.

"I want Kavi," she wept to Puran. "Why doesn't he come?"

Dallia had left the palace suddenly to go to her mother's deathbed. Puran had carried the news of the child's death to its grandfather. He sent his condolences to his daughter-in-law, but did not visit her, and without Puran saying so, Alinor learned that the Sheikh was deeply disappointed.

"Of course, if the child had lived, the Sheikh would have solemnized the marriage immediately, even without Kavi's presence, but now there is no need for hurry. It can wait for Kavi's return.''

Alinor still felt so stupid. "What do you mean?"

"Kavi explained to you, of course, that a Parvān royal marriage is not binding until after the birth of the first child. It is a formality—no king in living memory has ever repudiated a wife for barrenness, but still, the people expect the second ceremony and it must be done.''

"Are you saying that we aren't legally married?" Alinor pressed.

Puran shrugged unhappily. She had thought Alinor already knew. "No equivalent exists in the West. I cannot explain. A king must have an heir. And in Parvān there is monogamy, while in other Muslim states a man may take other wives.''

Alinor knew that. It was because Parvān had accepted Islam relatively late in its history. Monogamy had been practised among the tribes for centuries before the arrival of Islam.

But it was the first she had heard that her marriage wasn't legal until a second ceremony. And for such a semi-marriage, that state midway between engagement and legal marriage, Puran explained, one recital of the phrase "I divorce thee!" was enough.

She was horrified when she learned that Kavi had recited the *talaaq* to Alinor. "How angry you must have made him!" she cried. "Now the ceremony must be gone through again, with another waiting period. I am sure he regrets it already.''

"Has word been sent to him?" Alinor asked.

Word had been sent, but there had been no reply. She was sure it was because Kavi was trying to decide what to do with her.

And suddenly, Alinor saw that it was for her to take the step. She need not wait for the decision on her fate to fall from Kavi's lips. She had nothing to bind her here now— no child, no marriage, no one who loved her for herself. She would take matters into her own hands. She would go.

At first Puran said it was impossible, but even as she said it Alinor guessed that there was some way it could be done, and from that moment she did not rest.

At last the old woman admitted that, now that spring was come a way would be open through certain passes, but it was a long, tedious journey on muleback and Alinor was too weak still for such discomfort. She must wait a week or two, wait for Kavi's message…

That only hardened her purpose. She knew that Kavi would repudiate her, knew that Puran herself expected it, though the older woman did not say so.

On the third day after the death of her child, Alinor painfully mounted a mule and set off with a brigand of a guide who terrified her. She had money, food, and her passport, and for the rest she was in the guide's hands.

It was not to Kaljukistan he was taking her, that would not have been safe. He took her to the other border, but it was early in the year for such a journey, as the guide explained in his almost impenetrable accent. Some of the passes were so high she was delirious with mountain sickness, and so choked with snow and ice that she nearly froze to death.

"We have crossed the border now," he said to her one day, and for some reason she burst into tears. Until that moment she had not known that she was hoping Kavi would come after her.

After that, there was a desert, and the heat was so gruelling that she learned to think of the snow with longing. She was haemorrhaging, and her torn flesh, unmended after the birth, was a constant agony, walking or riding. She had never been so weary and depressed in her life, but she could only press on. There was no going back. Dimly she began to realize what a fool she had been, to understand that while she thought herself recovered, she had merely been at the mercy of a different set of emotions, a different kind of madness.

It was an evil, hellish journey. Her body bled from a wound that would not heal, her breasts spilled milk for a mouth that would never hunger, and her eyes spilled water for the child that had not lived and for those who would never now come into existence between her and Kavi, to fill that naked, aching place in her heart.

The guide rarely spoke to her, and even the mules did not bray. When at last they reached the city of their destination, he led her to gates emblazoned with eagles, and left her there.

She looked at the sign on the stone wall. "Consulate of the United States of America" it read, and this was the final straw. "No, no!" she cried, to the man who was already disappearing, with both mules. "I want the Canadian Embassy," she wept helplessly to the uniformed official who came out to her. "And now he's gone and taken the mule and how will I get there?"

Later she supposed that was the lowest moment of her life, when she was reduced to weeping over the lack of a mule for transport.

"Alinor."

She shook herself, trying to clear the misery that both past and present made her feel. How long had she been lost in reverie?

She turned to face Kavi, who had entered from another room in the apartment. He stood with a small child, a boy whose head was an angelic tousle of pale curls, marking his parentage as Kamrangi. His eyes were the same deep, dark green as Kavi's, however, and she frowned in perplexity.

For a moment they stood there, as frozen as a painting, while the child and the woman stared at each other. At last she whispered, "Kavi?"

But he addressed the child. "You have asked for your mother," he said gently. "Here she is, my son, as I promised."

"Mama?" said the boy, and smiled a smile like the sun on the Day of Glory.

Chapter 13

Everything around her went blindingly bright for a split second, as though the room was kindled with lightning sparking from every surface. She reeled, and then, mercifully, her brain asked no more of her and shut the world out.

When she was alive again, she found herself almost on her knees, with Kavi supporting her. Feverishly, she looked around. The child from heaven was still there, his glowing smile only just beginning to be transformed into anxiety.

"He lived?" she whispered, her voice hoarse and croaking like an old woman's. "He *lived?*"

"Did you doubt it?" Kavi asked.

"Is this my *son?*"

She pushed him off, knelt on the naked stone floor and held out her arms. The child stepped into her embrace as one who enters the Golden City. *"Pesaram hasti?"* she asked softly. "Are you my son?"

"Areh, Mama," he replied, and she wrapped him in her arms and drew him firmly against her breast.

For a long moment she held him like that, her head bent

over his, neither saying a word. Around her the world broke
apart and shaped itself into new patterns. On the small fair
head at her breast two diamonds glittered, and she marvelled,
not knowing that they were her own tears. Then she sat back
on her haunches and drew him onto her lap. He put his tiny
hand in hers, and she was riveted by its perfection. She stared
at it, turning it over, feeling the little mounds of the palm
with her thumb as if each were a separate and distinct miracle.

She kissed the palm, and then his cheeks and his eyes, and
saw both herself and Kavi in his makeup, and marvelled at
the perfection of this. She stroked his body, his hair, his face.

"My son," she said at last. "My child." Then she looked
up at Kavi, still standing there. In that moment she forgot
everything except joy, and the inexplicable miracle that their
love for each other had created this perfect child. She smiled,
her eyes glowing, and Kavi felt his heart kick in the old
response that he had sworn he would not again feel. "What
is my son's name?" she asked.

"Roshan," he said. "Roshan Kavād. I named him after
you and my father."

Not in the conventional sense, perhaps, but she understood
at once. Both "Roshan" and "Nur" meant *light*.

"Roshan," she repeated. *Your hair is like light*, he had
said to her once. Was it because the baby had her hair colour
that he had chosen the name?

The boy had begun to chatter, like any small child, telling
her something…she could scarcely follow him, with his
childish pronunciation. It stabbed her. She could not understand her own child's speech. She said something encouraging and looked back to where Kavi still stood, just inside
the door.

"Why was I lied to?" she demanded softly in English, so
that her anger should not frighten her son, and the sharing,
glowing smile that had captured Kavi a moment ago was
wiped out. "Why was I told such a foul and evil lie? On
whose authority? Was it yours?"

He was unmoved. "What lie were you told?"

"I was told...she said..." She began to weep, and she wrapped the uncomplaining child in her arms again and hugged him tightly to her. "They said he was stillborn. Kavi, *why?*"

He stared at her, one eyebrow raised, pitying but disbelieving. Before he could speak, Roshan stirred in her arms, and she released him.

He smiled up at her. "You are very beautiful, Mama," he said. "Baba told me it was so, and it is true."

Then she had to get to her feet and follow him to his own room, where he showed her his toys. And where Dallia, her old servant, sat stitching the collar of a tiny shirt and looking at her with frightened eyes.

She had dreamt of the baby, almost endlessly at first, but less as time went on. In her dreams he had Kavi's eyes and Kavi's black hair, and she held him and loved him and woke with aching, empty arms. Her family did their best to comfort her, but in truth there was no comfort to be had.

She had gone to the States to be with her family for a few months. Her mother had been horrified when she saw her. Alinor was thin to the point of emaciation, her hair was listless and falling out, and her body had been torn by the birth and not stitched, nor had it healed. And she was still intermittently bleeding.

She went into the hospital for repairs, and when she came out she had stopped losing blood and her body had been neatly mended. It was a long time before she started to eat, or to gain back any of the weight she had lost, but at least, as her mother said, she was looking human again.

In September she returned to London. She had lost a year of her degree, but this raised no eyebrows. All the college knew was that she had never registered at Shahriallah University, and there was no record of her ever entering the country, so they had not worried about Alinor when it came time to get their students home as war broke out. Students

were notorious for changing their minds without telling anyone and going travelling instead.

Lana was thrilled to see her. She had not taken another
roommate, and Alinor could move right in. And it was there,
in the comfort of friendship and the luxury of her old sur-
roundings, that she was able at last to piece the whole story
together, to see and understand what had happened to her.

"Don't you remember how dangerous I always thought
he was?" she told Lana. "The kind of man who could hyp-
notize people. I was so afraid of him."

"But then you fell in love," Lana pointed out. "I always
thought that meant you were just wildly attracted from the
start and reacted like that because you were afraid to fall in
love."

"But it was all a lie, don't you see? If he thought I was
you right from the start, of course he was going to pretend
to be in love, and of course I was going to think what you
just said. But some men do that, don't they? They make
women fall in love with them."

"Well, I've heard of people's stupid ideas of American
wealth," Lana said, "but I don't see how anyone who's been
educated in the West could really believe one man was going
to be able to finance a whole war and make a difference. It
would have taken fifty million dollars just to supply the
tribesmen with rifles, as far as I can see. My father has two
planes, and one yacht. I don't know how much these things
cost, but I really think a fleet of fighter bombers would have
been beyond his budget."

"It would have made a difference," Alinor insisted.
"They were armed with sticks and pitchforks at first. If
you'd been me, there'd have been money right at the first…"

"You never thought of trusting him?" Lana said. "I
mean, you never told him what that Puran woman said and
asked him about it?"

"Not directly. I knew it had to be true."

"You said you loved him."

"I thought I did. But Lana, we weren't even married. He

didn't tell me that. All that ceremony I went through was just a kind of engagement celebration. It was a trial marriage for him, but for me it was the real thing.''

Lana looked at her. ''Was it? Are you sure?''

''What do you mean?''

''I think it was a trial for you, too.''

The words hit home. It was true that she had fluctuated between trust and fear, that perhaps she had not really accepted the finality of what she was doing.

''Well, it's just as well, isn't it? He wanted me for money and for an heir, and I couldn't give him either.''

''I think Kavi loved you. The man I met was so crazy in love with you he couldn't see the ground in front of his feet, and if he was faking that for money and an heir, honey, he could have made enough to finance his war acting in Hollywood.''

''You don't understand.''

''The thing is, Alinor, you're still grieving about the baby. My mother says a woman's crazy for at least a year when she loses a baby, and she shouldn't do anything stupid like leave her husband during that year. Well, you didn't have my mother's advice, so you've compounded it now, and you've lost your husband and your home, too. Which is a thing that would make anyone crazy. If it were anywhere else, I'd say, go back, but you can't go back the way things are now, I guess.''

''I'm not going back. Anyway, he divorced me.''

''He didn't seem to make any attempt to spread the word that he had. If it was strictly between the two of you, how could it have any force? Maybe he just lost his temper. I've heard that Muslim men shout that a lot at their wives when they lose their tempers. It's supposed to make her straighten up and fly right.''

''I was pregnant. He shouldn't have said it.''

Lana sighed. ''Who are you trying to convince, me or you? He's fighting a war. And you were blaming him for a million things instead of helping him.''

"What was I supposed to do?" Alinor shouted indignantly. "Go on as if nothing had happened? Pretend to believe he loved me and let him make a fool of me?"

"Marriage is marriage," Lana said unarguably.

"*You* should have married him, I guess!" Alinor said. "You'd have been the perfect wife, *and* your father could have supplied the tribes with Kalashnikovs."

"I didn't love him," Lana said grimly. "And he didn't love me."

She ended up having almost as many arguments with Lana as she'd had with Kavi, and with equally unsatisfactory results.

But even if she couldn't convince her friend, it got clearer and clearer in her own mind. Kavi had been manipulating her right from the beginning. The way he'd stared at her, followed her—*stalked* her, really. And none of it had happened until she was living with Lana. As if someone had learned that a woman in that apartment was the Holding heiress, but had got them confused.

And whatever Lana said about trust and marriage, well, he'd never trusted her, either. He'd never confided his worries to her, he'd practically abandoned her in the palace, when he'd promised her there'd be work she could do…oh, it was all very clear. If she hadn't really trusted her marriage vows—whatever they had been—neither had Kavi.

When the message came, handed her by someone in the library who thought Alinor had dropped it—*Come home. You belong here*—she did not understand why it was sent, but she felt fully justified in ignoring it. And when no other message or action followed, she knew she'd been right.

"I want to know whose idea it was," she said to Kavian when they were alone.

He had spent the afternoon at the desk in their apartment, going over papers. She had gone down to the kitchens to prepare food, with the help of the cook, and when she had returned with it, he had smiled gratefully and come to sit down.

"This is nice," he had said. "I don't usually eat in the evenings."

"Why not?"

"Probably because I forget. During the war we got used to not eating. Supplies were scarce. Now we have the first early crops being harvested, and food is being imported. But I am not used to plenty yet."

She had learned one lesson, anyway. She let him eat the meal. His thinness had shocked her, and she could well believe he regularly forgot to eat.

At the end, she poured him a tiny cup of strong coffee, and as he sipped she said it. "I want to know whose idea it was."

He took a deep breath. "What idea?"

"Kavi, I was told my baby died in childbirth. Why? I want to know."

He put down his cup. "Are you sure you remember what really happened, Alinor?"

"What do you mean?"

"You rejected the child, Alinor. You refused to give it milk, you screamed at them to take the baby away."

"No!"

"The baby was taken away to protect him from you. You might have harmed him."

"That is not true!"

"It is not unusual when the pain of childbirth has been very great. It is a kind of insanity that sometimes happens to new mothers. Even animals will sometimes kill a newborn that has caused much pain in the birthing."

"You're making this up. I did not reject my baby. I did not refuse to give him milk. I never saw him. They took him away and said he had died."

"They took him away to give you time to recover. In a few days you would have been given the child again. But instead, you fled."

She looked at him, forcing him to meet her gaze. "Do you believe that, Kavi? Do you really believe it?"

"Alinor, it was a hard pregnancy for you. I saw you change before my eyes, from a loving, caring wife into a crazy woman. You accused me of terrible things—every time I saw you it was something new. This I saw with my own eyes. What do you now tell me—that everyone in the palace, Puran, my father, the servants—that all these people were in a grand conspiracy to steal your son from you? My father loved you. He welcomed you as his daughter. It broke his heart when you went away like that, without a word. Why would he have engaged in such a terrible conspiracy, not just against you, but against me and my happiness?"

He stood up, though he had not finished his coffee, nor touched any of the sweets she had arranged on a cloth in the absence of the little silver dishes they had used to use. For a moment he stood looking down at her. "Alinor, you are here because your son wanted you. He would not rest until he had seen you. Please do your best to be a loving mother to him. He has that right, is not that the truth? Can you deny that he has the right?"

She sat silent, not looking at him, letting the speech fall on her bent head.

"I never rejected my child," she said. But even as she said it she felt the first whisper of doubt invade her mind. Her isolation, her despair, the hormones of pregnancy, the nightmare birth—and then finally that dreadful, gruelling journey, at the end of which she had been practically certifiable. He was right. Women had gone crazy with the pain of childbirth. How sure of her memory could she be? How sure of herself?

She would stay in the old apartment with Kavi and Roshan. She had little immediate choice—to clean and furnish a separate set of rooms for her own use would take time. Besides, she wanted to be near Roshan.

That much was all right. But Kavi seemed to have made

no arrangement for a separate bed for her. Roshan had his own bedroom off the sitting room, the sofa was far too short for Alinor, and the only other bed was the ornately carved wooden frame and mattress that had been their marriage bed. The magnificently embroidered spreads and hangings, of course, were gone.

"You didn't sell this?" she asked.

He shrugged. "Things went piece by piece, the art and luxuries first, the necessities last. This bed would have gone in the next shipment, no doubt, if we had not been successful in driving out the Kaljuks."

She flinched from the thought of the daily anguish of watching the blood of your history drain away, drop by beautiful drop. "There's nowhere for me to sleep?" she asked hesitantly.

He shrugged. He was taking off his shirt in the glare of an uncovered electric bulb in a lamp that sat on the floor. Only the bed and the leaded glass in the windows showed any sign of what the room had once been.

She pressed him. "Am I—Kavi, are you expecting to share this bed with me?"

He was sitting on the bed now. He looked up at her. "I do not care," he said simply. "You can sleep here, or you can sleep on the floor or the sofa, or find some cushions somewhere in the palace. I will not touch you, Alinor, whatever you choose. I did not bring you here to restore what cannot be restored, but because my son wanted his mother."

"Good!" she snapped back. "You keep on your side and I'll keep on mine."

"What else?" he said.

She was wearing the lacy body stocking under Golnesah's *shalwar kamees;* it was the only underwear she had. For two nights in the tent she had washed it at night and slept naked, but she wasn't going to sleep naked tonight. She slipped out of the turquoise trousers first, and then, still wearing the tunic, glanced at Kavi.

He was sitting up, leaning against the wall at the head of

the bed, reading a sheaf of papers from a stack that sat on
the floor beside him. His chest was bare, the muscles of his
arms long, lean and hard. His ribs showed, and the scars had
destroyed the perfection of the body she had once known,
but it was still powerfully, dangerously masculine. More so
than ever, perhaps.

He felt her gaze and looked up from his work, meeting
her eyes before she had time to look away. She hadn't been
thinking anything, she protested to herself, but still she felt
the heat in her cheeks that told her she was blushing.

Kavi's jaw hardened, and he returned to his reading. The
message was obvious, and it angered her so that she forgot
the minor embarrassment of stripping off in front of a man
who was, after all, her husband, and who had been intimate
with every curve and fold of her body. Alinor pulled the
tunic up over her head, folded it carefully, and laid it with
the trousers in a corner.

When she returned to the bed he had forgotten his work
and was watching her. She stood stiff for a moment, caught
in the ferocity of his gaze.

The elastic lace of the body stocking, was, as Golnesah
had said, like embroidery on the skin. White flowers seemed
to have been scattered over the creamy beige of her body in
a curving pattern that concealed one breast but not the other.
Beside the strapless bodice, two wide armlets ringed her upper arms, the one thick with flowers, the other only net. It
was both innocent and erotic, emphasising the long slender
curves, the firmness of the muscles under the soft skin.

He looked at her, and in the harsh glare of lamplight, she
saw hunger flicker behind his eyes. Everything was changed,
but they were still a man and a woman in a bedroom where
they had each given the other the peak of physical pleasure
in a past whose bright, rich promise burned the brighter
against the sterility of the present. Much of what was gone
was irretrievably lost, but this much they could bring back,
if they chose, and as they stared into each other's eyes, they
knew it. Love was still possible. A country had been brought

to its knees, a way of life had been destroyed forever, the future seemed an unending stretch of bleakness ahead, but they could, *if they chose,* salvage love from the ruins.

Between them, he saw desertion in his hour of need.

Between them, she saw lies and betrayal.

"Did your body please him as much as it pleased me?" he asked.

She smiled. "Oh, more," she said.

She watched all the emotion leave his face—anger, torment, need...even the memory of love, and only then did she understand. If it was true that their marriage was and always had been valid, then out of her own mouth she had just condemned herself as the one thing a man like Kavian could never forgive. As an unfaithful wife. With one word she had killed all possibility between them, and only now, in its final death, did she understand how much she might have wanted it.

One word. And that word was a lie.

Chapter 14

She had spent three years in cold storage. Her life dwindled to the narrow circle of study and sleep. She made no new friends, and without Lana's bright presence her life would have been completely barren. Lana's common-sense acceptance of things was all that made life bearable.

She had met Gabe at a function at the Kaljukistan Embassy just after Christmas of her final year. Peace negotiations were then underway between Kaljukistan and Parvān, and looked promising. Gabe was on what the Foreign Office called "gardening leave," which meant he was waiting to be assigned to a new post.

He was immediately attracted to her and asked her out, but Alinor said no. A month later, when peace had been established, Gabe turned up at the college, as a student. The college taught language courses for Foreign Office diplomats, and Gabe, by then assigned to Kaljukistan, was taking a month's intensive study in Kaljuki before going out. Then he pursued her. He was so different from Kavi, gentle with her where Kavi had been hard, and yet, in some undefinable way, he had reminded her of Kavi. There was a bittersweet quality to every moment she spent with him, and for the first time, she felt as if her heart, which had until now felt entirely petrified, might one day lose that stony shell and become flesh and blood again. She both yearned for and feared the day when she would feel her heart live again.

Things moved quickly, and before the month was up Gabe was asked to go out to Kaljukistan. Until then, they had exchanged no more than kisses, kisses that had stirred a distant flame in her, but from which she had always drawn back. She could go no further than a kiss, but Gabe had known what he wanted from the first moment of talking to her. He asked her to marry him.

Somehow she could talk to Gabe. To no other man could she have said it, but she told Gabe, in hard, unemotional sentences, the facts of the year that had made her what she was. He said he understood, and that if she would marry him, he would be patient. He could wait. Under his loving care, she would, in time, heal. She would learn to love him.

She wanted to believe him. She *had* believed him. She did love him already, in a way, and given time, he would find the passion in her and make it live again. The thought of going back into Kavi's orbit frightened her more than she could express, she wished it had been anywhere but Kaljukistan that he was going, but something had seemed to warn her that it was now or never. She must choose to heal now, or be forever crippled. She had taken her courage in both hands and said yes.

Puran and Nargis were not in the palace. They had gone to Puran's husband's family, whose village had suffered badly, to help them through the aftermath. Of course they would return, but there was no saying when.

The most extraordinary thing about it, as far as Alinor was concerned, was the flood of relief she felt when she learned of this. It poured through her. She couldn't understand it at all.

* * *

She toured the city with Kavian on horseback. Until now, the four years since she had first come to this city had seemed an age, but now, seeing the dreadful changes war had made, it seemed impossible that so much could have happened in such a short time.

But there was an optimistic spirit among the people. Everywhere hardy souls were building their lives again, making homes amid ruin. Alinor was astonished at the ingenuity that created what was needed out of what was at hand. Rusted tank wheels became fireholders. A pink shower curtain served as a canopy over an ''open plan'' kitchen. Water was being routed along troughs pieced together of bits of wood, tin, plastic and steel. An entire room had been constructed of flattened plastic bottles.

It was tragic and ennobling all at once. For so much human effort and expertise to be devoted entirely to the basic necessities of water, food and shelter seemed the deepest tragedy. And yet human beings cooperating to overcome adversity was, surely, humanity at a peak it seldom reached?

They welcomed her back, their Shahbanu, politely if not ecstatically. They knew she had fled in the country's darkest hour; she saw the knowledge in their eyes. They even knew that she had abandoned the young prince, her own son. But they kept their opinions to themselves, out of respect for her husband.

It was a far cry from four years ago, when the faces that had greeted the new young Shahbanu had been wreathed in smiles, when gifts had been showered on her from every shop, every stall.

Even now, perhaps, they might have given her gifts, from the meagre store of what was on offer, out of the generosity of their own spirits rather than affection for her. But she had learned her lesson four years ago. She had learned then not to admire anything very extravagantly, for the next day she would find it delivered to the palace, and with no way of paying the giver that would not cause insult.

So she smiled now, and congratulated the shopkeepers on

their stores, without singling out any item for admiration. She could not bear it if, from their desperate need, they sent gifts to her.

They were a strong, independent people. They gave no one respect who had not earned it, and she could see that they doubted her now. Not that they blamed the Prince's wife for leaving when danger threatened; only that they would have respected her courage if she had stayed.

She saw and understood it all. It broke her heart. She remembered a time when there was nothing she had wanted so much as to be a part of these people, to deserve her position as their future queen. She had violated their trust, she had thrown her chance away on the wind.

"They were ready to love me once," she observed painfully to Kavian on the way back to the palace. "I've destroyed that."

He barely glanced at her. "Too much has been destroyed in their lives for them to notice the splintering of a few illusions about you, believe me." And she knew that he was not speaking merely of his people. He was speaking of himself. He no longer cared what she had done. It no longer affected him. He was polite, friendly, and unrelievedly distant with her. He would make her his queen without ever again wishing to make her his wife.

She shook off the gloom like a cat with water on its fur and sat up straighter on the back of the horse. But he was right. She was taking it all too personally. The fact that their future queen had failed them was the least of these people's worries.

Whatever had happened in the past was past. She would accept Kavi's verdict. There were things she could do *now,* and she intended to do them.

First on her agenda was to make a home out of the detritus for her own family. This much she had in common with all the women she had seen. Men could tinker and jury-rig the necessities, but when that was done, it was woman's portion to make the result a home. A heart that is burdened needs "those little anodynes that deaden suffering."

She began to troll through the palace, noting all those bits of furniture and furnishings that had not been sold. She had them all brought to the central hall. The palace was a huge place. Even one or two pieces per room was producing a substantial collection.

Kavi made no objection to her activities. He scarcely noticed them. Kavi was now Commander in Chief of both the armed forces and the police, and was largely preoccupied with the Kaljuk terrorists. Whatever they planned, they must be found before they carried it out. The country's manpower was too limited for good security on all the public buildings, standing or half-standing, that might be a target.

He was making up a map of the city from written reports that detailed what was still standing, what still in use. The map served two purposes: it tracked the progress of the tortuously slow house-to-house search for the Kaljuk terrorist cell, and it showed him their possible targets.

Signs of them had been found exactly where the Kaljuk prisoner had said they would be—in a cave beyond the city—as well as evidence of hasty evacuation. He believed that they were probably all still together somewhere, for to divide meant to multiply the chances of discovery by a vigilant population. But whether they had fled to another cave, or were somewhere within the city, was something he could not guess.

"Kavi, you need a break," Alinor said, and he lifted his head to discover her bending over him with a cup of something that steamed appetisingly, and a plate of hot bite-size snacks.

He threw down his pen and stretched his back gratefully, then reached to push some papers together to make room for her to set the tray down. But she held it aloft. "A real break," she said firmly. "Come and sit by the fire for five minutes."

He followed willingly as she sat in a nest of cushions by

the fireplace, where a small glowing fire took the chill off the evening. Not much had changed in the room, but it was inexplicably more inviting than before. The lights and shadows were softer. She had achieved much with little.

He sank gratefully down onto the cushions opposite her and reached for the cup.

"Have you found them?"

He chewed a morsel of food that was as he remembered food tasting, long ago. He shook his head silently, unwilling to burden her with his troubles.

"Tell me," she begged softly. Then he remembered their conversation in the tent.

"We found signs that they had been staying where the captured man told us they were. But they must have taken fright and changed their centre of operations at once. Now we must hunt them."

"He didn't look like a Kaljuk," Alinor said, and he nodded in acknowledgement. She had put her finger unerringly on one big difficulty: it was likely that the Kaljuk spies had been chosen for their physical characteristics as much as their terrorist skills. Kaljuks were predominantly Mongol-featured, so that one assumed it was a national characteristic. Of course there were many who did not fit the mould, but it was hard to overcome the prejudice that made the investigators instinctively more suspicious of someone with Mongol features, and less suspicious of anyone who looked like a Parvāni.

"I recruited my own spies entirely among Parvānis who looked like Kaljuks," he told her. "Naturally, they will have done something similar."

"What if you don't find them?"

He shrugged. "They know we know they are here. Whether this will make them strike quickly, or wait until our vigilance relaxes, I cannot guess."

"Golnesah said he said they were after the House of Parliament."

"I have increased security there. But if I were one of them, knowing that one of their number has been captured, I would suggest that we find another target now.''

"But which one?"

He sighed. "But which one." He let his head fall back on the cushion behind him. "Not much of this city is left standing, but I still do not have the manpower for full security on all possible sites. I must choose. What do you think, Alinor?" he said, raising his head to look at her. "What will they turn their eyes to, if Parliament is too well protected?"

"Something they're ideologically opposed to," she suggested. "They're trying to make a point, aren't they? But they're also trying to undermine those structures in this country that they disapprove of."

"Bookshops, libraries, the newspaper, secular colleges and schools, anywhere that employs or trains women," he agreed. "Which of those, Nuri?"

In spite of herself she felt warmed when he used that nickname to her. She smiled and shook her head.

"If you're hoping for some women's intuition, it's just not happening."

"If it does occur to you," he said, for intuition would at least give them somewhere to start.

"If it does." She sighed. "This is good. I wish you'd talked to me like this...before. I felt so isolated, so useless."

"I wish it, too," he said. "You are right—it is a comfort to share the worry. I am sorry if in protecting you from my cares I isolated you from my heart."

It was a bittersweet victory, like any that comes too late.

In the past, her old college had often made collections for countries in need: she remembered one of winter clothing for the Kurds, and another for Bosnia. She wrote to the registrar and asked if they would take up a collection of clothing, books, money—anything—when the new school year started. She mentioned their desperate need for building materials, medicines, cranes and earthmoving equipment. Everything that Western society took for granted.

She phoned her parents, too, of course, with the long impossible explanation. "I don't understand you," said her beleaguered mother. "First you were married, and then you weren't, and then Kavian divorced you anyway, and now it turns out you've been legally married all along, and I'm a grandmother. Well, I can't say I mind that, except that I'd like to see him. And all the papers are carrying a picture of him kidnapping you from a church. Was that posed, Alinor?"

"Not exactly."

"It looked posed. Is it because he's trying to get foreign money into the country? He certainly understands public relations—everybody's talking about how romantic it is. I've had two television stations wanting to interview me. What do you want me to do?"

"Soften them up with the romance and get their donations," Alinor said at once, knowing how much her parents would regret the devastation of a country they had visited and thought beautiful. "It would break your heart, Mom."

And she wrote Gabe, telling him that she had been mistaken in believing herself a free woman, telling him that, for better or worse, her place was here. Asking him to send word if he could, if he was well.

To Lana she wrote all the anguish of the tragedy that had befallen the country. She told her about the bombed cities, the damaged wells, the destruction of much of the tribal way of life. She wrote her, too, about the Arabian Nights palace that had been gutted of its treasures. All the things that she could not say to Kavian, because to be constantly bemoaning what was lost would be an added weight on his shoulders.

But she wrote, too, about her joy in her newfound son. About the pleasures of motherhood. She wrote about the pain of the loss of his first three years. And she told her what Kavi had said—that she had rejected her baby after the terrible birth, had refused to nurse or hold him, a moment she could not remember, however she tried, but which might have happened, all the same.

* * *

On her salvage operations, accompanied always by Roshan and sometimes by Dallia, she came eventually to the
oldest part of the palace, the central core of ancient stone
and dark passages built by the first King Kavād, and at last,
inevitably, to the "Bridal Chamber"—that room where generations of Kings and Princes had taken their new brides,
and where Kavi had brought her for their first nights together.

The sun was shining as they entered, throwing coloured
lights from the high, tiny windows all over the walls.

Nothing beside remained. The room had been filled with
the most priceless of antiques, the best pieces of generation
after generation. She remembered the bed, the cushions, the
carpets, even the wrought-iron charcoal brazier: all were
gone. The room that had been existed only in her memory
now.

Other things were gone, too, that this room had witnessed.
The passion between them. Whatever she had learned afterwards, whatever had been his reasons for marrying her, that
at least had not been a lie. He had desired her. She understood that now. Even the naked room had the power to remind her of what she had forgotten, what she had learned to
distrust, and she understood that if nothing else, the passion
had been true—and part of her yearned for it again, for the
brief shining moment when she had been loved, and had
known it.

Even the latticework wooden walls were gone, and the
carved doors, leaving nothing but bare stone. Except for the
light from the square of coloured windows around the bottom
of the domed roof, she could not have recognized the
place.

The light, and the memory of laughter that was borne on
the air.

"Why are we waiting, Mama?" Roshan asked. As far as
possible, he went everywhere with her.

She said, "This room is a very special room in the palace. One day you'll stay here with your bride on your wedding night, just as Baba and I did." And suddenly she was determined that it should be so. To this room, if nowhere else, she would restore all its ancient glory.

"Why?"

"Because it's our tradition," she said.

"Like the stories Grandfather used to tell?"

"Did Grandfather tell you stories?"

"Lots of them. Stories about our ancestors and our history." The last sentence was awkwardly recited, as though he had learned the difficult words by heart. "I liked them. Do you know the stories, Mama?"

She remembered the old man with sudden painful clarity. The rich, authoritative voice with its compelling tales. "Yes, I do know them. Grandfather told them to me, too. Shall I tell you them again sometime?"

"Yes, please."

Just here she had stood when her foot touched that other coin, the coin that foretokened death. Later, superstitiously, she had believed that it was the death of her child that was foretold in that moment. But her child had not died.... She bent and kissed Roshan, who was entranced with the red and green squares of light that fell on his hand.

"Then I will," she said.

She frowned, remembering something else. Dallia, saying in that urgent whisper, "Mistress, remember the coin! Remember the Enemy!"

She had been too ill, too distressed then, to hear it as anything more than another weight added to her misery, but now she understood: it had been a warning.

The warning of someone who feared to say more.

Alinor frowned. She had had an enemy, and Dallia had known it, and tried to warn her.

Who had her enemy been? And what had they done?

*   *   *

She went down to the market to buy certain items of clothing she had seen at the used clothing stall and elsewhere—an exorbitantly priced pair of bluejeans and a couple of plaid flannelette shirts, some pretty but serviceable *shalwar kamees*.

"What are you wearing, Mama?" Roshan asked, the first time she appeared in jeans and a shirt.

"Bluejeans," she said in English.

"Beloojeans," he repeated, frowning. "They are not pretty."

"No," she agreed with a smile. Out of the mouths of babes! Compared with the flowing, flattering *shalwar kamees*, bluejeans did nothing for the female figure. "These are work clothes."

"Are we going to work?"

"We are."

With Roshan at her side, she began to tackle the restoration. With all the spoils now gathered in the hall, she began to divide them and assign them to various apartments—some of the central reception rooms, the King's suite, Puran and Nargis's apartment, the servants' rooms, the apartment she shared with Kavi. Then, one by one, she made the rooms hospitable again.

"I don't believe you ever rejected your own baby, no matter how crazy you were with pain or anything else," Lana wrote indignantly. "A woman who is going to do that will show some signs of it in her everyday behaviour, and I just don't believe it. I'm sure Kavi believes it, but he wasn't there, was he? Who told him, and why? You'd better be watching your back, girl."

She sat with the letter in front of her for a long time, feeling its robust common sense give renewed strength to her own convictions. Lana was right. If she had rejected her baby—and such moments of insanity do sometimes strike even the strongest of people under unrelenting stress—at the very least she would remember it. But what she remembered, what she had never forgotten, what she had never succeeded in putting entirely out of her mind for one entire day in all the time since she had heard them, were the words *Your baby is dead.*

She had not imagined it. If she were crazy enough to have invented and sustained that memory, she would be crazy in other ways. What she remembered was the truth. Kavian had been told the lie that he had told her.

Puran had told her in cold blood that her baby was dead, and it had been a lie.

"How have you achieved this miracle?" Kavi asked her, on the evening of the day when it had been the turn of their own apartments.

"There were pieces here and there. And I'm afraid I took most of the furnishings of your hunting tent."

"I thought I recognized this carpet. The tent was in an outbuilding and overlooked. Otherwise all that would have gone also."

"Do you mind?"

"You have restored comfort where there was none. I am grateful, Nuri. How can I be anything else?" He looked around him. "I would not have believed so much was possible. It is more than the furnishings. You have made it...what it used to be. A place to come to from the cares of the day."

Her heart beat very hard at his words, and she turned away to hide the tears in her eyes. "I'm glad you like it."

She could have turned the fourth room of their apartment into a bedroom for herself, and slept there. She could have, but she didn't. She turned it into an office for Kavi instead, so that the sitting room could be a place to relax in.

She contented herself with putting a single bed into the massive bedroom Kavi used. Every night they slept a few yards from each other, but he never touched her. He never showed any signs of wanting to.

While Kavi was chasing down his enemies, she had a similar job. One day she asked Dallia if she remembered finding the coin. "I remember, Mistress."

"When I was ill, you warned me about an enemy."

The servant's eyes fell.

"Yes, Mistress."

"Who was my enemy, Dallia?"

No answer.

But the answer was obvious anyway. Now that she saw it, she was astounded that it had not been clear to her before. She began to collect her evidence, piece by piece.

Chapter 15

With the home front secured, Alinor cast her eyes further afield.

"Kavi, I want to do something."

He turned from his desk to smile at her. It was a smile that he might give to anyone, a smile of enquiry. She had just put Roshan to bed and was standing in the doorway to his office. "What is it you want to do?"

"No, I mean I want to do something to help. Surely you could use some assistance? Is there any way I could help you in the search for the Kaljuks?"

"It's a matter of house-to-house searches now, by police and soldiers."

"Well, there must be something. Or if I can't help you, do you think the girls' school could use another teacher?"

"You are giving Roshan his mother. That is enough."

She wanted to hit him. "No, it is *not* enough. In other times, maybe. These are extraordinary times, and I've got skills and talents that could help. And shouldn't you be making use of every resource you have?"

He paused, mystified. "Why? Why do you want to help?"

She gave an exasperated snort. "I wish you could understand me and my motivations just once! A long time ago we agreed that if I married you I'd find something constructive to do here, and I want to do it, dammit!"

He really did not understand her. She could see it in his eyes. He really imagined she would prefer to stand and watch him carry his enormous load without lifting a finger. "That was before you learned to hate this country," he said simply.

"If I said I hated this country, I'm sorry. I think I said a lot of things I didn't mean, and I certainly never meant that. But anyway, that was then, and this is now. This is your country, and my son's country, and whether you like it or not, it's my country, too. And it's bleeding, and here I am."

He was silent a moment. She could see that the words had scarcely reached him, or not in the way she meant them. But his human resources were scarce and he could not afford to waste any. "If you're serious, there is a job that needs someone who has both English and Parvāni. Such people are thin on the ground now. It's a very big job, Alinor."

Many of his Companions in the old days had had a foreign language, but half of those had not survived the war. She saw the shadow cross behind his eyes and wondered which childhood friend he was regretting now, to whom he would automatically have entrusted this task.

She crossed the room and sat beside his desk. "Yes. Tell me."

"The Red Cross are going to be sending in a team soon. I've had some enquiries from volunteer organizations who will come as soon as the Red Cross has established a presence. They'll be going into the villages and helping to rebuild wells and other work of that nature. Médecins Sans Frontières also want to come. Do you think you could liaise with all these people? There'll be a lot of coordination to do, otherwise we're going to waste people's efforts."

She took a deep breath. It felt hugely daunting, presented without warning like that, and it wasn't the kind of thing she was trained for, but it was without doubt the biggest contribution she could make. And other people before her had grown into difficult tasks. "That sounds fine," she said.

He turned back to his desk and lifted a thick file of papers. "We've been getting reports in for some time now, detailing what the worst problems are in every area. It will be necessary to match up the offers from charities and the volunteers' skills with the area that has that need."

"I understand." She began with difficulty to decipher the Parvāni scrawl on the top sheet. In a foreign language, she reflected, two things were always the last hurdle—infant speech, and handwriting.

"Your biggest problem is in the areas which were mined by the Kaljuks. Whatever their other needs, the most important objective is to make these areas free of mines. Otherwise, we can't allow ordinary volunteers to go in. We have two of our own teams working, but progress is slow, and casualties high. There is an organization offering help with that. They have advanced equipment. You might start there."

"Is your mother well, Dallia?"

Terror in the dark eyes. "My mother is well, Mistress, God be praised."

"She recovered from her illness?"

Silence.

"Your mother was very, very ill, was she not? I remember you had to return to your village to help the family."

The servant was on her knees, weeping. "Mistress, I did not want to go! He had asked me to look after you carefully, and I swore I would do so! But they told me my mother was dying and gave me money and a mule, so that I could go and come back quickly."

"And your mother? Dallia, please tell me," she begged, as the servant hesitated. "Please tell me the truth."

The young woman took a deep breath and glanced once into her face before hanging her head. "My mother was well. She had sent me no message to the palace. I returned at once, but the journey—so slow and dangerous in the war—when I returned, you were gone, Mistress, and—Prince Kavian asked me to nurse the child against your return.''

"You did not come to me to say your farewells before you left," she said. "Why was that?"

"Mistress, I was kept from your chamber," she whispered desperately. She was openly weeping now. "They said you were too ill, that you did not want to see me."

"Who kept you from my chamber?" Alinor asked in a hard voice.

"Golnaz."

Puran's personal maid.

Gabe wrote her. He was recovering from his wound, and, considering the shooting skill of Kavi's Companions, that must have been intended, for which, he admitted dryly, he was grateful. But as it was in his left shoulder, she would forgive him for typing the letter. She puzzled over that, until she remembered Gabe was left-handed.

"I spent most of an evening with your husband, Alinor. Perhaps I should tell you that, whatever his past sins, I believe that he loves you." Then he told her that she could always call on him if she needed anything, and signed off with a simple, "God bless, Gabe."

"Good afternoon, Princess! *Beh khoda tokel.*"

"*Beh Khoda,* Doctor."

"Do you come to make another round of my patients, or to consult me?"

"Just to ask you some questions, Doctor, if I may."

"I have five minutes. They are preparing a patient in surgery for me. Will five minutes be enough?"

"Two will be enough. Do you remember caring for me during my pregnancy, Doctor, nearly four years ago?"

"But of course I remember. It was difficult for us, was it not? I with only German. I speak a little English now, Princess, and your own grasp of Parvān has much improved. You have spent your time away from us well, I see."

There was no way to respond to that. "It was a very difficult time for us," she agreed. "Doctor, on the night I went into labour, you were too busy with war casualties, I think, to come to the palace."

"*Chera?*"

"My memory may be at fault. Did you not send word that you could not come?"

"Not come to attend a premature birth of such a nature for the heir to the throne? *Khoda*, what could have been more pressing than such a life in the midst of so much death?"

"But you did not come, nonetheless. Was there another reason for this? You were perhaps ill?"

He was looking closely at her now, frowning. "Princess, I was not sent for. We knew nothing of the birth here till many days after it had occurred, when the infant was close to death and the Prince sent for me to prescribe for it. Naturally I demanded to know why I had not been sent for." He paused and massaged his chin. "It was explained to me that you had refused to have me attend, and that you were in such a state of panic it was thought better not to risk violating your wishes. Had I been informed of this at the time, of course I would have insisted on speaking to you. But I knew nothing."

The next two days were spent finding another desk and chair and getting organized in Kavian's office. She had telephone lines installed, too, late one night, by an overworked engineer. Kavian was, astonishingly, impressed when he discovered it. Up till now there had been only one working phone in the entire palace, which had been kept going somehow throughout the war. Kavi had got used to the inconvenience. "How did you manage this? There is a waiting list months long," he marvelled.

She looked at him. "Kavi, you're the Prince Regent,

among other things. Don't you think that gives you the right of priority?''

"I never thought of it that way." She believed him. The Durrans came from a tradition of sovereign as servant of the people rather than the other way around.

"Well, fortunately your subjects saw it my way. All I had to do was ask. They had no idea there was only one working phone line here, and they saw at once how urgent it was.''

"Western thinking has its uses," he said, and they laughed together for the first time in so long it was almost painful.

They sometimes relaxed together for half an hour, late at night in their sitting room when they had both worked themselves so hard no more was possible. Then, as always, they spoke as friends engaged on the same pressing task, but no more. Still, she looked forward to such times. She had never had conversations like this with Kavi in the past.

"The war changed things very quickly in Parvān," she said one night, when they had discussed some problem she had been told about that day on a tour of one of the nearby villages.

"Undoubtedly," he said dryly.

She smiled at her own stupidity. "I meant, the attitude to women. No one resents me going among them now by myself.''

He raised that one inquisitive eyebrow. "When have the people of Parvān ever resented your going among them by yourself?''

"Well, you know, I was always supposed to have a male escort for fear of offending them.''

"Alinor, what are you talking about?''

She frowned impatiently at his wilful misunderstanding. "But that was why I could never go out, wasn't it? I needed an escort, and it wasn't fair to be always asking for one, when everyone able-bodied was mobilising for war.''

"You were afraid to go alone. You said so.''

"I never said so! I was only trying to obey Parvān custom."

"Parvān custom, as you call it, has not prevented women from walking alone for decades."

"Not women—just the Crown Princess."

"Alinor, what is this about? My own mother used to go into the city to do her shopping, and that was thirty years ago."

"But...Puran said..."

"Puran has old-fashioned ideas. She always disapproved of my mother, too. Her husband was a Muslim husband of the old school—or maybe now I should say, the new school—and she did not struggle against his dictates. But whatever she told you, I had already promised you, while we were still in England, that you would be a free woman here."

She dropped her head. "Yes, you did," she said.

There was silence in the room.

"But you did not believe me," he said quietly. "Why, Alinor?

"I don't know. I don't know."

There were two kinds of mine, Alinor discovered. Ordinary anti-tank landmines, of the kind she had seen lying in the desert sand, and anti-personnel mines of various types, the worst of which were the "butterfly" mines. The last were bits of high explosive designed to look like anything at all—ballpoint pens, strands of grass, a mirror, a toy. If you picked one up, you lost a hand or an eye. If you stepped on one, a foot. If you walked through a bush where one was lying on a branch, any part of the anatomy at all: eye, knee, breast.

Where the mines had been sown on level stretches of ground, as in the desert, it was a simple, if tedious operation. You drove an anti-mine tank up and down that stretch of land and eventually the space could be considered cleared.

The high ground and the valleys were almost impossible to clear entirely. Every blade of grass, every cobweb was suspect, but every blade of grass and every cobweb could not be combed through.

She could keep the volunteers out of the unsafe areas, but she could not keep the citizens out. They wanted to go home, wanted to return to their villages and herds. And so each day brought news of some casualty: a woman had opened the door of her house and been blinded by an explosion when she had set off the butterfly mine that had been draped over the latch. A young boy had had his hands destroyed when he tried to clear out a bombed well. Men and animals were constantly in danger as they tried to plough the hungry fields. Children under three could not be taught not to touch the pretty, shiny toys they found in the grass...

"I wouldn't mind so much if they were honest about it," she said to Kavi one night, reading yet another report. "If they would just call them 'anti-baby mines' or 'child-crippling mines.' Anti-personnel seems so clinical. Why can't they at least be honest about what they are?"

"When is the military ever honest about anything that it does?" Kavian replied. "If they spoke the truth, they would have to stop what they do. But what is the problem? We know, if we are willing to face the truth, that since the dawn of history, all military organizations on earth, without exception, have been formed and carried on entirely for the purpose of killing and maiming human beings, and for no other. If we accept their lies that say otherwise, the responsibility is our own."

"The purpose hasn't always been to kill and maim civilians. It used to be soldiers only, didn't it?"

"When you consider the actions of victorious armies in the past, does this seem true?"

"Well, I hate them. I hate everybody connected with these filthy, evil mines."

"Then you hate a lot of good, decent people."

They were sitting at their desks, in the circle of light from two lamps. There was silence all around them, for few noises penetrated the ancient stone walls.

"What do you mean?"

He looked at her steadily for a long moment. "Do you know that about half of the anti-tank mines out there in the Central Desert have been manufactured in England or by English subsidiaries?"

"What? I don't believe you!" But it was a reaction of revulsion, not real disbelief, and he seemed to recognize the fact, and carried on.

"Do you think that the workers, men or women, who go to work every day in such factories to make those mines, say to themselves in the morning, 'Now, how many innocent people in the world can I cripple today'? Of course they don't. They do their job and bring a paycheck home to feed their family, and that's the right thing to do, isn't it? They're decent people."

She sat in righteous, indignant silence.

"And the Prime Minister of Great Britain, when he refuses to sign an agreement to limit the export of the landmines that these people make, is that because he wants a whole generation of Parvānis to be maimed and crippled for the future?" He shrugged. "He's trying to prevent factories from closing in some depressed area and keep up the nation's balance of payments. It's the human condition, Jānam."

Jānam. My soul. He had called her that, long ago.

From the other room, there was a murmur and a sighing breath as Roshan moved in his sleep. They both turned, listening for a moment.

She said quietly, "It's war against children. Kavi, I read these reports, and I think, they're the same age as Roshan…and what would I do if it happened to him? How would I live if…I've suffered it once, it's hell, it's the worst thing in the world, Kavian. But then—it turned out it wasn't true, it was only a bad dream, just as I used to pray. And somehow, that makes it worse. I got through it once, but I know I couldn't go through it again. Do you understand that? Some things, you get through them, and you think, well, I've learned how to cope with that if it ever comes my way again, but this isn't like that! I've been through it, I've lost him once, and now...I can never, ever lose him again. I couldn't live through it a second time."

She was weeping, she had been under too much unspoken stress for days, and suddenly he was holding her, pressing her into his shoulder, stroking her hair. He murmured unintelligibly, letting her cry, and she wept and wept, until it seemed that there was nothing left in her.

At last she drew back, digging in a pocket for a hankie, and wiped her face and blew her nose.

"Better?" he asked gently, smiling.

"Better," she said. "Thank you. Kavi?"

"Nuri?"

"That's the first time you ever held me when I was crying, and comforted me."

"Is it?"

"Why didn't you ever do that—before?" She wasn't blaming, she just wanted to understand.

"Maybe because before you were usually blaming me for whatever it was that made you weep. Shouting at me. It didn't seem to me that it was comfort that you wanted."

"I'm sorry." He was right. Ever since she had learned why he married her, she had always been secretly blaming him.

"Hello, Arash."

"Alinor!" The two Companions whom she had known at college in England had continued to call her by her first name when they spoke in private. She had enjoyed such familiarity from those two, when so many around her spoke formally. Now there was only one; Jamshid had not survived the war. But Arash kept up their friendly private custom, and she welcomed it as a sign that he, if no one else, did not judge her for the past.

"How's it going?" he said in English.

She grinned wearily. "About the same for me as for you, I guess. How are you?"

"Pretty well. What can I do for you?"

"You can pour me a cup of that, for a start."

He laughed, his strong teeth white against his darkly tanned skin. Arash spent most of his days out of doors, though it was hard to keep track of all he was doing. He was closely in Kavi's confidence. He poured her a tiny cup of the mud-like coffee he was addicted to, sugared it for her, and lifted it over his desk.

"My friend Lana sends her regards. She asked after you."

Before she took hold of it, he let go, and the little cup and saucer fell, hitting the edge of his desk and spilling its contents over her shoes as it hit the floor.

"Ah, Alinor, forgive me! So clumsy!"

She pulled out a tissue and wiped her shoes, picking up the cup. For a couple of minutes they were preoccupied with the cleanup. It seemed just one of those moments when two people's coordination had not matched, but…Alinor had seen the flicker of—alarm?—in Arash's eyes in the moment before the muscles of his hand failed him.

She sat back, watching him. Had it started here, then? Was this the clue? She was silent, waiting for him to find a way to prevent the conversation getting back where it had been.

There was a long pause while Arash stared blindly at the papers in front of him.

"So you write her," he muttered at last, and Alinor sat back in astonishment as an entirely different suspicion from the one she had just been entertaining struck her. Arash cleared his throat and looked at her again. "Is she—well?"

"Very well," she said slowly. "She's been travelling in Europe this summer, and enjoying herself very much. She doesn't seem eager to get back home."

His eyes drifted again. "Of course, she does not have to think about finding a job." He glanced at her again. "Has she—" He thought better of whatever he had been going to ask.

She fought to speak casually over her mounting tension.

"Most people have to think about finding a job. Why not Lana, specifically?"

He did not answer.

She waited. Then, "Did everybody know, Arash?"

"Everyone? No. We knew."

"'We'? You and Kavian and Jamshid?"

"I—" He cleared his throat. "We told Kavian, yes. Such a thing cannot be hidden easily when one goes looking."

"You went looking?"

His eyes were embarrassed, sorrowful, ashamed, knowing she was after something, and thinking he knew what it was. "When we saw the way it was with Kavian—even before you...before he told his father about you, Jamshid and I knew how it was. It was part of our job to protect him, Alinor. Forgive me, but you were studying Kaljuki...we worried about who you might be, whether you had been sent to entangle him...we checked your background, and that of your friend...of Lana. He knew nothing of it. He would have been angry...he *was* angry, when he discovered it. Very angry. Please understand how it was. War threatened. We had to know."

"I understand. Of course you had to check up on me. So you all knew who Lana was almost from the beginning?"

"Oh, yes," he said bitterly, almost to himself. "Oh, yes, we knew."

"And you loved her."

He twisted his head in a tiny shrug.

"Did Lana know? Did you—tell her?"

He shrugged and shook his head.

"Why didn't you—?"

He laughed, interrupting her. "Why didn't I? A woman as rich as the old Mughal Queens of India, and you ask why didn't I?"

"You are a member of the Parvān royal family, after all," she pointed out. It might be a distant relationship, but she knew he came from an aristocratic background, and most branches of the aristocracy had married into the royal family at some point in their history.

He shrugged. "I knew there would be war. Kavian believed that it would be averted, but I knew in my heart. I thought—if the war does not come, if the Sheikh's negotiations are successful, we will return to England. Then, perhaps, I told myself. And now, what is there? My family has lost everything. My country has lost everything. I walk with a limp. What shall I offer such a woman?"

A little later, she thought to ask, "Who did you tell about it, Arash, when you returned here?"

"I told my sister. She said I was a fool. She said a man who is afraid of money is as weak as a man afraid of gunfire. Perhaps she was right. When you ran away, I told myself that between Kavian and myself, I suffered the less. But now you have returned to him. He does not suffer anymore. I can have no such hope."

Later, alone in their bedroom, she looked at the ruin of her life, and the full horror of the plot against her fell on her. From the beginning, from the very first day, Puran had worked to undermine the marriage, to destroy her. She had been lied to about everything, had had her trust, her love for Kavian so poisoned that every action, every word out of his mouth became suspect. No longer did Alinor doubt, and wonder whether in the pain of childbirth she had rejected her baby and then forgotten the fact. Now she was certain of what had happened.

But the central fault lay with herself. She saw that, too. Now she could look and see that if she had trusted Kavian as she should have, as a woman should trust her husband, none of it could ever have happened. Whatever had been done to her, she had conspired in it all. She had betrayed Kavi in every possible way.

But even that was not important. What was important was—was there any way back?

Chapter 16

She wanted all the time she could get with Roshan, and although she spent two hours every afternoon with him, and put him to bed at night, the most important thing seemed to her to be the fact that she was working right next door to his own room.

She was working harder than she had ever worked in her life, harder than she would have believed possible. She had a team working with her now, but they were in offices elsewhere in the palace, and she stayed where she was.

Roshan could run in to see her from his play whenever he wished, he heard the sound of her voice...it was security for him. Kavian was often there, too, but the child was already sure of his father. It was his mother's presence he needed to remind himself of.

"I have hair like yours, don't I, Mama?" Roshan said one night, toying with the long strands where they lay on her shoulder, and as his little hand unconsciously brushed her breast, she was reminded of how the milk had streamed from them and how she had been deprived of those first joys of motherhood, and her heart twisted.

"Yes, my darling, you do. And what colour is that?"

"The colour of honeycomb," he lisped.

"Honeycomb!" She was enchanted by the child's poetry. "And where have you seen a honeycomb, my darling?" Such delicacies were rare now in Parvān.

"I've never seen one," he said sadly.

"How do you know the colour of it?"

"Baba told me."

Her heart simply stopped beating for two seconds.

"Did he?"

The boy nodded.

"What else did he tell you?"

"He said you were a beautiful princess and you loved me very, very much but you was sick and you had to go far away to get better, like Grandfather. And one day you would come back and be very proud of me, but I had to eat all my breakfast so I would grow up to be a strong prince and Mama would be proud of me," he said all in a rush.

"Well, he was right. And you did grow up to be a handsome prince, and I'm very, very proud of you."

"Were you bad sick, Mama?"

"Yes," she said softly. "Or I would have come much, much sooner. I didn't want to be away from you at all, I wanted to be with you so badly. I dreamt about you at night, and in my dreams I watched you growing up, so I was already proud of you, because I knew how big and strong you were growing."

He smiled, and it was the sun in the sky. "I dreamt about you, too, Mama. You kissed me."

"Of course I did." She kissed him now. "That was because I love you."

"When are you going away again?" he said, with deceptive casualness, playing with her wristwatch.

"I won't go away again," she assured him.

"Never?"

"Not to stay away. Only for short visits, the way I go to the villages. I'll always come back."

"You won't go far, far, far away again?"

She wondered what sort of life she was setting up for herself, making such a promise. A loveless marriage all the rest of her days?

She kissed him again. "If I do, I'll come back quickly. I couldn't stay away from you now, could I?"

She felt tension in the air, and looked up to see Kavian in the doorway, with a face like stone. There was no knowing how long he had been there.

"Here's Baba," she said quickly, before he could turn away, "come to say goodnight."

He came into the room then, like a stranger, his eyes softening only when they came to rest on his son. Alinor stood up, and Kavian took her place on the bed, putting out his hand to caress Roshan's head. For the briefest moment it was unsteady as it touched the fair hair, and her heart clenched. He had once loved her as much as that, and what had happened to that love?

Overwhelmed with sorrow, she slipped down to kneel on the floor beside the bed, and, not looking at Kavi, smiled at Roshan as he chatted to his father about his day. Hardly noticing what she was doing, she raised an arm and rested it on Kavi's knees to support her chin.

She was made aware of her action with a jolt, because she might as well have been resting on rock. There was no movement, no answer to her in his flesh. He went on talking to Roshan, and then, when their goodnights had been said, he lifted her arm away and stood.

There was nothing in his touch but distaste, and a bone-deep unwillingness to feel her flesh against his.

Over time, as the pain of her loss was transformed by the joy of Roshan's presence, as the tendrils of love that had been her right since his birth formed and bound the two of them closer and closer in that unique loving bond found only between mother and child, she felt less bitterness about missing his infancy. Perhaps it should have increased, but all Alinor could think was that she had found her son alive when she had believed him dead. And even though she had lost three and a half years, this was so much better than if he had really died, she sometimes hardly remembered what had been done to them, the lies that had been told.

In spite of having his mother's hair, he was very like his father. Those intense, thoughtful, green eyes had Kavian's slightly exotic tilt, the creamy pale skin was his, the generous, firm mouth—touched with an innocence which his father's mouth had lost now, but which she remembered all too clearly—was Kavian's when it smiled or spoke.

Such things touched her heart twice over—in her love for Roshan, but also in her love for Kavi. She had been weak, mistrustful, she had not known how to love properly, but she had loved him desperately, and whatever she had told herself, she had never stopped loving him.

She was older now, she had learned about life in a hard school since. She knew she could love him better now. But Kavi did not want her love. He could respect her as a working partner, as someone dedicated to the restoration of his country, he could admire her hard work, her stamina, he could approve of her loving commitment to their son. But he wanted no more from her. He never betrayed by so much as a glance that he regretted what they had lost, or that he looked forward to a future when they might clear up the misunderstandings of their past and be husband and wife again.

She wanted to fight his indifference, wanted to force him to listen while she explained what she knew and what she had discovered. But their days were full of other things. They worked long hours that were exhausting mentally and emotionally as well as physically. After a tour of a village where people were trying to rebuild their homes and lives from nothing and with nothing, after a discussion of yet another poisoned well, after an afternoon of seeing women in the traces pulling a plough because there were no cattle, after a visit to yet another underfunded orphanage, after an afternoon of reading about desperate need on the endless stained sheets of paper that arrived daily on her desk, and knowing when she gave up for the day that Kavi had had a day exactly the same in essentials, she had nothing left for overcoming Kavi's resistance.

In fact, she quailed from it, because of what she would have to explain. That his own aunt had worked to destroy what he held dear, had lied and betrayed him for an unknown reason...how could he accept that, with the little proof Alinor had? And if he could believe it, would it bring relief, or would it merely exchange one burden of pain for another?

She watched him. She knew how he suffered with the pain of his people, how he bled for his country. What would he suffer to learn of Puran's deliberate, coldly-plotted increase of his anguish in his darkest night?

Alinor woke with a start and sat up in the moonlight, her heart beating with urgency. What had aroused her? Roshan? Had he called?

As swift as the thought, she swung the covers off her legs and stood up.

"Nuri! *Nuri!*"

Alinor gasped as the cry came again, and looked at the bed opposite. Kavi lay in a shaft of moonlight, his face beaded with sweat, grimacing with pain. "Nuri!" he cried again.

She stepped over to his bed and sank down on it, instinctively putting her hand out to feel his broad forehead. Icily cool. The sweat was not from fever. She sighed and dropped her hand to his bare, hard-muscled shoulder, gleaming white in the moonlight. "Kavi," she whispered gently.

He moaned. She bent closer. "Kavi."

He strode through the long corridors, and always the soft silk of her dress flicked around a corner just ahead of him, just out of reach. He called her, begging, pleading with her to stop for him, but always she eluded him. He knew the dream of old, he knew that he would find her when they reached the centre, and so he followed, half-despairing, half-hoping, for he did not remember what would happen after he caught her.

He chased and chased, but always she was faster; and then there they were, the doors he had seen before, with that flicker of grey gauze just disappearing through. With a powerful effort he reached them, dragged them open, and she was there, in the room with no exit, her beauty perfect; and now he remembered the end which he had not remembered at the beginning, now his heart was all despair, for he knew that even so, she would escape him.

"Nuri!" he begged, all his love in that one word, and reached for her and wrapped her in his arms. She opened her mouth, and quickly he bent to kiss her, for he knew that if he waited she would elude him yet again. He smothered her speech on her lips, and held her more tightly than he had ever held her, out of fear, and the passion of his longing burned out of his being into hers.

And then it was all new, and he felt what he had never felt in the dream before as she lifted her arms up around his neck, and her breasts behind the thin gauze pressed against his chest, and her mouth was warm and firm and wet, and she did not disappear.

Now, suddenly, they were in bed, and it was dark, and she lay with her pale hair glowing like honey in a shaft of moonlight. The perfume of her body filled his nostrils, and his sex was painfully hard against her. Hard and seeking, so that by the time he understood that he was awake he was already deep inside her, and she was grunting with the mingled pain and pleasure of his entrance.

"Kavi," she whispered. "Kavi!"

He remembered only that she had not been there, and now she was, and his body was ferocious with the long time of need. He swept a hand up over her, pushing away what covered her, and then her breasts lay open to his gaze, smooth and perfect in the moon's gleam. He raised himself over her and began to thrust his body into her, and although he understood the reality of the hot, soft wetness that enclosed him with every stroke, he understood nothing else.

He both felt his body's own movement, and saw it reflected in her face, for she opened her mouth with pleasure at each thrust, and shut her eyes, and cried the high cry of seeking and pleasure that had used to thrill him, long ago.

Her hands stroked him, caressed him, his face, his hair, his shoulders and arms and back, wherever she could reach, pressing and urging him, painting him with fire; and now she lifted her legs to encircle his hips, giving him the deepest access to her body.

He drove all the way then, deep, she could take the full length of him now, and the pleasure was everywhere, brain and muscle, sinew, skin and hair—suddenly there was too much, it overwhelmed him, and he began to cry his pleasure to heaven. She pressed up against him, crying too, and writhed there in the way he had learned to understand, and he thrust hard once, twice, pushed hard against her. As the involuntary spasm of her muscles closed on him, sensation exploded all around him, and he called her name, and wrapped her in his arms, and drove the last drop of his pleasure into her.

"Alinor," he said in another voice entirely, when memory began to trickle back. He drew himself up away from her, and when she lifted a hand and would have stroked his hair, he caught it and prevented her. "What happened?"

He felt her flinch. "It's pretty obvious, isn't it?" she said.

He rolled away from her. "I was dreaming," he said.

"Yes. What were you dreaming, Kavi?"

He avoided that. "And then, you were there. What are you doing in this bed?"

She couldn't tell from his tone whether he blamed her or not. "You called me. You were sweating and calling my name. And then—you grabbed me."

"I'm sorry," he said.

It was like a slap. "Are you? Why?"

He didn't answer. She felt him retreating from her, to his own inner mountain territory, where she could not follow.

"You know what?" she said conversationally, holding up her hand in the moonbeam and watching the play of silky soft light on it. "You love me."

He went as cold as death against her. "Alinor," he said warningly.

"I don't expect you to like it, but it's the truth."

"Whatever I may feel for you in a moment of sexual weakness, it makes no difference between us, Alinor."

"Why not?"

"Because I do not choose that it should," he said.

"And what are we going to do with the rest of our lives, Kavi? Or haven't you thought it out that far?"

"We will find some arrangement when there is leisure to think of ourselves."

She wanted to cry for the waste, for the loss, for the hurt she had caused him and he her, for impossibilities. "What do you mean by 'arrangement'? That we'll both take lovers, or something?"

She saw his jaw clench in the pale moonshadow. "I will not discuss it now."

"If that was what you planned, Kavi, why didn't you just let me marry Gabriel?"

"It was not possible, whatever my personal wishes were. You are married to me."

"A fact nobody knew, before you made such a noise about it. I would have thought you'd have more pride."

He leaned over, turned on the lamp, and stared down at her, his eyes black with reined-in anger. "My whole country knew it. Do you count my people as *no one?* What was more shaming to me, as a man? To let my wife marry another man in a bigamous ceremony in front of the world, or to show the world that I, as a man, would not allow it? You tried to shame me, Alinor, and you failed. It was no shame to me to tell them what I will and will not allow my wife to do! And now, do you try to shame me again, by telling me that I still love an unfaithful wife, a wife who has left duty, home, child and country for the sake of another man? I do not love you! If I desire you, that is a testimony many men give to beauty."

She was silent and horrified under the stream of angry words, not knowing which accusation to refute first.

"For another man?" She struggled to a sitting position, her back against the wall. "I didn't leave you for another man! What are you talking about?"

"The man whom you wished to marry—was not he stationed at the British Embassy in the very city that you fled to after the birth of our son?"

"*Gabe?* No! At least—was he?"

"You did not know it, my wife?"

"I don't know it now! And whether he was there or not, I didn't know him, and I didn't go there to meet him, if that's what you're trying to say!"

He looked at her, and she burst out, "For God's sake, Kavi! I loved *you,* remember?"

"I remember that I believed it. Oh yes, you pretended well. I remember how you used to stare at me with those wide, frightened eyes, and then run when I came close, till I was crazy to have you, till I was out of my mind for you.

"But I have not forgotten, either, how you tried to get to Kaljukistan as soon as war was declared. I have not forgotten how many questions you asked, or how angry you were when you were pregnant with my son. Or how you hated him when he was born..."

"*No!*" she cried desperately.

"...and how you fled, leaving him to die. Was there someone for whom you did all this, eh, my wife?"

She was mesmerized by his black eyes, by the rammed-down ferocity that wanted to lay violent hands on her but did not allow himself. "Who?" she whispered confusedly, staring at him.

He smiled, no smile she could ever have wished to see. "Who, you ask? I don't know. There were some who said the Kaljuks paid you."

She slapped him. Hard, across the cheek. "Shut up!" she said flatly. His eyes changed as she struck him, and she was suddenly terrified of him. She scrambled out of the bed and stood looking down.

"I'm sorry, I shouldn't have done that. But neither should you. You have no right to speak to me like that, Kavi. If you suffered, so did I, and you will have to learn to respect that."

"You suffered?" he asked, as if he did not believe it. "What did you suffer?"

She turned her back and left the room.

Alinor paced for hours, thinking.

She had had no idea how deep it had gone with Kavi, but tonight had made a lot of things plain. It was much worse than she had imagined. He had rewritten everything, since the beginning, just as she had, saw himself as her dupe, saw all she'd said and done from the beginning as a lie. Just as she had. Even suspected that she might be a spy, imagined that those questions she had asked she had been paid to ask.

How different was that from what she had done? Her heart wanted to get indignant, to dwell on how little he'd trusted her—but she had believed equally awful things about him, on the word of one woman.

They had a lot of thinking to do, both of them. A lot of talking. And it was going to be uphill work, because Kavi did not *want* to love her, whereas she wanted to love him. She did love him. She had fought it at first, but once the evidence was there, she had no reason to go on resisting the truth that her heart knew.

The list of her betrayals which he had recited to her was long and ugly, and if she was going to refute them, Kavi was going to have to listen, and accept.

He loved her. He must, she told herself desperately. The passion with which he had held her...she melted at the mem-

ory of it, of the sound of his voice in her ear. He might say
that it was only the tribute any man would pay to her beauty,
but she did not believe him. She couldn't believe him.

Once she'd have said that if only they made love, all
would be solved. They had always had that, or if not always,
she remembered sadly, at least till near the end. Once, sex
had broken down any barrier between them, but at the end
it had been good sex, but no more. There had been a meeting
of bodies, but not of minds or hearts. And then even that had
gone.

So it had been optimistic of her to hope for that to resolve
things. She'd thought if they made love Kavi would be able
to listen. But he hadn't wanted to listen an hour ago.

On the other hand, he had told her more about his feelings
than she had learned since the day he'd kidnapped her. So
perhaps it did still work, only that Kavian was unwilling that
it should.

Had Gabe really been in the British Embassy where she'd
fled? Or was this another of Puran's inventions? If so, it put
a huge difficulty in the way of her telling him the truth about
Gabe and herself.

When she thought now of the wanton lie she had told
about Gabe, she could have killed herself. He had such pride,
and she had said the one thing that was unprovable either
way. Damned out of her own mouth as a faithless wife. It
might stick in his throat forever.

She had been worse than a fool, telling Kavi he loved her
in that stupid way. Of course he had to repudiate the charge.
Why had she been so smug, so sure? It must have sounded
like triumph. With what he imagined about her motives, he
was probably telling himself that she had deliberately pro-
voked the incident in order to prove that however badly she
had treated him, she could still get under his skin.

In the morning, in their office, it was as though nothing
had happened. He treated her exactly as he had before, like
an efficient colleague he could count on. No memory shad-

owed his eyes, no tenderness softened the line of his lips. Around the eyes she could see that the sexual release had eased some of the perpetual tension he carried, but he did not look at her as though he was grateful for it.

Alinor mentally gave up then. If he had showed her any feeling, anything at all as a result of what had occurred last night, and the confession he had made of how she had hurt him—but he was not even indifferent. He was exactly what he had been yesterday at this time.

I was wrong, she told herself. *And Gabe was wrong, and Lana. He does not love me. His love is dead.*

Chapter 17

One evening, as they sat over a late dinner, talking about their work, Kavian said, "I have had a letter from Puran this morning."

Alinor shivered, and found herself saying brightly, "That reminds me—Lana phoned today! She wants to come out, but they've refused her a visa. She's hoping you can intervene with the consulate in London. Can you?"

"I'll speak to Rusi about it." Rusi was the government minister responsible for tourism. "A word from him will do it. When does she come?"

"Next month, she says. She says she's got a surprise for me but she has arrangements to make."

Kavi only nodded. He seemed to have forgotten his letter, and part of Alinor rejoiced. She could not bear to think or speak about Puran. She wanted to forget the woman existed.

But she had to know. Puran had proved how dangerous she could be, and to avoid listening to information on her would be the action of a fool. She couldn't hide her head in the sand, or who knew what would happen?

As Kavi was about to stand, Alinor put out her hand to him. "I interrupted what you were saying about Puran. What did she say?"

"Nothing important. A few stories about the village and how her family is coping. She'll be home next week."

Her brain took refuge in ignorance. "Home? What do you mean? Where is she now?"

He smiled. "Home, Alinor—that means here. She and Nargis are coming back next week."

"No!" She was swamped by such a wave of revulsion she nearly lost her dinner. Swallowing convulsively, she stared at Kavi, who was looking astonished. "No!" she said again. Her voice was hoarse. She took a breath. "No!" It seemed to be all she could say.

Kavi frowned, then raised his eyebrows. "What is the matter?" he asked without heat.

She tried to speak calmly over the thudding, ugly fear, the animal terror that suffused her. "She is not coming here, Kavi. I will not have her, I will not speak to her or look at her. She's not coming!"

"This is her home," he said mildly.

"No, it is not, it's my home, mine and yours and Roshan's, and I will not share it with her." She knew her voice was going higher and higher; she was not calm. She was starting to sound like an hysteric. She couldn't control the feelings that swept through her.

"She has her own apartments, Alinor. If you're angry with her over some imagined slight, you don't need to have more than minimal dealings with her."

She jumped to her feet. "I don't need to have *any dealings whatsoever* with her! And I won't! She is not coming here, and if she does, *I will leave!"*

He was silent for the length of a deep, controlled breath. "Do not start this again, Alinor."

Oh, God, what had she said? "I'm sorry, I'm sorry! But you must understand, Kavi! That woman stole three and a half years of my son's life from me, and she wrecked—!"

"Alinor, stop this!"

"I will not stop! I will not have this!"

It descended into a shouting match where nothing coherent was said, or listened to. At last Kavi stormed out of the apartment, slamming the door with a blast that blew the candles on the table out. Alinor sat down in her place, trembling from head to foot, sick with fear and worry.

"Mama?" The door to Roshan's bedroom stood open a crack, and he peered through, as if afraid to open it all the way.

"Roshan! It's all right, darling! Come here," she said shakily.

He pushed the door and ran to her, burying his face against her. She sighed and stroked his hair, and calmed herself. Every time she looked at this precious piece of humanity she was amazed all over again.

"Did you hear Baba and me shouting? Is that what the trouble is?"

He looked up, nodding, his green gaze troubled, like a stormy sea. "Why were you shouting?"

"Because we were very angry with each other."

"Do mothers and fathers shout when they're angry?" he asked, looking for a ruling on the nature of the world.

"Yes, they do sometimes. But they still love each other."

"Oh," he said, accepting it. "Are you going to shout at me?"

"I hope not, darling, but it might happen. People lose their tempers, and then they shout at the ones they love." She stroked his head. "But I wouldn't want to lose my temper with you ever."

He was satisfied with this. "I lose my temper sometimes," he said, practising the words. They embarked on a discussion of the various times when Roshan had felt angry, and then he was calm enough to be put back to bed and fall instantly asleep. His mother, meanwhile, returned to the sitting room and sat thinking for hours.

What a mistake it had been to put off talking to Kavian

about what she knew. She should not have waited. She should have presented her case to Kavian before there was any threat of Puran returning, when she was thinking clearly.

She was not thinking clearly now. Like a torture victim who hears the step of the torturer in the corridor, she felt helpless, panicked, as though to be anywhere near Puran must mean falling into her power again.

She was also in the grip of deep and ugly emotions, almost too violent to handle. Rage at what had been done to her blazed through her, giving the lie to all her belief that she had come to terms with losing Roshan's babyhood, with almost losing him forever. She had never felt such a fury in her life. It terrified her. It was like being insane. She thought, with what seemed like diamond clarity: *If Puran comes here, I will kill her. I will pick up a knife and stab her through the heart, and that will destroy us all forever.*

She had to stop her coming. She had been a fool to give in, to accept that Kavi did not and never would love her, to accede to the death of her marriage when she loved him. She should have been fighting all this time. She should have made him listen and believe while she still had time.

"We need to talk," she said. She had gone to bed before him, but she had lain awake in the darkness until he came in, knowing he would not come in till he thought her asleep. Then she sat up and put on the lamp beside her bed.

He glanced at her across the length of the room. "Do we?"

She supported herself on one elbow. The sheet fell away from her body. She was wearing a singlet, but in any case his eyes were not caught for an instant. "I want to explain something to you. Well, lots of things."

"Problems with one of the volunteer groups?"

"What?" She fought against the little burn of anger. It was his way of dismissing what was too hard to handle. "No, this is about us, Kavi," she said firmly.

His face was shuttered. "It is not necessary to explain

anything to me, Alinor." Since that night in his bed he had never called her Nuri again. He turned away and began to strip off his clothes as if to have her watching was of no more significance than if a cat did.

"Yes, it is! But you won't know that unless you listen! Kavi, can't you listen? Please, there's so much misunderstanding between us."

"I see no misunderstanding between us. It seems to me we understand each other very well."

"If you are intending to let Puran come here, Kavi, we do not understand each other at all," she said levelly.

He stood looking down at her. "My aunt's place of residence is no concern of yours."

She cursed herself for drawing up the battle lines so quickly. Confrontation was not what was needed. She took a deep breath, struggling for calm.

"Kavi, if I could just make you feel a little bit better about me...could make you stop despising me..."

"What are you talking about? You are an excellent worker, with more stamina and brains and ingenuity than any ten others. What makes you think I despise you? If I gave that impression I'm very sorry."

"This is like talking to a tank!" she exploded, losing it suddenly. She sat bolt upright. "Earth to Kavi! Is there anyone in there, or are you just a thick hide of bombproof metal?"

Now she wished she hadn't jeered, for he turned, and his eyes when they met hers were as deep and deadly as a cup of hemlock.

"Alinor, whatever you want, believe me when I say that you will not find it in me." He bent down and reached a hand towards her lamp. "Now, shall we put the lights out?"

She caught his wrist, preventing him. "Kavi," she said desperately, all her carefully constructed outline of this scene in tatters. "I lied to you when I said Gabe and I had..." She cleared her throat. "Had been lovers. We never were. Not physically."

He raised his eyes to hers in distant interest. "How short-sighted of him. But he was not to know." Gently he lifted her clinging hand from his wrist and straightened.

She flushed. "I *mean* it. I know I said we did, but that was just because I was...so angry. And hurt."

"What did you hope? To make me jealous? I did go through many torments, imagining you in other men's arms, but that was long ago."

"No one, Kavi. *No one.*"

"I am not the man to take the edge off your hunger," he said coldly. "However it may have seemed."

She flinched away.

As he moved again, she remembered her original plan of procedure, and drew a breath. "Kavi, was there any reason at the outset why your aunt would have been opposed to our marriage?"

"You asked me this once before, Alinor. What—"

She gasped with surprise. "I *did?*"

"Yes, you did. And I—"

"When?" she demanded.

"When we were first married," he said.

She didn't remember it at all. "And what did you say about it?"

"I told you to put it out of your mind."

She sank back on the pillows, astonished at the wave of feeling that washed over her. "I suspected then, so early? Oh, my God. Oh, God, yes, I do remember. I tried to talk to you...." She looked up at him, to find the first glimmer of responsiveness in his gaze: it was frowning surprise, but that at least was a start. "And you told me to forget it, to put it out of my mind. And I did."

She sat for a moment in silence, as the last cog slipped into place, then sighed in deep, useless remorse. "What a pair of fools we were. Oh, God, why didn't you tell me the truth then? You knew, didn't you?" She could see it all now. She sat up, bent forward and pressed both hands to her face, then looked at him again. "You knew she hated me, and you just didn't want to tell me so."

"I did not know she hated you. She did not hate you. But she was at the beginning opposed to my marrying a foreigner. She tried to convince my father to withhold his consent, and she wrote me a letter outlining my duty. Why was it so important that you know this?"

"Because I might have been on guard against her machinations. And you're wrong, she did hate me. Does. Oh, how she must hate me! Oh, God, Kavi! Did we ever confide in each other about anything, back then?" She wanted to weep, but her heart was too heavy, like stone, and her eyes burned with dryness, not tears. "You put me off my guard, and then I forgot that first suspicion…what a mess we made of it, eh? What a stupid, bloody, hopeless, useless mess we made of life and love and marriage and hope and parenting and everything."

"Stop it, Alinor!" Kavi said roughly. For the first time he was shaken, he was not proof against the terrible despair that came from her. He sat beside her on the bed, clasped her shoulder and shook her a little. "Stop this! What is the matter?"

She could hardly bear to look at him. "If you knew what Puran had done," she said, shaking her head. "If you knew."

"What could she do? You were my wife." She noted the use of the past tense, and shook her head again in hopeless despair. There was a long moment of silence, in which she could sense decision in him.

"Tell me, then."

She thought that he had only decided to humour her, to listen to her paranoid ravings. But whatever his attitude, he was listening. She had to make her points now.

She drew a deep breath. "When I first got here, Puran was all I had, you know? After our—our honeymoon, you were away so much, and I knew nothing about anything—palace life, my duties…"

"Your duties?"

"Yes, you'll say now I had none, but first she buried me under that..." A floodlight went on in her brain, and suddenly she was clear, could see it all as if it were woven in a tapestry, all the slow, hideous campaign of lies, could explain it with a clear accuracy. "She made me feel guilty wanting to go out in an ordinary way, down to the city, because I'd be taking a man off important duties to accompany me. I was so cut off from everybody except her and Nargis...I can see now how she did it, step by step...."

His eyes were dark, but she could not read what was written there. "Alinor, it was you yourself who did not wish to go into the town without an escort. You were afraid."

"Is that what Puran told you?"

"I am sure you told me yourself."

She shook her head. "No, *no!* I remember complaining to you about not being able to go out, and you got very frustrated and said, Well, then, go by yourself, and I thought—I thought that was you giving in in exasperation. I thought it was you saying, Well, then, violate all the customs and traditions of this country if you must be so selfish. And..." She shrugged. "I didn't want to do it that way, I wanted..."

"What did you want?"

"I wanted some sign of support from you! I wanted you to tell me that things were old-fashioned here but that you were committed to my being a free woman, and that you'd stand up for me if I violated your people's traditions."

"My people do not have such traditions. Or only a segment of the population. I told you so from the outset."

She hung her head. "Yes, you did. And if only I'd believed you...don't you see the worst was the way Puran played on my expectations? She couldn't have done it without my help, I'm not saying she could. But I see now I was *expecting*—in spite of what you'd told me I was subconsciously expecting that there would be restrictions on my life here because I am a woman...if I'd trusted you, Kavi, if I'd believed your assurances, she'd never have made me accept it...."

"Why did you not trust me? What reason had I given you not to trust what I had told you?"

"I know it doesn't make sense. And yet...you were never here, and Puran was all I had. She became my authority on everything. Now you've reminded me, I remember that very early on I did mistrust what she was telling me, but what reason could there be for her to lie? That's the point—it's facing up to the possibility that a person who pretends to be your friend is really your worst enemy. Is coldly, deliberately, telling you lies. That's not easy to accept, Kavi. And when I *was* suspicious, when I did ask you, you told me I was imagining things."

He shook his head. "Alinor, you're imagining *this*. Puran was opposed before she met you, but once meeting you, getting to know you, she realized her mistake and accepted you were the right wife for me."

He did not say that Puran had been right the first time, but the words seemed to be in the air anyway. She had to remind herself that it would be as difficult for him as it had been for her to accept that his aunt had a motive of deliberate malice. More so. She bit back an angry retort.

"Who told you so, Kavi?" she asked softly instead. "Puran?"

"Puran came to the palace in the year after my mother died. As far as she could, she took my mother's place in my life. She loved me like her own son, and why should she want to do evil to me?"

Alinor heaved a sigh from the depths. "Yes, why shouldn't you have believed her? And why shouldn't I have accepted your reassurances? But once I'd learned to ignore what my instinct was telling me, what defence did I have? And then—when she was my authority on everything, when I was really dependent on her, and not until then—she let it out that you thought I was Jonathan Holding's daughter."

"Who is Jonathan Holding?"

"My friend Lana's father. He's—" She cleared her throat. "You know, he's very rich."

"I remember. I never thought you were Jonathan Holding's daughter," he said frowning, as though she had accused him of it.

"No. I believe you. But until that moment I'd had no idea you knew anything about Lana, and when Puran said that—how could she have known about a computer heiress at the college, except through you? She pretended to think that it had been an explicit agreement between you and me, that you would make me Princess of Parvān in exchange for my father's financial support in the war. She seemed so shocked and disapproving when she discovered that I wasn't party to it, as if it had been wrong of you to pretend to me...and at the same time so brokenhearted over the fact that there'd be no money after all...."

"Alinor, think what you're saying. How could she think you were a party to such an agreement when your father was not Jonathan Holding?"

She rubbed her head in exasperation. "Oh, for God's sake, Kavi! Can you just open your mind for one second? She was trying to make me think that you had also lied to her when you told her I had agreed to it. That you wanted to hide from her what a monster you were being, marrying me for money and pretending you loved me!"

"And a fool, too, if I told her all that!" he responded angrily. "Everything contradicts itself, Alinor! I never said anything to Puran about your friend, why should I? It was information that held no interest for me. Then how could she have known anything about it, unless you yourself told her?"

"Kavi, if we can't trust each other now—after all that's happened if we can't believe the other even wants to tell the truth, what's the point?"

"I have never said there was a point to this discussion," he said flatly.

"No, you haven't." She looked up, full into his face. "But

wouldn't you rather trust me, Kavi? If I could explain things, wouldn't you prefer that to thinking what you now think?''

''You left, Alinor,'' he said. ''You left me, and you left your newborn son. What can explain that?''

''Can't you wipe out what you think you know about me, just for the next half hour? Forget everything you were told about me and about what I said and did, and just listen with an open mind? What if I'm right, Kavi? What if what you believe is wrong and what I'm saying is right?''

''If I accept that, the rest of reality has to stand on its head.''

''Well, put it on its head for half an hour. Can't you do that? We have a child to think of. For his sake, could you listen to what his mother is trying to tell you?''

He was silent, not looking at her. After a moment, he said, ''Go on.'' And for the first time there was a tone in his voice, a hint that something in him had shifted, that he was at last willing—able—to listen.

''I accepted that that was why you'd married me, why your father had approved. I believed you had confused me with Lana and married me in order to have money to finance the war. And that's—the night she told me that was the night you came back to the palace for the first time in ages, and I told you I wanted to leave you.''

He whispered a curse through his teeth, as if the memory still had power to hurt him.

''It was the one thing that made sense of everything…made sense of the world as Puran had explained it to me. Why you'd lied about my freedom here… You weren't there, Kavi, and when you were—we never talked, you never told me anything, and after a while I thought…'' She broke off, sighed, and began again.

''I got pregnant so quickly, and I was so vulnerable then. And Puran began to make sure I was really, seriously isolated…I'm sure it was she who arranged that the doctor who came to look after me was a man who had trained in Germany and spoke almost no English, even though I've found out since there was an American-trained doctor on the staff at the time. You know how limited I was in Parvāni then. I couldn't explain anything, he couldn't tell me anything, unless Puran was there to translate.

"And then she told me your father had taken a bad turn and I couldn't visit him again. At the end she sent even Dallia away. It was—like being in prison, in solitary confinement. And Puran was my only outlet. My jailer. I was completely emotionally dependent on her."

He wiped his hand over his eyes and sighed heavily. "And why did you never tell me any of this at the time?"

"I didn't see what was happening then. What should I have told you?"

"The doctor, why did you not say to me that you wished for a doctor who spoke English? When I asked you about your doctor, you said he was very good."

She looked at him until he returned her gaze. "Kavi," she pointed out gently, "you were fighting a war. I didn't want to bother you with things you could do nothing about, and when I did, if you'll recall, you weren't very patient."

"You shouted at me once that the doctor spoke no English. I thought it was just another excuse to leave me and return home, and I would never see you or my child again."

"Well, no one could accuse us of having clear lines of communication," she said, and laughed mirthlessly. "Oh, Kavi, we were sitting ducks! We might as well have sent out embossed invitations to anyone who might want to cause trouble between us!"

"Yes, I did not do well with you," he said abruptly, and it was the first sign she had seen of a crack in the facade. He didn't reject blame for himself, it was Puran's share he couldn't accept. "A man should understand that when his wife is pregnant she will have many fears and worries that seem foolish to him. I did not want to understand this. From the day you threatened to leave me I wanted to punish you. I thought you had never loved me. I thought you only wanted to be queen of Parvān until you saw that life would be more difficult than you had imagined.''

"I'm sorry,'' she said. "I was so hurt that night, I forgot to think of you. If only I'd confronted you with what she'd said, instead of…''

He rubbed his face with both hands, as if it were a gesture he had used often, to stop himself weeping. "All right,'' he muttered, his face still buried. "Tell me what you have to tell me.'' He sighed heavily and looked up.

"The night I went into labour, Puran said the doctor sent word that he was too busy with casualties to come. When I asked him a while ago—he's still at the hospital—he told me he was never sent for.''

Again he swore under his breath. "And the midwife?''

"She didn't come, either.''

"My aunt told me you had the midwife, that you had preferred the midwife to the doctor at the last.''

"I didn't prefer anything, I was too far gone. All I wanted was something to take the pain away. I wouldn't have cared if the vet who looked after your horses had administered it! Puran found another midwife. I couldn't understand a word she said. She left before—I don't know when she left, I only know she wasn't there afterwards. I've never seen her again. I never knew her name. Now I wonder if she was a midwife at all.''

"What?''

She drew in a breath, and prayed for courage. "I think now Puran really hoped the baby—that Roshan would die. But when he didn't, Kavi…she told me he had.'' Now, at last, the tears came. "Oh, Kavi, please believe me! If you could understand what that's like, it's the worst pain in the world, first you hurt and hurt and then at the end, there's nothing to show for it, and you're just so empty. Oh, if only you'd been there! I cried for you, I wanted you so much, I didn't care who you thought I was, or whether you loved me, I just wanted you there to take the pain away.''

She sobbed wretchedly, and he took her in his arms and whispered, "I'm sorry, I'm sorry," over and over.

Then she wiped her tears and went on, because it must all come out, he must know it all. And because she herself was seeing the full enormity for the first time, and had to know it, had to get it straight at last, to fix it in memory. "And then, when I was almost blind with pain and misery, then your aunt told me that you and I weren't really married, that a Parvān royal marriage wasn't binding until a proper legal ceremony after the first child was born, and that now you could repudiate me, since I wasn't rich and the baby was dead…and I believed her, because you had said the *talaaq* to me. And she said that after the preliminary ceremony we had gone through, even one recital of the *talaaq* legally meant we were no longer tied to each other."

"These are the ancient laws. I have told you before such laws have no force now. There was no reason for her to recite such nonsense to you." His voice was hard.

"Somehow she put it into my head that I had to get out, that I could get away from it all and forget everything and be all right. That I didn't have to wait for you to repudiate me publicly because you'd effectively already done it.… She found me a guide and mules, and…oh, Kavi, what a journey that was…" She choked and started to cry again. "Before I was halfway down the hill I was hoping you'd come after me, but it was too late then…I'm sure I left three trails of liquid all the way, blood and milk and tears."

"Blood?"

"You don't think I'd recovered enough to travel, do you? I was haemorrhaging, and bleeding from the tearing, too. I'd had no stitching. You should have heard the doctor at home cursing out Middle Eastern medicine when he saw the state I was in."

His face was as black as the smoke over a battlefield.

"She moved fast, she had to, while I was still crazy with grief, too sick to think clearly…oh, what a trip! That awful guide, I was terrified the whole way that he was going to slit my throat and leave my body behind a crag…and then he dumped me at the gate of the American Embassy and went off with both mules, and I stood there weeping over a mule, Kavi, because there was no way for me to get to the Canadian Embassy!'' She began to laugh then, through the tears, the laughter of despair. ''I think that was the lowest point, when I was reduced to crying over that stupid, uncomfortable, miserably stubborn mule! I don't think I remembered at that point that cars had even been invented. My whole world was reduced to one mule.''

He did not laugh with her. He comforted her, and then, when she had wept herself into silence and something a little like peace, he sat staring into the distance, his face haggard, his hand absently stroking her arm. At last he looked at her. ''Go to sleep now,'' he said. ''No more tonight. We'll talk in the morning.''

Obediently she lay down. She was mentally and physically on the edge of utter exhaustion. ''Do you believe me, Kavi?'' she whispered.

''I…believe you.'' But whether it was true or not he himself didn't know. ''Good night, Nuri.'' He bent and put out the light, but then he did not get into the other bed. In the darkness she heard him dress, and open the door, and go out.

Chapter 18

She awoke to the sound of an explosion down in the city, and stirred lazily. She had a bit of a headache, probably the result of all the emotional spillage. She could tell by the sun that she had slept late, but when she reached for her watch it fell to the floor.

Explosion?

Alinor leapt up, but there was nothing to see from the window. Kavi's bed was empty. Calling for him, she raced into the sitting room. Empty. She tore open the door, ran through Roshan's room, where the boy still lay in undisturbed sleep, and into the office.

He was not there, either. The door into the corridor was wide open. Alinor ran back to the bedroom and threw on jeans and sneakers and a sweatshirt, then dashed out into the corridor, up some stairs, and out onto a terrace.

The city lay far below, alive with early-morning activity...and with a pillar of sinister black-and-white smoke rising from one building. She could not tell from this distance what building it was. It was certainly not the parliament

buildings, which were in a spacious square much further to
the east. But Kavi knew the city well. He would know at
once. She looked down into the courtyard. He was opening
the door to the truck.

"Kavi!" she shrieked. He looked up. "Wait for me!"

She tore down the stairs, along the hall, threw open a door.
"Dallia!" she cried to the startled servant. "I'm going down
to the city! There's been a bomb! Roshan's alone!" Then
she tore out again, running flat out, faster than she had ever
run in her life, her heart sick within her.

He was waiting with the engine running, the passenger
door open, and let off the brake even before she closed it.
"Where is it?" she gasped.

"Bostān-i Dokhtar, I think," Kavi said briefly. The Girl's
Garden. It was a secular school for seven- to fourteen-year-
olds. Alinor bit her lip, but said nothing. He needed all his
attention for the newly-rebuilt road down. It wasn't yet finished, and was full of machinery, and potholes and humps
that might send them over the edge at this speed. To save
time, she turned around in her seat and scrabbled for the hard
hats that were always there and pulled two onto her lap: she
had toured so many damaged sites it was second nature to
her now to wear one.

"What time is it?" Kavi asked, when they had got past
the worst part.

She hadn't stopped to find her watch. "I don't know. Eight
o'clock, maybe."

"God send there were no students there yet."

Alinor said nothing. She had visited the school more than
once, and she clearly remembered the headmistress telling
her, "Our girls are very eager, some of them come in early
in the morning to read, because of course we have not
enough books for them to take home."

The high white wall around the perimeter of the property
was curiously serene and untouched, the only sign of what
had happened a layer of plaster dust that whitened the green

rose leaves twining over the gate. Through the gateway, they could see that the southeastern quarter of the small school building had been the site of the blast, the facade crumbled away in a shockingly large pile of rubble, the floor of an upper-storey room gone, the rest drooping, several rooms and part of an upper corridor exposed. As Kavi brought the vehicle to a slamming stop, another desk fell from the second storey to join its fellows on top of the pile of rubble.

The smoke was acrid, bringing tears to their eyes as they flung out of the truck. More bricks fell. Somewhere there was the sound of glass shattering. A few people, stepping gingerly in the rubble, with little regard for the danger of falling brick, were already stoically beginning the task they knew so well: moving the bricks and stones, pausing to call and listen, moving more bricks and stones.

"I'll go inside and get out anyone in the building!" Alinor said, and set off up the brick-and-glass-strewn front walk towards the gaping, silently screaming mouth that had been the front door.

It was not like the other bombed buildings she had seen; they had been like corpses, while this one, still alive, was like a wounded man, pulsing with agony. Alinor shivered as she stepped warily through the rubble, an eye to what was above as well as what was underfoot.

"Kasi injā hast?" she called, as she moved through the downstairs rooms. "Is anyone here?" At the back of the ground floor was a kitchen, with food in the midst of preparation, a knife lying on the floor. Whoever had been here, thank God, had escaped. Alinor retraced her steps into the hall and gingerly tested the staircase. It looked stable enough to get her upstairs, and if it collapsed after that, she could always jump from a window. She went up quickly, but without running, testing her weight only briefly on each step as she went. As she ascended the walls around her disappeared, and she emerged into the open air.

She kept on calling. Her blood shivered when she heard an answer, but thank God it came from a room at the rear.

The headmistress's office, Alinor remembered. Before she reached it, a woman staggered to the door, leaning against the wall for support, holding her head. "What has happened?" she muttered dizzily. It was the headmistress. There was blood dripping down her forehead. Alinor went to her side and wrapped an arm around her waist.

"Mrs. Bahram," she said calmly. "You're hurt. Can you walk?"

"Yes," said the headmistress. She was blinking, and her head was obviously clearing. "It was a bomb?" she asked matter-of-factly.

"Yes. We should get out as quickly as possible. Is there anyone else in the school?"

"Are the girls out?"

Her heart sank. "I don't think so. Are they upstairs or down?"

"Downstairs. In the Class Five classroom." Alinor swallowed and sent up a prayer. "Nasrin, Mojgān—I heard a third girl arrive, but I did not see who she was. And Mrs. Vahnoz in the kitchen. Are they safe?"

"Shall we go down? Can you manage the stairs by yourself? It's probably better if we don't put our combined weight on them."

"Yes, of course. I am not hurt, only a shelf of books above my desk fell." Holding the bannister, she began the descent. "It knocked me unconscious, that is all. I heard your voice, it woke me right away. How bad is—?"

She broke off then, because as she descended the devastation of the Class Five classroom became evident. Then those who worked to clear the rubble came into her view. She cried something aloud, and then was silent, stepping quickly down the rest of the way and running to join them.

When Alinor had made the descent the headmistress was talking to Kavi and Mrs. Vahnoz, the cook. A fire truck had arrived, and many more people were helping to clear the rubble. She arrived as the headmistress was saying to them all, "Three girls were in the room." They could now hear a banging coming from somewhere under the rubble, so one at least was alive. Alinor joined the workers, the rough stones tearing the flesh of her hands until someone—Kavi, she thought—stopped her and pushed a pair of workgloves into her hands.

They worked till her back was breaking and every muscle screaming, and then, just when it seemed that the pile of rubble would never be depleted, someone uncovered a hand lying between two bricks.

But the owner was not a girl, and he was not alive. The hand lay pathetically lifeless, brown, with grimed nails and black hair on the knuckles. Long before the entire body was uncovered they knew that this was the body of a young man.

"He came yesterday to fix the electricity!" exclaimed Mrs. Bahram, who had refused to go to the hospital until her girls were found. "I thought he had finished. Why did he come back?"

"Perhaps because the bomb had not gone off," Kavi said. Spilled under one side of the body there was an open suitcase, and all the wires and tools so essential to a terrorist bomber's kit.

Shortly after that they heard cries added to the banging from under the rubble, a girl's high voice, and they worked more quickly now, in silence, exactly over the spot. There was a larger pile here, and the relief was almost singing joy when they reached polished, if crumpled, metal and understood that the voice had come from underneath the teacher's desk.

It was the girl named Nasrin, filling them all with jubilant high spirits as she poked her smudged little face up to the hole they soon made in the rubble. She was tucked underneath the desk, in the kneehole, and although rubble had spilled in after her, she assured them she was unharmed.

"My eraser rolled under Miss Dara's desk!" she told them as soon as she was free. "And I went after it, and then there was a big roar, and it was dark and raining rocks."

Alinor was leading the child towards the road, where by
this time there was a battered ambulance waiting, with the
German-trained doctor in attendance. He agreed with the girl
that there were no bones broken, but put her in the ambulance to rest. She was certainly suffering from shock, he
confided to Alinor. Or would be. The headmistress was already there, her head bandaged now, but she still refused to
be taken away. She greeted Nasrin with tears of relief.

They began to work with new vigour, inspired by the suc-
cess of Nasrin's survival, and when a lifted brick revealed a
naked foot, with a shoe nearby, it was a moment before they
realized that the seeming movement of the foot had been
caused by the shifting of the brick itself. Subdued and silent,
they dug away to reveal the body. There had been no protection for this child. The force of the blast had blown her
backwards onto a desk, and the ceiling had rained down on
top of her.

They put the body on the grass, covered her with a sheet,
and kept on digging. Alinor, her muscles by now numbed
into submission, her mind dulled, was working like an au-
tomaton—bend, lift, throw; bend, lift, throw. A man was
working opposite her, on the same mound of rubble, in sync
with her own motions, so that when she bent, he was throwing, and vice versa, in a rhythm that kept them out of each
other's way. The man was Kavi, but although she was aware
of the bare fact, she was incapable of taking it in.

They found her together, first one brick and then another
being lifted to reveal the bright red of a sweater that moved
gently with the regular, blessed pattern of human breathing.
They shouted in unison, and others came swiftly and carefully over the ruins and aided their efforts.

She was unconscious, but alive. Her head had fallen between the legs of a chair that was lying on its side. In the
ordinary course of events, the chair would have offered no
protection; there would have been nothing to shield her head
from the fall of bricks. But a large chunk of masonry had

been the first to fall, neatly over the two legs, creating a little roof. It was an amazing thing to happen, little short of a miracle that the legs had not given way, dumping the heavy fall of masonry on her head.

For the rest, her body was cut, bruised and broken. But she was alive.

The girl was gently lifted out, put on a stretcher, and at last the ambulance, carrying all three survivors, drove away.

The rescuers, their backs breaking, their faces filthy, tears in their eyes, stretched painfully after hours of bending, called out farewells, and began to disperse. On the grass, the bodies, of the bomber and his victim, lay in mute condemnation of human madness.

Alinor, standing near Kavi, looked down at them as the numbness left body and spirit, and she was swamped with a mixture of anger, pain, love, sorrow, and an intensely personal sense of loss. She thought with distant surprise, *These are my people now. This is my country and my home.*

Kavi ordered the terrorist's body to be laid out in one of the city's buildings, and radio and mobile car broadcasts asked everyone who could to go and look at the body to see if they recognized it. He hoped by this means to get some lead on the rest of the group. And because, if they had not already left, they might now be trying to leave, he ordered that roadblocks be established on all routes out of the city.

The citizenry responded. All that evening they lined up four deep, to file past the body of the Kaljuk, and at nightfall it was necessary to keep the building open, for the crowds only increased as word spread through the city.

Alinor returned to the palace beaten, shattered, more tired than she could remember being since the night of Roshan's birth. Suddenly it all seemed to be catching up with her. She realized she hadn't taken a day off in weeks. She would do no more work tonight. She'd take some time to rest. It would be stupid to work herself to exhaustion.

She took a long bath, letting the grief and grime and fa-

tigue seep out of her pores, and then Dallia, catching sight
of her bruised and torn hands, put ointment and bandages on
them for her. Roshan was already asleep; she had missed his
bedtime ritual.

Stretching out on some cushions with a cup of coffee and
a book Lana had sent her weeks ago, she found the words
swimming before her eyes. It was not reading her mind
wanted, but rest.

Kavi, meanwhile, worked himself well over the edge of
exhaustion. The police and army were fully engaged in man-
ning the roadblocks and otherwise dealing with the repercussions of the terrorist bomb, and Kavi's Companions had
taken on the work of following up leads from those who
viewed the body. Arash sat by the body, listening to anyone
who thought they might recognize the dead man, taking notes
and names. Kavi and the others, in several teams, chased
down the leads.

It was pretty fruitless work. Someone had seen him on a
bus, in a particular shop…a prostitute had serviced the man
two weeks ago, and when he had reached his climax he had
cried out something unmistakably in the Kaljuki dialect. She
had spat at him and refused payment, throwing him and his
clothes after him out of the room. She had not known about
the terrorist threat. If she had, she would have reported the
incident then.

Kavi listened, and smiled at her as gently as he knew how.
Her voice told him that she was educated. She was young,
not even twenty, probably just at an age where the war had
interrupted her education in a final way, too old to consider
starting again now that the war was over. And doubtless
without the means.

"Do you believe me, Lord?" she whispered pleadingly,
when her story was ended.

"I'm very grateful you came forward. The information
you have given is very helpful. We will put extra searches
on in Takht-i Kava." The man had said something that made

her think he lived or worked in that area of the city. "Is there anything else you can add?"

She shook her head. "And do you believe that I—that I took no money from him? Do you believe me when I tell you this? I took no money from him, Lord, I swear, nothing! He was an enemy of my country, and if I starved first I could not take his filthy money!"

He felt drained of all emotion, all feeling, and yet this girl had the power to reach him. His heart moved in something like pain. *Do you believe me?* Why did the question affect him so? *Do you believe me?* She was like Alinor with that urgent gaze, demanding something from him that he had forgotten how to give. Demanding that he respond with his heart, when he no longer had a heart.

"Of course you took no money from him," Kavi said. "You are an honourable woman, and you have acted honourably. I believe you."

She burst into a storm of weeping that shook him. "Lord," she said. "Do you call me honourable, knowing what I do?"

"The war has made many of us other than what we wished," he said grimly, and knew that it was true.

He drove back to the city centre, and found that the long line of people to see the body had all but disappeared. Fifteen or twenty were there. Arash had gone. An old man sat by the body in his place.

"Good evening, Father," he said.

"Prince Kavian?" said the old man, peering at him in the gloom. The city was subject to odd, random power cuts in various areas, and it seemed one had happened here. The overhead bulb glowed dully orange, and around the corpse now its faint light had been fortified with lanterns. "Is it you, Lord?"

"It is. What has gone on here, old man? Has everyone gone home?"

"Someone came who knew this man. I perhaps knew him myself, but my eyes are too dim now to see a face clearly.

I need the voice now. It was your voice I recognized. I was there when you led the defence of the city. I wasn't much use, but I was there. And if I didn't kill any Kaljuks, at least I didn't kill any Parvānis, either." He cackled. "I didn't fire a shot. Well, I had no bullets. Many of us did not."

"Old man, what has happened here tonight?"

"Someone knew him as a neighbour. A man. He began to curse and leap in the air, swearing that he knew where the whole lot of them were, in a house near his own. Well, next thing was, the whole line-up was determined to go with this man and arrest the Kaljuks before they had a chance to escape, and off they went. Some of your Companions were here, tried to stop them, but it was no good." He paused. "Never is, when a mob's got their blood up, like that. I've seen the sort of thing before. So the best they could do was follow along."

"Where did they go?"

The old man sniffed. "Well, now, in all the shouting, I couldn't just pick it up. Somewhere over in the Takht-i Kava area, if you ask me."

They were almost at the prison when he found them. A large number of citizens, in their midst Arash slowly driving a Land Rover carrying four handcuffed men, and several of his Companions marching alongside it, rifles carried in a manner that looked casual. But Kavi's eye told him they could be firing in a second.

Nima stepped over to his vehicle. "Good evening, Lord, you come at a good time."

"So I see. What went on, Nima?"

The Companion shook his handsome head. "Your citizens practically took the house apart stone by stone before we got there. We saved the Kaljuks, but not before they had learned to fear for their lives. They are not in the best shape. Now the elated citizens are personally delivering them to the prison. We had to swear by God Arash would drive at a walking pace. Meanwhile, one of them bleeds to death."

Kavi smiled grimly. "Perhaps when the story is told, it

will make the Kaljuks pause before they offend us again. I'll meet you at the prison.''

Alinor, dozing on the cushions, awoke when he entered the apartment. "Did something happen?" She took in the dark circles around his eyes, the pallor of his skin, the fatigue that he would not give in to. It was very late.

"They've been captured. They're in prison."

"Thank God." She asked no more. He was ready to collapse. "Come and eat something," she invited, getting up and leading him to the cushions she had plumped up for him hours ago.

He allowed her to comfort him, being too worn to resist, sinking down and not moving again while she brought a tray with lighted candles under the food, and served him. He hardly knew what he was eating, his body so hungry that he wolfed the food uncontrollably for a few minutes. Then, with the gnawing edge of hunger sated, he could relax and eat more slowly.

"Tell me how you found them," she said then, recognizing the moment.

"Not I. Someone who has lived beside them for several weeks and recognized the body as one of his neighbours. He led half the city to the place, where, in spite of the protests of my Companions, the door was broken down and all the Kaljuks dragged out into the street. There they were attacked, with a singleness of purpose which astonished my men. In the end they confessed to being Kaljuk terrorists, and begged for the protection of the law, and then for mercy. They were not shown mercy. One of them will almost certainly die. All of them are in the prison's hospital ward.''

Alinor set down a forkful of food, her stomach heaving. "How dreadful," she whispered.

One eyebrow went up. "Dreadful? Why?"

"Don't you believe in the rule of law, Kavi? Of course you do. This is like a...like vigilantes. A lynch mob."

He was weary, with a sorrow that went to the roots of his soul dragging him to a place in himself he had never been.

"There is a deeper law than the rule of law," he said. "It is the law of a nation that will not put up with any more. The Kaljuks met that law tonight."

"It's barbarism."

"What the Kaljuks did to Bostān-i Dokhtar—what is that?" he asked with deceptive softness.

"That's barbarism, too."

He nodded and sat up, and suddenly his face was very close to hers. "Listen, my wife," he said. "Do not confuse my people's instinctive justice towards the murderers of children with the acts of those murderers. It is not the same. These Kaljuks sought to continue the war. They made the city a battlefield again, and one must prepare to be wounded on a battlefield. A man may not invade a sovereign country to kill its inhabitants in what he terms a holy *war* and then demand the protection of that country's peacetime laws. In war, one does not put the enemy on trial. One kills him. So be it. We are a strong, independent, mountain people, and we protect ourselves wherever and however necessary, with the means at hand." He paused for a moment, but she made no answer. He was aware, though not quite in full possession of the fact, that there was more feeling behind what he said than that anger which belonged to the team of Kaljuk terrorists.

"In our past we have driven off the British, and then the Russians, and we made such a mark then that later the Soviets never even tried to subdue us, although they wished it. And now the Kaljuks have been driven off, but see at what cost. My people tonight have sent to the Kaljuks a message: either the war is over, and we are the possessors of our own land, or it is not over, and we will deal harshly with the enemy. Choose which it is to be."

She was moved in spite of herself. She could hear the feeling packed in behind his voice, and it called to her own deep sorrow and restless fury at the ruin of this tiny, once happy nation. "Pretty ferocious, all the same, Kavi."

"Yes, ferocious. They are lions when life calls for lions, Parvānis. And your son is one of them. One day he will be their Prince, their King. Learn to accept the ferocity of my blood, for I will not have my son trained up a weak man."

Chapter 19

She stared at him wordlessly. She had never seen Kavi like this, with his feelings so near the surface—or at least, not since her return. Something—perhaps the cumulative experiences of the past thirty-six hours—had shaken him out of the armour he had placed around himself. His eyes had lost the wariness she had come to expect when he looked at her, and he seemed much closer to the young man he had been, a lifetime ago.

"Kavi," she whispered, but she lacked whatever words it would take. He looked at her, and a muscle moved in his jaw, but he did not speak. "What is it? What happened tonight?"

He shook his head. "I'm a little fatigued."

A breath of laughter came out of her, not that she was laughing at him. "You are always exhausted. What else happened?"

Without knowing why, he reached into his breast pocket, pulled out a piece of paper, unfolded it with one hand, and sat thoughtfully gazing at what was written there for a moment.

Alinor watched as he absently turned the page over and glanced at the blank reverse. Then he handed it to her.

Rohani Rudagi
10 Tajeskandar Road

Alinor read it twice and looked up. "Who is she?"

"Now? A prostitute."

She tried to think what there was in a name and address that had done this to him. "And before?" she prompted.

He shook his head. "Probably a child in school. Her age was difficult to guess. We went to interview everyone who left their names after viewing the corpse. She had—the dead Kaljuk had visited her, she recognized his body."

"Is she how you found them?"

"No. He had mentioned Takht-i Kava, and she thought he might live or work there. But in the meantime a neighbour had also recognized the man." He began to tell her about his interview, how the girl had wept for her honour, and suddenly, he found himself choking on emotion. And for the first time since the night he had come home to find that his wife had left him and his abandoned newborn son was not expected to live, Kavi felt tears burn his cheeks.

He stood up abruptly, but she was on her feet, too, and pressed herself against him, holding him tightly. "Don't go!" she whispered, as if her heart was breaking, too. And the unjudging understanding in her voice was too much for him. He wrapped his arms around her, bowed his head over her, and wept. For the girl, for the war, for the ruin of his marriage, for everything.

"My country, Nuri, my country." The words, the emotion choked him. He was incoherent, scarcely aware himself of all that he was saying and wished to say. "My people—what has been done to them? What have they become? Such a proud people, honourable, hospitable, and now they tear men apart in the street like animals. You are right, it is barbarism, yet how can I call it wrong? They do what must be done; this message must be sent to the Kaljuks. They know it."

"I know. I know. You were right, I was wrong. It's self-defence. I didn't see that before," she murmured, meaning it. What had happened could not be judged in a preconceived way, as if there were no other truth than the one she had learned.

"This girl—she was an ordinary girl, she longed to study, to marry and have children—and instead she is a prostitute—for men whose wives have been killed and for crippled soldiers who will never have wives. All she had left was that I should believe her word. This is what we are brought to! We have won a war, but it has destroyed us, Nuri! I look around me and see nothing but a victory that did not come in time to prevent us being burned to the ground. How can we call that victory? There is nothing left."

"Oh my darling," she murmured, for there was nothing to say. Her job now was to listen. She clung and listened with all her heart as he stroked her hair with a trembling hand and then pressed her closer to him.

"She reminded me of you when she asked me—'Do you believe me?' I thought of all the times I had not believed what you said, all the times I believed things about you that I should not have believed. If I had loved you the way a man should love his wife, would I have believed that you would try to harm our child? That you would abandon him to die? If I had refused to accept it, as a man should, would not the truth have come out then?

"My aunt, my aunt who was so close to me, Nuri, my mother's own sister! How could she do the things she has done? Now she is lost, too; more lost to me than if she had died in the fighting. Nothing is left, Nuri!"

It flooded him then, he could no longer speak over the sobs that shook him, and with an oath he gave himself up to it as she held him with all the love she had, her heart breaking, her own face wet with tears.

When the storm abated, he lifted his head, and looked into

her face, and she sniffed and smiled up at him. He lifted a hand and drew a thumb across her cheek, where a last tear fell. Then he bent and gently kissed the place where the tear had been, then one damp eyelid, then the other, gently, sweetly.

"Nuri," he said. "My light."

And his voice was the voice she had used to hear, that she had longed to hear again, of the man who loved her. She smiled at him and reached up to offer him her lips, and as he bent to meet them, her arms slipped up around his neck, and she sighed with all the relief of a lost child who has at last come home.

His kiss was slippery with the tears they had both shed, warm, gentle, loving. But as she responded with all the pent-up love in her heart, all the sorrow, all the pain, all the pity, all the need, wrapping herself deep in his arms against his body, his mouth became gradually less tender, more demanding. And then, with an abruptness that shook the world, every feeling in each of them was suddenly translated into burning, hungry, physical need of the other. There was one release, one expression of all that was between them, a communication they had hungered for for weeks, months, years; and now their beings clamoured for it, body, soul, heart and spirit. Passion struck them, a wave from an invisible sea, so that they gasped and even staggered a little under the power of its blow.

He lifted her, like a man who snatches triumph from the ruins, like one who unexpectedly brings his most precious jewel from the flames of destruction, and carried her to the place they were both desperate to be.

Afterwards, lying in silence, he lifted her hand to his mouth and kissed it. "Thank you," he said. Then they lay side by side, talking about many things, and about the bombing, about the girl.

"She is a symbol of something," Kavi murmured. "A symbol of all that we are, what we have lost, and what has become of us. Perhaps that was why..." *Why she touched my heart when I thought it was dead.*

She understood that he had built a wall of non-feeling around himself—had had to build it, in order to be able to fight a war; that she had been beating her head against that wall without realizing what it was. But now it was down.

"Then the future is full of hope," Alinor said softly, "if she is the symbol of Parvān spirit. She did what she thought was right without thinking of the cost to herself. She threw him out without taking the money she probably desperately needed, and she faced you and admitted what she was because it might help you find him. How could you ask for a better future than to rule a people who, even after all you have been through, are so unselfishly devoted to the good of the country and to what is right?"

"Nuri, Nuri, how did I live without you for so long?" he said.

They talked long into the night, and for many nights after that, drunk on their newly re-found love, determined that it should never again be buried under the weight of mistrust or starved by the inability to communicate which they had once allowed to overtake them.

It was not Puran's fault that she had been allowed to come between them, and they both saw it. If they had been talking, listening to each other, she would have been powerless.

"I wish I could see why she did it," Alinor said. They were in bed on a rare morning when they had decided to take a day to be with each other. Later they would take Roshan somewhere, but for now they were alone. Kavi was leaning against the wall as they talked, with Alinor alternately leaning on one arm, or resting against his chest. "Was it just pure xenophobia? She just didn't want an outsider in the family?"

Kavi shook his head. "No. I thought so at the beginning, when she wrote me her letter of protest, but after you left, she began to urge me to divorce you so that I could marry again, someone of our own this time, someone who would not betray me by running away when I needed her most, someone who had a stake in the country and the family.... She was careful. It was only after two years that she came to me with her sudden inspiration—that I should marry her daughter, Nargis. What could be more natural? she wondered. How could we have overlooked the obvious so long?''

"She actually said something about it to me—very early," Alinor interjected. "I'd almost forgotten. About how if Nargis hadn't been too young for childbearing, you'd have married her, because with the war coming your father wanted to ensure the line."

He grunted. "It was never my plan, nor my father's. But now I believe that it was her plan from the beginning, perhaps from the moment of Nargis's birth. When her husband died, leaving her with a new daughter, she wrote my father begging to come and live here with us. Of course he did not refuse, but there was no reason for such a request. Her husband left her well provided for. Perhaps she was planning it even so long ago. I wish I had seen it before this."

"And then, after fifteen years, when it looked as though she might be close to the goal—off you went abroad and brought home a bride to destroy all her hopes and plans."

"I think so."

"Would you have married Nargis, Kavi?"

He shrugged. "If I had learned for certain that you were out of my reach—who can say? I have never loved her except as a sister, but war changes our priorities. We want to clutch at certainties, at security. Perhaps marriage with Nargis would have come to seem like security to me."

"Maybe that was why you came for me," she suggested. "Maybe you thought it was your last chance to avoid that marriage."

"I was not yet so close to the trap, *jānam*," Kavi pointed out mildly. "I believed then it was for Roshan's sake, because he began to ask for you...because I felt he needed his mother."

"But who had described me to him? Who had made him long for his mother?"

Kavi smiled. "This is easy to see now. But I did not foresee at the time what result my descriptions of you would have, or at least, I could be wilfully ignorant. Then I believed my only thought was to hide from him the fact that his mother had left him as a matter of choice. As for us, I was determined that there should be nothing between us, that I would never ask you to be my wife again. But this was a lie I told myself. The thought of you marrying another man, whether you were married to me or not, enraged me, but I would not look at what this meant."

Alinor smiled, and dropped her head to kiss his bare shoulder. "What did it mean?"

He caught her head between his hands and gazed at her, while two tiny black flames of passion in his eyes seared her. "It meant that you were mine, and I knew it, and I had laid claim to you and would never let you go."

Then he drew her forcefully to him, and kissed her hard, letting her feel his physical strength and his determination, as though some wild part of him was still compelled to teach her that she belonged to him.

She did not resist his power. His masculine passion melted her. Kavi tasted the responsive desire on her lips, and the animal in him stirred ferociously to life. Sensing it, she took her lips away from his, and with another smile, as though to prove to him that she had power of her own, that he belonged as much to her as she to him, bent low over his aroused body. His hands were still on the back of her head, and now they tightened, and he held her there, and then, with scarcely controlled passion, pushed her where she wanted to be.

"Yes," he whispered, "you are right," although she had said no word; and then her hungry mouth enclosed his flesh and he gave himself up to pleasure.

"Ah," said Kavi one morning, opening his mail. "A letter from Puran. Perhaps you would like to read it."

He had written his aunt, saying that now that Alinor was returned, it was not convenient for her to return to the palace just at present. It was all he said, but she might read between the lines if she chose. If confrontation could be avoided, he preferred it. If the unspoken knowledge that her machinations had been exposed and that her plans had come to nothing was enough to ensure that they were free of her, he believed it was better. To repudiate her, publicly or even privately, might be to cause unpredictable repercussions. And Kavi wanted peace.

"You tell me what she says," Alinor said, for the thought even of touching a letter written by Puran filled her with a repugnance that she could not overcome.

"This letter invites me to congratulate her. She has arranged a very good marriage for Nargis with the son of Puran's cousin, a young man named Bizhan who already owns property in the village. He is rebuilding his house there. Puran hopes we will understand that she prefers to stay and spend her remaining years beside her daughter and future grandchildren."

She said nothing.

"Nuri," he said softly. "Is this enough for you?"

She lifted her shoulders. "What else could you do?"

He smiled at her, as though the sight of her was enough to lighten the burden of unpleasant things. "If she were a government minister or ambassador, I could appoint her to the embassy in Kaljukistan. But as it stands—I can think of no punishment more painful to her than banishment from my father's palace. There is no law under which she could be prosecuted—she has done nothing illegal. I think it would serve no purpose to expose her, but if you wish it—"

"How inadequate human laws are," Alinor observed dispassionately. "All that dreadful malice, all the anguish she caused, but she broke no human law."

"Shall we leave her to divine justice?" Kavi asked gently.

Alinor took a breath. To expose Puran would mean rolling in the same hatred again, becoming obsessed with what she only wanted to forget. She had to let it go, if only for the sake of her own spiritual well-being. And Kavi wanted peace, and after so many years of war, what would it gain to force him into a distasteful confrontation that would, in the end, solve nothing, except her own hunger for revenge?

"Let's forget it, Kavi," she said. "Let's go on with the future and forget the past."

A weight seemed to lift from her heart.

A letter had arrived from Lana by the same post, naming that day for her arrival in Shahr-i Bozorg. "I've caught a ride on a relief flight that's bringing in equipment and supplies," she wrote. "I've always wanted to ride in a Hercules."

Alinor checked her lists, but could find no record of the relief flight. "Have you got something coming in that I don't know about?" she asked Kavi.

There was no trace of the flight, nor of who might have financed it. "Thursday we have something coming in," was all Kavi could offer. "Perhaps she wrote the wrong date."

Alinor went to the airport at the stated time, just in case. She had missed her friend, and the prospect of her arrival showed her just how much she was looking forward to seeing her again.

She saw the big Hercules circling to land as she arrived, and was out on the tarmac as it cruised to a stop on the only working runway. The huge bay at the plane's tail opened impossibly slowly, so that Alinor was practically jumping with impatience by the time it had touched the ground and the screeching, red-haired figure was allowed to dash down the ramp and into her friend's arms.

"Oh, it's so wonderful to see you!" Alinor cried, hugging her fiercely. "I'm so glad you came! Come on, let's get you through customs and all that. Where's your stuff?"

Lana let out an irrepressible giggle. "There's actually quite a bit. We won't be able to carry it all."

Behind her, a huge yellow Caterpillar was slowly coming down the ramp, and Alinor was momentarily diverted. "Oh, wonderful! We can sure use that!"

"I know you can," said Lana. "You said so in your letters to the college."

Alinor didn't catch on. "You know, we have no record of this shipment at all. I sure hope—oh, *look!* is that another minesweeper? And—oh, I don't believe it! Oh, thank God!— Lana, do you mind waiting around a bit while I sort this out? Oh, I hope this isn't some mistake!"

"There's no mistake," Lana giggled. "It's all for you."

She understood then. Turning away from the enthralling vista of the equipment they so desperately needed to focus on her friend's impishly mischievous face, Alinor paled.

"Lana!" she whispered. "What did you do? What have you done?"

"I went shopping, that's all! I explained it all to Dad, and luckily I picked a moment when he was in a really generous mood. I had a great time doing it, too! I've never bought heavy machinery and tons of timber and building supplies before. It was more fun than buying a sweater and boots at Harrods, let me tell you!" She took her friend's arm and drew her towards the metal cornucopia that was pouring its plenty into the hungry land.

"And I've brought a very, very special piece of equipment just for you and Kavi," she said. "I wasn't sure I'd find exactly the right thing, but we tracked it down eventually, and, Alinor, it's been said before, but never with so much truth—I just know you're gonna love it!"

All the heavy equipment having unloaded, a forklift truck was now beginning to off-load the supplies. And first off were two massive flat wooden crates with FRAGILE stenciled redly across them in two languages.

"That's for us?" Alinor breathed. "What is it?"

Lana hugged her arm. "Come and look!" she commanded, dragging her closer, and then, as Alinor stared speechlessly, she pointed out the sticker plastered to the crate. "Sotheby's Antiques," it read. "Contents: walls of Parvān Royal Bridal Chamber."

"Hello, Lana."

"Hi, Kavi! Great to see you again!"

He understood the unspoken message in that, and accepted it with an amused flicker of his eyelashes.

"It's good to see you, too."

"And these two experts on landsweeping are Jock Hardy and Andy Smith. Guys, this is Crown Prince Kavian."

"Hiya, Prince," said Jock, instantly revealing himself as an Aussie.

"Hi," added Andy. American.

Kavi shook their hands.

"Jock's invented his own portable butterfly-mine detecting and sweeping system, and he thought this would be the place to try it out," Lana explained.

"Well, we can offer you lots of scope for experiment," Kavi said dryly.

"So Oi've hed."

"Yeah, I told him already. They're on a two-year prepaid contract to start," Lana explained. "I've bet them a year's additional salary as bonus that they can't get the country clear of mines in that time. They think they can."

They did not tell Kavi about the Bridal Chamber. In secret the two friends worked on the restoration, aided by Alinor's memory, and when that failed, consulting Dallia.

"Of course I couldn't trace all the carpets and furniture," Lana explained, as they worked out the jigsaw puzzle of the carved wall panels. "Oh, look, isn't this neat? A little door, and behind it a mirror! Boy, they really knew how to live!

Do you know Sotheby's dated most of this workmanship to the seventeenth century? Look at this bird! Isn't it beautiful, his beak right in the flower? Don't you wish we had artists who'd do stuff like this nowadays?''

Alinor didn't answer. When her friend looked up, she was wiping her eyes. "Honey, what's the matter?"

"Nothing, nothing! It's just that—oh, I was so sick about this room, I thought it would be years before…and I still don't know how you managed it! It's like a little miracle. I thought it would all be in private collections by now, panel by panel."

"Yeah, it's not everyone who wants to line a room this size! It was a bit of luck, and a lot of detective work, I guess. I had a dealer who asked around for anything that had come from the Parvān Royal Palace. I mean, they keep a record of what they call the provenance. Some of the furniture and stuff was actually labelled Bridal Chamber, I guess because it sounds so romantic and makes people want to buy. But the walls were a real stroke of luck. Someone who bought them a year ago and then found they just couldn't be made to fit the room he bought them for offered them back to Sotheby's and…well, the rest is history.''

"I wish I knew how to thank you, Lana," Alinor said.

"You know what?" Lana said. "Some gifts there's just nothing you can do about. You just have to accept them. I think this panel with the drawers fits beside the mirror one. Is that what you remember?"

A few days later the first snowfall of winter fell on the city. Alinor settled Roshan for sleep, then, with Lana's help, dressed in a beautiful robe of dark green silk shot with gold, and draped a matching gold scarf over her hair. She sprayed herself with her favourite floral perfume, combed her newly-washed hair, made up carefully.

When Kavi came in she met him at the door, waved to

Lana, and led him out into the corridor again. "Lana's baby-sitting tonight," she explained.

Kavi kissed her. "You're very beautiful," he murmured. "You look like a bride. Where are we going?"

Alinor smiled mysteriously, took him by the hand, and led him down endless corridors.

Suddenly he recognized where he was: in his dream. He blinked and shook his head as the gauze of her scarf, carried by the slight draft always present in the older part of the palace, flowed over him. The silence was total, for here no sound pierced the walls.

At last, she paused, and he recognized the wooden doors of the Bridal Chamber. "Now, my Lord," she whispered.

He picked her up in his arms, enwrapped in all the magic of the first time they had stood here. He could remember his own hungry passion, the fierceness of anticipation, the pride of possession, and the totality of love. Not questioning her, he moved towards the double doors. They were on the latch, and, in the absence of the two Companions, now dead, who had once performed this service for their prince, his bride reached out and opened the doors.

It was only as he passed through the ancient doors that he remembered they should not be there, but that wonder was drowned in the next moment. "Alinor," he said.

All the lost magnificence of the Royal House of Durran seemed to him to be resurrected in that room. The ancient glory of the room was restored—the centuries-old bridal bed, the chests, the hangings...carpets of splendidly rendered birds, flowers...in the fireplace a brazier glowed, and near a nest of inviting tapestry cushions a table covered with a treasured engraved silver tray groaned under the weight of a host of dishes of traditional bridal-night food.

Prince Kavian of Parvān set his bride on her feet, drew the long, delicate scarf away from her hair, and then, taking her beloved face between trembling hands, he kissed her gently on her perfect mouth.

He knew there would be explanations to hear. He knew that her friend's generosity was the cause of this. But all that would come later. For now he was intent on what that generosity had provided: the chance to re-dedicate his love and his marriage in the place where, long ago, it had promised perfection.

* * * * *

Silhouette's newest series

YOURS TRULY

Love when you least expect it.

Where the written word plays a vital role in uniting
couples—you're guaranteed a fun and exciting read
every time!

Look for Marie Ferrarella's upcoming Yours Truly,
Traci on the Spot, in March 1997.

Here's a special sneak preview....

1

Morgan Brigham slowly set down his coffee cup on the kitchen table and stared at the comic strip in the center of his paper. It was nestled in among approximately twenty others that were spread out across two pages. But this was the only one he made a point of reading faithfully each morning at breakfast.

This was the only one that mirrored *her* life.

He read each panel twice, as if he couldn't trust his own eyes. But he could. It was there, in black and white.

Morgan folded the paper slowly, thoughtfully, his mind not on his task. So Traci was getting engaged.

The realization gnawed at the lining of his stomach. He hadn't a clue as to why.

He had even less of a clue why he did what he did next.

Abandoning his coffee, now cool, and the newspaper, and ignoring the fact that this was going to make him late for the office, Morgan went to get a sheet of stationery from the den.

He didn't have much time.

Traci Richardson stared at the last frame she had just drawn. Debating, she glanced at the creature sprawled out on the kitchen floor.

"What do you think, Jeremiah? Too blunt?"

The dog, part bloodhound, part mutt, idly looked up from

his rawhide bone at the sound of his name. Jeremiah gave her a look she felt free to interpret as ambivalent.

"Fine help you are. What if Daniel actually reads this and puts two and two together?"

Not that there was all that much chance that the man who had proposed to her, the very prosperous and busy Dr. Daniel Thane, would actually see the comic strip she drew for a living. Not unless the strip was taped to a bicuspid he was examining. Lately Daniel had gotten so busy he'd stopped reading anything but the morning headlines of the *Times*.

Still, you never knew. "I don't want to hurt his feelings," Traci continued, using Jeremiah as a sounding board. "It's just that Traci is overwhelmed by Donald's proposal and, see, she thinks the ring is going to swallow her up." To prove her point, Traci held up the drawing for the dog to view.

This time, he didn't even bother to lift his head.

Traci stared moodily at the small velvet box on the kitchen counter. It had sat there since Daniel had asked her to marry him last Sunday. Even if Daniel never read her comic strip, he was going to suspect something eventually. The very fact that she hadn't grabbed the ring from his hand and slid it onto her finger should have told him that she had doubts about their union.

Traci sighed. Daniel was a catch by any definition. So what was her problem? She kept waiting to be struck by that sunny ray of happiness. Daniel said he wanted to take care of her, to fulfill her every wish. And he was even willing to let her think about it before she gave him her answer.

Guilt nibbled at her. She should be dancing up and down, not wavering like a weather vane in a gale.

Pronouncing the strip completed, she scribbled her signature in the corner of the last frame and then sighed. Another week's work put to bed. She glanced at the pile of mail on the counter. She'd been bringing it in steadily from the mailbox since Monday, but the stack had gotten no farther than her kitchen. Sorting letters seemed the least heinous of all the annoying chores that faced her.

Traci paused as she noted a long envelope. Morgan Brigham. Why would Morgan be writing to her?

Curious, she tore open the envelope and quickly scanned the short note inside.

Dear Traci,
I'm putting the summerhouse up for sale. Thought you might want to come up and see it one more time before it goes up on the block. Or make a bid for it yourself. If memory serves, you once said you wanted to buy it. Either way, let me know. My number's on the card.

Take care,
Morgan

P.S. Got a kick out of *Traci on the Spot* this week.

Traci folded the letter. He read her strip. She hadn't known that. A feeling of pride silently coaxed a smile to her lips. After a beat, though, the rest of his note seeped into her consciousness. He was selling the house.

The summerhouse. A faded white building with brick trim. Suddenly, memories flooded her mind. Long, lazy afternoons that felt as if they would never end.

Morgan.

She looked at the far wall in the family room. There was a large framed photograph of her and Morgan standing before the summerhouse. Traci and Morgan. Morgan and Traci. Back then, it seemed their lives had been permanently intertwined. A bittersweet feeling of loss passed over her.

Traci quickly pulled the telephone over to her on the counter and tapped out the number on the keypad.

* * * * *

Look for TRACI ON THE SPOT
by Marie Ferrarella, coming to
Silhouette YOURS TRULY
in March 1997.

In the tradition of
Anne Rice comes a
daring, darkly sensual
vampire novel by

MAGGIE SHAYNE

BORN IN TWILIGHT

Rendezvous hails bestselling Maggie Shayne's vampire
romance series, WINGS IN THE NIGHT, as
"powerful...riveting...unique...intensely romantic."

Don't miss it, this March, available
wherever Silhouette books are sold.

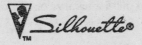

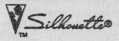

**This summer, the legend
continues in Jacobsville**

A LONG, TALL
TEXAN SUMMER

Three BRAND-NEW short stories

This summer, Silhouette brings readers a special
collection for Diana Palmer's LONG, TALL TEXANS
fans. Diana has rounded up three **BRAND-NEW**
stories of love Texas-style, all set in Jacobsville,
Texas. Featuring the men you've grown to love from
this wonderful town, this collection is a must-have
for all fans!

*They grow 'em tall in the saddle in Texas—and
they've got love and marriage on their minds!*

Don't miss this collection of original Long, Tall Texans
stories...available in June at your favorite retail outlet.

In April 1997
Bestselling Author

DALLAS SCHULZE

takes her Family Circle series to new heights with

TESSA'S CHILD

In April 1997 Dallas Schulze brings readers a
brand-new, longer, out-of-series title featuring the
characters from her popular Family Circle miniseries.

When rancher Keefe Walker found Tessa Wyndham he
knew that she needed a man's protection—she was
pregnant, alone and on the run from a heartless past.
Keefe was also hiding from a dark past...but in one
overwhelming moment he and Tessa forged a family
bond that could never be broken.

Available in April wherever books are sold.